A Novel by TINA MONSON

This is a work of fiction. The characters, names, places
and dialogue are not to be construed as real.

tina@soundsofzion.com
visit us at www.soundsofzion.com

Printed in the United States of America
First printing August 2004

ISBN: 1-933098-00-7

10 9 8 7 6 5 4 3 2

Acknowledgements

Moroni's Treasure is a result of persistent children. Carson, Carter, Sierra, and Bristol's encouragement and enthusiasm for the Book of Mormon inspired me to write this book. And to my illustrator, best friend and husband, who patiently waited countless hours for my attention — Thank you.

Special heartfelt thanks go to Suzette Jensen. Words cannot adequately express my appreciation for her support, patience, long hours, and efforts on my behalf.

To my family and friends — thank you for sparking ideas and showing entertaining personality traits that shine through the characters in the story.

My sincere gratitude goes to Doyl Peck, who could see beyond the rough draft to an exciting Book of Mormon adventure. And to all the talented people at Sounds of Zion who have, in many ways, assisted in the preparation and publication of this book — Thanks.

MORONI'S

EASURE MAP

Chapter One

Earl sat motionless, watching through the bars of his jail cell window as the dark, black fog mysteriously rolled toward him. He felt clammy, cold and almost frightened of the storm that had crept over the valley. He was hopelessly lost in thought about the events to come.

"The rain and thunder are so loud, I can hardly think!" exclaimed Eddie, as he covered his ears.

"Maybe it will help us tonight," said Earl, abruptly brought back to the moment. "We could use a little help."

"Be quiet," whispered Eddie, as he frantically looked around to make sure no one was listening.

Eddie Dyer and Earl Thunstrom had been planning for months to escape from their ten-foot by ten-foot, block-wall, gated prison cell.

For nearly six years, they had been roommates in the Timber Creek Correctional Facility. It was not the most desirable place, with its run down, yellowed, dirty, dingy cells, and dark gray metal, bars. Earl, unlike Eddie, had somehow made this place home.

Judge Judith H. Wilson had shown the duo no mercy. She sentenced them both to twenty years behind bars for their crimes — the maximum sentence allowed by law. Earl could not help but wonder why they had ever tried to rob that bank, especially with a toy water gun.

Eddie was short and stocky, but he made up for his lack in stature by always being in charge. His eyes were dark green, almost the color of jade, and they got even darker when he was scheming. He had ragged, brown hair, and before his incarceration, always wore a gray knit cap embroidered with ECHS for El Capitan High School. The cap was a sore spot with Earl, as it was how the duo had been identified and apprehended so easily.

Before his incarceration, Eddie usually dressed in style. He always wore faded blue jeans, a white t-shirt, mahogany penny loafers and a black leather jacket. Earl thought that Eddie wanted to be a modern-day "Fonzie". But since their capture, Eddie was required to wear bright orange coveralls, a white t-shirt, and slip on tennis shoes — which he loathed.

Eddie had no patience, which occasionally caused his temper to flare. His social skills were rough at best. And because he did not always understand what people were talking about, he was easily offended.

Eddie continually concocted the most hair-brained schemes. And Earl, timid as a mouse, would mindlessly follow. But this time, Earl felt Eddie's plan was way out of bounds. No one had ever escaped from Warden Willard's reign of terror. Actually, not even one inmate had ever attempted to escape from the Warden's maximum-security prison in twenty-five years.

Eddie was desperate to get out of prison, and Earl knew it. Not a single day went by that Eddie did not mention his plan to escape. His idea consumed every moment. Earl always listened, but he never really thought Eddie's plans would come to life. After all, Eddie had been talking about escaping since the two had been sentenced to jail six years ago.

As the duo quietly made final arrangements for the night's dangerous escape, they quietly discussed each and every detail. Suddenly the prison lights dimmed, casting a soft, spooky, glow around the dingy cell. The duo watched in horror. The lights flashed brightly, dimmed again, and then the room went dark. Sirens sounded, inmates began yelling and the prison dogs barked. Between the thunder and lightning, the guards screaming and the dogs barking, the noise made a dreadful choir.

"Silence! Stand at attention and face the wall!" yelled Warden Willard over the loud speaker. Quickly the inmates moved to do as told. They knew from past experience that the warden ruled with an iron hand and punishment would be severe for not immediately following his instructions.

The Warden's outrageous temper had been the reason no one had ever attempted to escape. As Eddie quietly moved toward the wall, he realized, now more than ever, that he wanted to be free. Escape was all he could think about.

Generators soon kicked on, providing just enough light for the inmates to move safely to the walls in their cells. A power failure had happened before, and the duo knew the routine. The inmates would stand facing the wall, and the guards would move slowly from cell to cell and inspect each inmate for anything suspicious.

Eddie and Earl waited patiently at their wall for inspection, still feeling very nervous that something might give away their escape plans. As they waited, Eddie's remaining calm nerves quickly frazzled.

"This won't work at all. The guards will be watching even closer tonight," he whispered. "We need to have power!"

"It won't be out for long," replied Earl calmly. "Be patient. Everything will be alright."

"Don't tell me what to do, Earl," replied Eddie. "I want this escape to happen tonight."

"Sorry, Eddie," Earl replied fearfully.

Earl had always been the peacemaker of the pair. He loved sports, but never played them much. His favorite was volleyball, although he struggled with his ability to play the game. He enjoyed relaxing games like ping-pong, badminton, and anything non-confrontational. He especially liked Parcheesi and was actually good at the game. Earl had very little motivation and was content to just hang out — a trait that Eddie despised.

Earl met Eddie in high school. They instantly became the best of friends. Earl had uncontrollable, curly, bleached-blond hair, and soft, baby-blue eyes. He was tall, lanky, and clumsy on his feet. Needless to say, he had not been part of the cool and popular crowd in high school. Earl never stood up for himself. He continually let Eddie do the talking and boss him around. Earl had not been surprised when he could not talk Eddie out of the bank heist.

After the guard's quick and lackadaisical inspection, Eddie paced around his cell. He clomped from one side to the other, and then back again, until Earl was almost crazed.

"Please sit down," Earl asked timidly. "Everything will be alright. The power is never out for long."

Worriedly, Eddie flopped down on his bed. He listened to the rain and thunder pound the walls outside as he wished for night to come. He was suddenly afraid of the dark and scared of the night's adventure ahead. He sat there, trying to focus on their escape, sketching every last detail in his mind. Several long nervous hours passed, until the power flickered, shined for a minute, and went out again. Finally, at long last, the power came back on to stay.

Eddie, still lying on his bed, breathed a cautious sigh of relief, knowing that the storm could knock the power out again at any moment. As no further outages occurred, the tension slowly drained from his face. Everything seemed to be returning to normal — just in time.

"What a night to plan an escape! Thunderstorms. Power outages. What's next?" whispered Earl, for the first time not really sure he wanted to go through with the breakout. "What if we just stay?" Earl asked. "We are only a year from being paroled. We are going to get into more trouble if we break out and get caught, especially with Warden Willard in charge. Can you even imagine how angry he will be?"

Eddie just scowled at Earl and continued with his jail-break preparations.

At ten p.m., the guards flashed the lights in the cells and called for lights out. The inmates knew they had five minutes before the cell doors locked. Finally the time had come to put the duo's plan into action.

They brushed their teeth faster than usual. Then they climbed quickly into bed, just like every other night, and pretended to fall asleep.

Around two a.m., the prison was exceptionally quiet. Most of the inmates were asleep, and the guards had just finished their last shift change for the night.

Eddie whispered to Earl, "You ready?"

"I guess," replied Earl nervously.

"Well, let's go then!" Eddie commanded.

Eddie quietly moved toward the metal bars of the cell and cautiously checked the corridor for guards. He looked down the hall at the clock and said, "Exactly twenty-two minutes before the guards come again."

Earl hesitated for a moment and Eddie said, "Come on, Earl. What are you doing? We gotta get moving."

Earl quickly pulled what looked like two big rolls of toilet paper from under the sink. As he unwrapped his creations, he remembered how proud the art teacher was of his papîer-mâché heads. He had even talked her into bringing fake hair and allowing him to attach it to the heads.

He showed Eddie the heads and said, "Well, what do you think? These otta work, right?"

"They're great," Eddie said without looking. "Now let's get out of here."

Earl, disheartened at Eddie's response, dropped his head and let out a deep sigh. He looked at the job he had done on his head, half smiled and shrugged his shoulders. He placed the fake heads carefully in between the covers and the pillow, fluffed the blankets and used his extra clothes to shape the covers to look like a body.

Eddie again glanced at the clock and said, "We are right on schedule. Let's go."

Earl looked at Eddie and apprehensively asked, "Well, what do we do now?"

Without a reply, Eddie quickly went to work. In the floor under the bed was a cold-air intake vent. It was covered with un-removable, titanium steel, powder-coated metal, and had an engraved key-code lock on the cover. Eddie crouched down on one knee and eased onto his stomach. Then he slowly slid under the bed.

Earl said, "Eddie, you can't get the cover off without either the key or the code. If this is your plan, we are doomed from the start."

Within minutes, Eddie had removed the cover and frantically motioned for a bewildered Earl to quickly follow him. With Eddie in the lead, they slipped into the darkness of the vent.

Earl carefully slid the cover back onto the vent so that

no one would notice it had ever been removed. Then they slithered through the vents as quietly as possible.

Eddie, as always, led the way. He had meticulously memorized the vent layouts after he stumbled onto the prison blue prints in the library. Warden Willard had no idea that the ventilation system map and the vent codes had been accidentally filed in the prison library.

Several days later, Eddie had smuggled the blueprints into his cell in a book titled, *Handy Do-it-Yourself Home Repairs,* a book he thought no one would look at in prison. He cautiously and methodically studied the entire air ventilation system. Eddie knew exactly which turns to take to get them closest to the fence outside.

Eddie and Earl were now on their way to the first-ever breakout from this maximum-security prison. Eddie chuckled at the thought of Warden Willard's face when he found out that they had escaped.

However, after all of Eddie's careful preparation, he had not counted on the amount of time it would take them to get through the vents as slowly as they had to move.

They made it to the furnace room much later than Eddie had planned. This room was located next to the final security fence. He had hoped they would already have been tunneling for nearly an hour now.

Frantically, Eddie looked at the clock on the wall in the furnace room and said, "We have less than two hours to get out of here before the next cell check. We spent ninety minutes in the vents. We need to hurry!"

"What do we do now?" asked Earl, climbing down out of the air duct.

Eddie quietly unscrewed the cover on the storm drain, stood up, turned to Earl and said, "This is where you get your hands dirty. We have to crawl to the end of the unfinished storm drain and dig our way to the surface. That will put us outside the fence. Hopefully we will only need to dig a foot or two. We better hurry, we're already behind schedule," Eddie said.

"What do we dig with?" asked Earl naively.

Eddie looked at Earl, held up his hands and asked, "You have two of these, right? Now hurry. We can still get a few hours of running in before the guards do roll call."

Eddie and Earl started digging, trying to be as quiet as possible. They knew if anyone came into the room, they would be caught. And the warden's wrath would be severe.

As the dirt started to pile up, Eddie said, "I think we're almost there."

He slowly continued digging upward. Within a few minutes, mud began caving in from the surface. Rain pounded through the small hole. They could hear the wind howling and blowing fiercely outside.

Eddie turned to Earl and said with a huge smile, "We've made it. We're free!"

He quickly turned back and took a few more strikes at the dirt, making the hole big enough for them to crawl out. He slowly stuck his head through the small hole and saw the prison guards only a few hundred feet away.

"They can't see us from here," he whispered. "Especially in this rain. Let's go!"

Eddie slowly slipped out of the hole, with Earl close

behind. Keeping their heads down and bodies close to the ground, they crawled slowly and cautiously through the mud toward the cornfields about fifty feet away. Suddenly, the prison sirens sounded. The lights started flashing and swirling around the prison yard.

"They've seen us! They've seen us!" yelled Earl, ready to give up.

"Just hurry!" yelled Eddie. "Get up and run! We can still make it!"

Eddie grabbed Earl's jumper and pulled with all his might. Running as fast as they could go, they raced into the cornfield. The torrential rain made everything hard to see. They could hear the prison dogs barking just behind them. Helicopters were flying around and sirens were still blaring. Their hearts were pounding so loudly that Eddie was sure the beating could be heard for miles. Their labored breath sent out puffs of white smoke floating slowly upward from the chill in the air.

"Quick, Earl. Break down some corn stalks and cover up!" ordered Eddie.

Just about the time they were completely covered, they heard officers with dogs moving closer and closer.

Earl nervously whispered, "We're gonna get caught. Let's run!"

"No! Wait!" said Eddie frantically. "Just wait! They won't find us if we don't move. Stay still. Please!"

As the officers moved closer, the prison dogs went crazy barking. Officer Barney J. Nelson, annoyed, jerked his dog's leash.

"Tiger!" he yelled. "You better hold still boy. And quit that barking. There's nothin' up here but corn."

"He must smell rabbits or something," said Officer Roscoe P. Cahoon. "Let's get back. I'm sure they've rounded up the decoys for tonight."

"Are you sure?" asked Officer Nelson. "We haven't found any of them decoys. I was hoping we would at least have a chance to cuff one of them jail-breakin' varmits tonight."

"Well, they were just decoys. We would have found one, if it had been a real escapee," replied Officer Cahoon confidently. "Besides, I'm getting soaked. If this were a real jailbreak, it would be different. I'm freezing. Let's go."

The officers walked west toward the prison. Tiger, still growling and barking, whimpered as he received a stiff pull on his leash. Eddie and Earl breathed a long sigh of relief.

"What a night to have a drill! You have got to be kidding. I thought they had us for sure," said Earl, wiping the sweat and rain off his brow.

Eddie, nervous that the officers might return, slowly stood and cautiously took a look at their surroundings. Then he hunched back down on his hands and knees.

He turned hastily toward the city lights and said, "I'm not really sure where we are, but I think we're only a few miles from town." He pointed toward lights in the distance and said, "Let's go find a safe place to hide before they discover we have broken out and really come after us."

They crawled through the cornfield for several hours, hoping the bad weather would cover their tracks and foil the search for them.

And they were right. By morning, when the guards discovered the prisoners were gone, the weather was noticeably worse. The police scoured every inch of the area. Officers in helicopters, cars, and on foot, along with several police dogs, began searching for the two escapees.

Despite Warden Willard's stern decree for silence, someone had leaked the breakout information to the media. Local news crews were everywhere, and even civilians were searching for the infamous duo.

But no one was having any luck, not even the police dogs. Every clue had been destroyed by the night's weather. With the drill during the night, Officers Nelson and Cahoon could not believe the prisoners had not been caught. And neither could Warden Willard, whose red face and angry scowl left the rest of the prisoners and guards ducking for cover. As for Eddie and Earl, they were safe and sound, hiding somewhere in the sleepy town of Timber Creek.

Chapter Two

For the eighth straight day, the clouds grew darker. They brought with them an air of mystery as they slowly rolled over the Skarpal Mountains and settled in the valley. A gray mist hung at the foot of the mountains, and static filled the air. Thunder and lightning threatened to disrupt the uneasy peace that had momentarily overtaken the valley.

The Skarpal Championship Baseball Tournament was finally supposed to start today. But with the fields soaked, minutes seemed like hours as the Timber Creek Titan's, consisting of Hero, Bubba, Runt, Tater, Stick, Butch, Bean, KP and Red, waited nervously on the balcony of their treehouse, contemplating just how long it would actually be before the games were canceled.

They somberly watched rain slowly drip from branch to branch and then leaf to leaf, counting each drop as though somehow they might make a difference as to whether or not the games were canceled. The clouds pushed together, slowly climbing the east face of the mountainside. Suddenly, the sky became frightfully dark, as the wind swirled unruly above the Team's heads, howling with the might of a wolf pack. Lightning joined the stage, with thunder instantly following. Finally, the rain fell again. The Team sat dejectedly, not wanting to believe that the rain was determining their future.

As the rain grew steadily stronger, Hero dropped his head and breathed a long heavy sigh.

"Team!" Hero's mom broke the silence with a call on the Team's walkie-talkie. "I just got the call. The games are all officially canceled today," she stated.

The Team moaned in unison.

Bubba responded, "Mom, it's only nine o'clock in the morning. What are we suppose to do now? We can't even practice!"

"Well," said Mom matter-of-factly, "why don't you and the Team keep true to your promises and clean out Mr. Jensen's attic?"

The Team moaned again. Everyone except Tater, who excitedly said, "Great! Let's go eat breakfast." He smiled, lifted his eyebrows and looked around at everyone for approval.

Runt looked at Tater, shook his head and moaned again.

"Come on, Team.You've been promising him for weeks that you would get it done. There won't be any baseball today, and a promise is a promise. Besides, it is a great day to be inside," mom said in a cheery voice.

Hero and Bubba's mom was right. Mr. Jensen had done a lot to help the Team with the Treehouse. He had carved out old tree branches and skillfully made the lamp, table, a couple of chairs, and a chessboard. He had even built a trophy case for the big trophy they were supposed to win today. As payment, they had promised to clean his attic.

Hero, as Team Captain, raised his hand and asked, "All in favor say 'aye'?" The vote was unanimous. Like it or not, today was a great day for the Team to clean the attic.

"All right, Team," Hero said. "Hurry home, change out of your baseball uniforms into work clothes, get your cleaning supplies, and meet back here at the Treehouse at nine thirty sharp."

Nine players and one mascot made up the Team. Hero, the Team Captain and pitcher, and Bubba, the left fielder, were brothers. With their love for baseball, the two boys had been excited that everyone in the neighborhood wanted to play. Hero and Bubba organized everything the Team did, including the tournaments, practices and even fundraisers.

Hero, with his slim build, was average height for his age of thirteen. He had fine, sandy-blonde hair with two cowlicks — one in the front and one right on the crown of his head. Under each of his baby-blue eyes he had three freckles. Very athletic and intensely competitive, he loved all sports, but his passion was baseball.

Bubba had a stockier build. He was always in competition with Hero, no matter what they were doing. He had thick, dark-blonde hair, soft-blue eyes that twinkled when he smiled, and one dimple on each of his cheeks. He had a small cleft in his chin, which he thought attracted all the girls to his ball games. He always had a pocket full of food or candy to eat. When the Team was hanging out in the Treehouse, easy-going Bubba was usually the center of attention. He loved to make the Team laugh.

Everyone on the Team moved into the neighborhood around the same time and had been playing together for just a few years. They had all become the best of friends in a short time. They built the Treehouse together, and now they were ranked first in the state and set to win the Skarpal State Championship Baseball Competition.

They had searched and searched for the perfect place for a clubhouse, and then chose the tree in Hero and Bubba's backyard. The tree was an old and twisted Oak. It was more than twenty feet around at the trunk and nearly one hundred feet tall, with leaves and branches growing in every direction. Each gigantic branch and all of the leaves provided several large secluded areas. Only the most experienced tree experts, and of course the Team, could attempt the treacherous climb.

This tree provided some of the very best adventures in the neighborhood. In fact, the Team had used the enormous tree to play hide-and-seek and sardines. Even after countless games and hours of searching, new secret hiding spots were still being discovered.

The tree was an ideal place to build a secret tree-house and a perfect place for the Team to meet in private — away from Hero and Bubba's little sister. Squeaks, tiny for her age and quite sneaky, made a habit of informing Mom of the Team's secrets. The Team had worked hard on the Treehouse all spring. They had finished the balcony just in time for the spring baseball season and a summer of fun.

Hero and Bubba walked slowly in the rain toward the house.

"I can't believe the game's been canceled," said Hero, shaking his head.

"I guess we could have fun at Mr. Jensen's," said Bubba, shrugging his shoulder and scrunching up his nose.

Hero looked up and started laughing. Reaching over to grab Bubba's shoulders, Hero said, "You are such a goof."

The boys ran to their room. They took off their baseball uniforms and threw them on the floor with the rest of their clothes. Frantically, Bubba searched the room. "Where is my favorite pair of shorts?" he mumbled.

Meanwhile, Hero quickly put on a pair of baggy shorts and his tennis shoes. Ten minutes passed as Bubba continued to search and Hero watched.

Finally Bubba looked up at Hero and said, "Do you know where they are?"

"Where what are?" Hero asked.

"My shorts! You know, my shorts," answered Bubba, pointing to his legs.

Hero looked at him with the straightest face possible. "I have no idea what you are talking about."

Bubba, sensing that Hero was hiding something, took off running straight toward him. "Where are they?" he yelled, as he tackled Hero.

Hero struggled but was laughing too hard to escape. With tears streaming down his face he squealed, "I really don't know. I promise!"

"Come on, man. Tell me where they are," Bubba pleaded, as he climbed off Hero and let him get up.

Hero stood up, brushed off his shirt and looked at Bubba. Hero pointed to the shorts he was wearing and ran out the door asking, "Are you looking for these?"

Bubba jumped up and took off after Hero. "Give me those," he yelled, as he chased Hero up the stairs, through the living room, down the hallway and straight into the kitchen.

The room was filled with the rest of the waiting Team. They quickly backed against the wall as Bubba chased Hero around the table yelling, "Give those back to me! Give those back to me!"

Just then, Squeaks, their little sister, walked into the kitchen. "Mom, Bubba and Hero are fighting again," she yelled.

Hero stopped, panting on one side of the table and Bubba gulped for air on the other. Mom walked in the kitchen and casually said, "Hi, Team." Then she turned to her boys and said, "I will make the two of you clean the attic without the rest of the Team if you don't stop fighting."

Hero replied, "We're not fighting, Mom."

"Well, then why is Bubba chasing you around in his boxer shorts?"

The Team laughed as Bubba's face turned red. He quickly headed downstairs, yelling as he left, "I'm gonna get you, Hero. You better watch out!"

The Team was still laughing when Bubba returned – dressed. Always the good sport, he smiled and bowed as he entered the kitchen. "Real funny, guys. Come on. Let's head up to the Treehouse and make our plans for the day."

Eddie and Earl had successfully made it east to town without being caught. They had even sneaked inside a secluded, somewhat rundown house, where they hoped to stay safely hidden until the search was called off. Besides, the weather was really working in their favor. With all the rain and dark skies, the hunt for them had still not moved out of the cornfields, miles away from the town.

Officer Nelson and Officer Cahoon frantically searched every inch of the cornfield. Each additional minute that the duo was on the run added another minute for Warden Willard to become angrier and angrier. They were soaked and exhausted, but neither one wanted to face the Warden without at least one of the escapees.

"Can you believe they escaped?" asked Officer Cahoon.

"Did you see how mad the Warden was?" replied Officer Nelson. "His face was so red, I thought he was gonna have a heart attack."

"What should we do?" asked Officer Cahoon.

"We've got to catch 'em," replied Officer Nelson.

"How? Every trace of their escape has been washed away by the rain," Officer Cahoon said, pointing to the clouds.

"Do you think Tiger spotted them last night when he was barking?" asked Officer Nelson.

"It makes me sick to think about the possibility," replied Officer Cahoon. "But probably so."

"Maybe we should head into town and start searching there," said Officer Nelson.

"We will have to get permission from the Warden," said Officer Cahoon nervously.

"He's always liked you; you ask him," instructed Officer Nelson.

Officer Cahoon thought for a few minutes and said, "It sure would be great to catch them and bring them back to the Warden ourselves."

"It would be the best thing we've ever done. We'd be heroes" replied Officer Nelson.

"We'd get medals for sure," Officer Cahoon said. "Come on. Let's go talk to him." He marched out of the cornfield and back toward the prison.

As they got closer to the Warden's office, Officer Cahoon's hands became clammy, perspiration dripped down his face and he felt sick.

"Maybe we should just wait for the Warden to give more orders," Officer Cahoon said, as he hesitated outside the Warden's door. Suddenly the door flew open, knocking Officer Nelson to the floor. Officer Cahoon was left to face the Warden alone.

"What do you want?" bellowed Warden Willard. "Have you found the prisoners?"

Officer Cahoon trembled. "Not yet, sir," he quietly answered.

"Then, what are you doing here? Get out there and search the fields!" roared the Warden, as he started to walk down the prison hallway.

"I…I…I, have a request, Sir," stammered Officer Cahoon.

Warden Willard turned his six-foot stature, jutted out his barrel chest, and focused his dark brown, see-right-through-you piercing eyes. "What did you say?"

A little bolder, Officer Cahoon responded, "I have a request, Sir."

The Warden stood motionless and expressionless. Finally he snarled, "So what is it? What do you want?"

"Sir, could Officer Nelson and I go to town and search for the prisoners? We have searched the fields, and we are convinced they are no longer there."

"Why would they have gone toward town?" demanded the Warden. Why wouldn't they try to get away from town?"

"Just a hunch, Sir. We thought they might have gone looking for shelter from the weather," answered Officer Cahoon.

The Warden turned his back on Officer Cahoon and replied, "Go ahead and search the town. But don't come back here empty-handed. And this time don't mess up!"

He turned and disappeared down the hall, discussing the situation with Governor Storrs on his cell phone.

A huge grin spread across Officer Cahoon's face. He turned to Officer Nelson, who was crumpled on the floor behind the door. "Come on. Let's go! We have some prisoners to catch."

As the two Officers drove toward town, they made plans to search every house, every business and anything that looked like it could be a hideout. They were certain they would catch the escapees — dead or alive!

Chapter Three

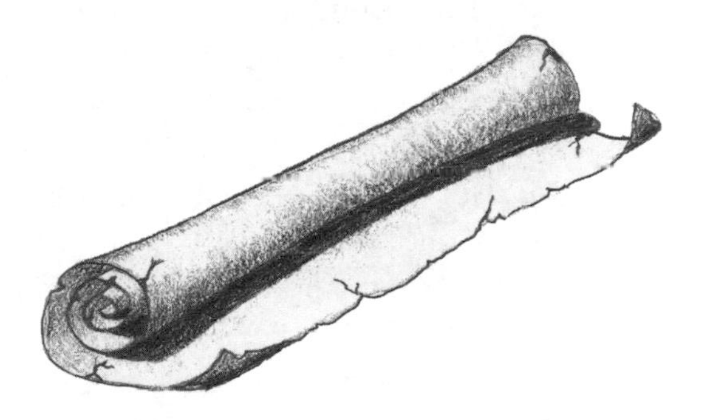

Luckily, the weather cleared for a few minutes around ten o'clock, as the Team prepared to leave the Treehouse on their preferred mode of transportation. Their bikes gave them the freedom to get everywhere, including to games, without having to be driven by their parents. Today, their bikes would take them the few blocks to Mr. Jensen's house, located right in the middle of the older part of town.

Mr. Jensen lived down a narrow dirt road. His yard was overgrown with tall trees, bushes, creeping vines and waist-high weeds. The dark, ominous clouds piled up again and the wind blew stronger. This had to be the spookiest ride the Team had ever taken. Every noise they heard left them wondering what might be behind the next bush.

Red, the first baseman, being incredibly mischievous, continually played tricks on the Team. Riding his bike just ahead of them, he started plotting another prank. The wind flapped his baggy shirt against his body and brushed his thick, red hair off his round, freckled face as hastily he invented a new plan.

Spotting a mud puddle ahead, and trying to lighten the nervousness of the spooky ride, Red saw a chance to play another joke. He quickly calculated the possibility of splashing the Team and hurried to get positioned. He waited patiently as the Team approached the mud puddle. Then, just as they reached what Red determined to be the splash zone, he jumped on his bike and, with his stocky, muscular legs, furiously pumped the pedals to reach top speed. He leaned his bike to the side and tried as hard as he could to surprise the Team with a nice, big, muddy splash. Unbeknownst to Red, a large rock lurked just below the surface of the muddy water. Without warning, Red was launched from the seat of the bike over the handlebars and thrown face first into the mud.

The Team raced to his aid, fearful that he might be hurt. Before they could reach him, Red pulled his head from the mud with a 'pop' and sat up. His unruly, red hair spiked out around the edges of his helmet and his face was covered with thick, dripping mud. At first Red heard a few snickers, and then the Team laughed so hard that Bubba fell off his bike.

Even Stick, usually the most sensitive player, was laughing uncontrollably. "It's a good thing you had your helmet on!" he chuckled, as he patted Red on the head and helped him off the ground.

Red nursed his wounded ego and sore tailbone as he sulked back to pick up his bike out of the mud puddle. "Don't worry. I'll get you guys next time," he said confidently to the Team.

They rode the remainder of the way up to the old house, still laughing and teasing Red about his failed plan and muddy face. Luckily they parked their bikes under the eaves of the house, just as the rain started to fall again. This time it was coming down harder than the Team had seen in the past few days. The rain landed on the ground with loud thumps, as the storm seemed to be getting stronger and stronger.

Hero moved quickly under the eves of the house and nervously rang the doorbell, almost hoping Mr. Jensen would not be home. But after a few seconds, the door creaked open — so loud that the Team covered their ears and cringed in pain. The sound was worse than fingernails down a chalkboard.

"Hi, Mr. Jensen," the Team said in unison.

Mr. Jensen answered, "Well, hello." He looked shocked to see the Team, but his smile was as beautiful as ever. "I didn't expect you today."

Mr. Jensen was ninety-two years old and still had a driver's license. He had large veins in his hands from years of hard work, but still exercised more than any of the Team's dads did. Silvery-white hair circled around both sides and the back of his head, leaving a bald area on the top. His speckled, blue eyes were hard to see through his dark glasses. He always wore a bolo tie, a cowboy belt and carried a harmonica in his shirt pocket, ready to play at a moment's notice.

"We are here to clean and straighten the attic — as promised," said Hero proudly. The grinning teammates held up their rags and cleaners for him to see.

Mr. Jensen smiled. "Great timing. Come in out of the rain and follow me, Team."

The house looked as though Mrs. Jensen had been a wonderful interior decorator. Everything seemed to be a collector's dream of amazing antiques. An old phonograph played a familiar tune in the background. Paintings and framed photos hung on the walls. A beautiful grand piano was opened as though someone might play it soon. And as they walked down the hallway, they noticed a trophy case a lot like the one Mr. Jensen had built for the Treehouse. It was filled with over a hundred baseball trophies.

Surprised, the Team gathered around the case, looking in awe at the gigantic collection of signed baseballs, hats and gloves — not to mention all of the rookie cards from the early nineteen fifties. No one said a word; they simply stared. Hero was seriously jealous of all the cool baseball memorabilia.

As the Team continued through the hallway, Bubba, leaned over to Bean and asked, "What's that smell? Do you think he has a water leak in here?"

Bean, the center fielder, hastily twisted her long, dark brown hair tightly and tied it into a knot. Ignoring Bubba, she shrugged her shoulders. Her beautiful emerald-green eyes tried to concentrate on reading the names on the ball that was signed by the Georgia Peaches, one of teams from the Women's Professional Baseball League.

Hero stopped Mr. Jensen at the end of the hall and asked, "Did you play professional baseball?"

"Just a little," Mr. Jensen replied. "A long time ago."

Just then Red shouted in a strange, nasal voice, "Mr. Jensen, could I bring over some air freshener for your house?" He pinched his nose closed to avoid smelling the stench.

The Team and Mr. Jensen just laughed.

"Red, you goof," chuckled Runt. "Mr. Jensen is canning corn."

Red shrugged and said, "Sorry, I didn't know canning smelled like this."

Mr. Jensen had reached the back room and pointed to the staircase saying, "The attic is up those stairs. Be careful climbing up and down."

As he turned for the door he said, "I don't like to climb up those stairs any more, so bring everything down. Then you can separate the items into piles. Put the books on the shelves, place any pictures on my desk, and throw away any trash or broken toys. If you see something you are not sure what to do with, holler for me, and I will let you know where it goes. There is a ton of work to do up there, so try to have lots of fun in the process!"

As he rounded the corner and disappeared down the hallway, the Team looked at the stairs.

Then KP, the second baseman, oldest and most level-headed of the Team, broke the silence. He climbed up the stairs and said, "Let's get it done."

KP had a large frame and a stocky, solid build, which helped him stand his ground on second base. His quiet smile subtly revealed bright silver braces. He was quiet and reserved until required, and then he commanded attention and respect.

Everyone watched, not moving an inch, as KP climbed the stairs and poked his sandy-blonde head into the dark, cave-like attic. He stepped timidly into the pitch-black room. Cautiously, he moved forward two steps, searching for a light. He stumbled over an old pair of shoes. Trying to catch himself before he fell to the floor, he frantically grabbed for something to break his fall. He found the cord to the only light in the room. With a sharp snap, the light flashed on, just as KP fell forward and landed on several old books. Pulling himself to his knees, he scanned the room with his dazzling blue eyes and was instantly amazed at its contents. KP sat staring at a room filled with the coolest stuff he had ever seen.

He frantically yelled to the Team. "Hey, get up here quick. There is great stuff up here. Everybody, come look!"

Broken from their trance, the Team raced up the stairs and found a room full of old treasures. As they scanned the room, they saw paintings, pictures, books, shields, swords, arm bands, odd clothing and farm tools. Red found an old world globe and was determining how fast it could spin on it axis. Bubba draped an amazing old costume robe over his shoulder.

"Why would anyone have all this stuff?" asked Runt.

"Maybe his family owned a costume shop," suggested Red, dressing up in a Native American costume and holding a sword.

"I wonder if his family was in theatre," said Bean, modeling a piece of intricate jewelry.

"You're scaring me, Bean," said Butch, making fun of her modeling attempt.

Butch was not afraid of anything and was very adventurous. His flat-top haircut defined his personality. Anxiously, he opened box after box. Searching for anything peculiar, he said, "I bet we could find some old baseball stuff in here."

Anxious to explore, the Team searched the room, excited that they might find a treasure.

Hero found a picture album and was turning page after page of pictures with people dressed up like characters from the Book of Mormon.

"Hey, everyone come check out these pictures. These are the coolest costumes I have ever seen," Hero hollered to the Team.

Bubba looked at the photos and exclaimed, "There's my robe!" He twirled in a circle, showing off the robe he was still wearing.

Bean moved quickly over to look at the album, and said, "Do you think any of these pictures are real? I mean actual Indians and stuff?"

Hero replied, "I don't know for sure, but these are the closest to real that I've ever seen." He set the book down and moved on to another.

Stick looked around and said, "We better start cleaning. This is a huge job. Besides, I can't find any real jewels or cash anywhere."

"This is going to take us forever," complained Red, as he lost interest in the spinning globe and scanned the attic.

"Well, we gotta do it for Mr. Jensen. We are already here, and he has been really good to us," said Bean. "Let's dig in and get it done."

She rolled up her sleeves and started giving orders. "Butch and Runt, start pulling everything away from the walls. Stick and Red, please start emptying all the boxes." She paused a moment, looked around, took a deep breath, and then continued, "Hero and Bubba, pull down all the pictures. KP, you and Tater carry down all the toys, bicycles, and big stuff."

"You betcha," replied Tater, holding up his arm and flexing his muscles.

Bean smiled sweetly and then rolled her eyes.

Then Runt, wanting to be helpful and always the inventor said, "Let's form an assembly line down the stairs. I bet we can get it done faster that way."

The Team agreed it was a good idea. They easily carried everything down to the room below in three short hours.

"Now, let's just do a quick, final pick up and sweep," said Bean.

As Runt and Butch collected the trash and took it downstairs, Bean finished sweeping the floors. When she bent over to pick up the dustpan, she heard a clanging noise — almost like clothes hangers hitting together.

Startled, she looked around but saw nothing. Hesitantly, she continued. She was almost finished filling the dustpan when she heard the noise again. This time, she scanned the attic anxiously and then asked, "Did anyone hear that?"

KP replied, "Hear what, Bean?"

"I thought I heard something," she replied.

"I didn't hear anything," KP said.

"Me neither," added Tater. "Ya'll must be hearing the rain. I think it's coming down hard again."

"I bet you're right," replied Bean, as she hastily gathered up the broom and dustpan. She scanned the dimly lit room one more time. Then she moved a little closer to Tater for comfort — still a little nervous.

"Let's take one last look for anything we might have missed," she said.

The attic looked great. The job, which originally promised to take all day, had actually only taken a few hours. With nothing more found, they were all about to move down when Bubba tripped over the rug and flew head first toward the wall. Tater, as usual stepped over just in time to cushion Bubba's fall.

"Nice catch, Tater," said Stick, as Bubba picked himself up off the floor. "That fall would have left a mark."

"Hey, something is stuck on my shoe," Bubba said, as he sat down and pulled at it. With a wrinkled nose and an exasperated look, he called to Hero. "This won't budge. I think I might have ruined my shoes. Will you please help me pull this off?" he asked, pointing to the metal pin and wire sticking out of his shoe.

Hero took hold of the wire. With a soft tug in the right direction, the pin easily popped out. "Your shoes are still good," he said.

Hero started winding up the wire to throw it away before they headed downstairs. But as he reached the far wall, the wire seemed to be stuck in the floor. Again he gave it a gentle tug, but nothing happened. Frustrated that the wire would not budge, he gave it a little firmer tug. Then suddenly, he was unexpectedly starring into the black opening of a small vault in the wall.

"Look at this!" Hero said in amazement.

"What is it?" asked Tater.

"I think it might be a secret hiding place," Hero replied excitedly.

"Is there any money in it?" asked Stick.

Hero just looked up at Stick and said, "Come on Stick, give us a break."

Stick just smiled and said, "Today just keeps getting better and better!"

Hero looked up at Stick, shook his head and laughed.

"Maybe it's food storage," Tater, the Team's catcher, said as he bent his Mack-truck body down to look inside the small opening. "Hey, everybody. Wait! There really is something in here."

Red stated the obvious when he said, "Hey look, it's an old box."

"Can you get it out?" asked Hero.

Red quickly took hold of the small box and pulled with all his might, but the box refused to budge.

Embarrassed, Red said, "It is heavy. I think it must be

full of gold."

"Maybe even rubies and diamonds?" wondered Stick, outloud.

Tater chuckled at Red's struggle to move the box and said, "Get out of my way. Let me do it."

Red smiled and moved aside, allowing just enough room for Tater to slide by him.

Tater, big, solid and stocky, reached inside the small vault and pulled at the contents. He has strong, muscular calves, which are the size of tree trunks, and tussled, sandy blonde hair. Tater loves all kinds of food and generally has a hefty supply available for the entire Team.

Tater provides the Team with security and always stands up for the underdog. He is very resourceful and strong. He is often referred to as the gentle giant, because sometimes just a look from Tater will ward off confrontation with other teams.

In a few short seconds, a large brown chest sat in the middle of the room. It had leather hinges, a metal lock that opened with a key and small engravings on the front.

"Take off the lock!" Bubba yelled, excited at the prospect of what might be in the chest.

"Shouldn't we ask Mr. Jensen first?" asked Bean.

"Do you think he even knows this secret vault and box are here?" asked Butch, as he scanned the box for a way to open it.

"I doubt it," replied Runt. "I don't think he would have let us clean the attic if he was hiding stuff."

"I agree," replied Red. "Besides, he has let us sort all of his other stuff. Why wouldn't he let us sort this, too?"

Silent for a moment, Hero finally chimed in and said, "Red is right. I don't think Mr. Jensen would have a problem if we open the box. Does everyone agree?"

Unanimously, the Team agreed.

Tater, being the strongest, used all his strength and pulled on the lock, but it would not open. He rubbed his hands together, clapped twice and took hold of the lock again. He pulled with all his might, straining every muscle in his face and arms, but the lock still would not open. The rest of the Team watched in amazement. Everyone except Bean took turns trying, but as hard as each person tried, the lock would not open.

Stick was getting impatient. "It must be gold! Let's just break it open," he urged.

Butch said, "No, let's pull the hinges off the back."

"Let's just cut a hole in the bottom where no one can see it," Bubba suggested.

"Oh, great idea, Bubba. No one will ever notice that," said Hero sarcastically.

Bubba shrugged his shoulders and smiled. "Just trying to help."

Then Bean, who had been looking carefully at the lock, said, "I can do it. It's easy!"

She pulled a safety pin off her tennis shoe, opened it, and jiggled it into the lock. She twisted it once left and twice to the right and with a little effort, the lock popped open.

"There you go!" she said, pointing to the lock as a very large smile spread across her face.

The rest of the Team moaned and rolled their eyes.

After a few seconds of grief, Bubba said, "Good job, Bean."

Stick, frantic to find money, did not wait for pleasantries. He pulled off the lock and dropped it to the floor, right on Runt's foot. Stick barely noticed Runt hopping around, holding his foot and screaming in pain. He quickly threw open the lid, letting it bang loudly into the backside of the box.

"Stick, slow down buddy," Hero yelled. Be careful! This isn't ours. Runt is hurt and Mr. J. will be up to check to see what we have broken."

To Stick's disappointment, his first glance in the box revealed a few carefully folded old clothes. With a scowl, he quickly threw them aside. Underneath were several old pictures. Frustrated he muttered, "Where are the gold coins?"

Refusing to accept the discouragement creeping into his mind, he quickly moved those things aside, still looking for something of value. Unfortunately, he found nothing — just old jewelry, photos, and an acient Native American feather. Nothing in the box seemed to be of any real value to the Team, especially not to Stick, who reached the bottom and looked up dejectedly.

Hero tried to sound positive. "Well, I guess it is just an old locked box of memorabilia — not any treasures or old gold coins in here. But we did have fun looking."

"Bummer, I thought we might have had something with that secret door," said Bubba.

"Man," said Stick. "I just knew we were going to be rich."

"Why would anyone lock and hide a box full of old junk?" asked Runt, sounding heartbroken.

"It's probably not old junk to Mr. Jensen," responded Bean, disappointed herself.

"I'll bet Mr. Jensen didn't hide this box," said Bubba.

They were carefully placing everything back into the chest when Butch noticed a piece of leather hanging off the back of the lid.

"Hey!" said Butch excitedly. "I think Stick might have knocked something loose when he opened the box."

"What is it? What is it?" yelled Stick eagerly.

Butch carefully picked up the rolled piece of leather. It was yellowed and frayed around the edges. He began to slowly unroll the leather, being careful not to tear it. As he opened it, he noticed that the material was thick — more like animal skin. It was fairly soft with a silky, smooth texture.

"Painters canvas or maybe even treated leather," Butch thought to himself.

It was approximately one-eighth inch thick and had two small holes just to the right of center. It had strange writings all over it. But to the Team's surprise, three words were written in English, and those had been scribbled in below the title. It read:

Moroni's Treasure Map

Their eyes stirred with excitement as they looked around at each other.

"Could this really be a treasure map?" asked Bean.

"I know who Moroni is," said Runt assuredly.

"We all know who Moroni is," said Hero. "We have all heard stories from the Book of Mormon."

"But why is a map about Moroni in Mr. Jensen's attic?" questioned Bubba.

"Could it be real?" asked Runt.

"It looks and feels real to me," responded KP, as he ran his fingers over the map.

"Could this be a map that Moroni actually made?" asked KP.

"It sure would be cool if it was," stated Butch sounding unconvinced.

"After all, he was one of the greatest prophets in ancient times, and he is my favorite hero from the Book of Mormon," said Bubba with a huge smile on his face.

"How could something that old be here in Mr. Jensen's attic?" asked Red.

"This map can't be real. Can it?" asked Bean.

Not exactly sure what to do, the Team stared at the map in silence.

After a few minutes, Stick yelled, "Waaaahooo! We are gonna be rich!"

KP replied, "It's not our map, Stick. What do you mean, we're gonna be rich?"

Butch said, "Well, let's ask Mr. Jensen if we can have it. I don't think at his age he will be out looking for treasure anytime soon!"

"He's not going to let us have it," said Hero.

"Well, let's just ask him," said Bean. "It's worth a try! Maybe he will let us borrow it."

"It's probably just a pretend map. Besides, why do

you think Mr. Jensen would have a real Book of Mormon map with Moroni's name on it?" asked Runt.

"Well, I'm sure I don't know, but it would be fun to look for treasure. We won't be playing ball for a few days," said Bubba. "Let's find us a treasure instead! What if the map really leads to great Book of Mormon stuff? We'd be famous, and that's better than being rich!"

"What a great adventure this could be!" exclaimed Hero.

The Team quickly closed the small secret door and carried the old box and its contents downstairs.

In their haste, the Team had completely missed the small closet in the dark, back corner of the attic where Eddie and Earl were hiding among the old, musty-smelling clothes. They had nearly been discovered.

"What luck," whispered Earl. "We're still safe."

They had been listening intently from inside the closet. When they could no longer hear the kids, Eddie slowly opened the closet door.

"Did you hear that Earl? We're gonna be rich!" he said.

"We don't have that map," said Earl. "And who is this Moroni guy anyway? What kind of treasure would he have?"

"I don't know, but he must have been rich," said Eddie. "I bet those kids learned about him in school. He's probably some great king or something."

"How are we gonna get the map?" asked Earl.

"Were going to follow those kids and take it away," replied Eddie.

"What if that old guy doesn't let them have it?" asked Earl.

"Then it will be really easy to take it from the old man," replied Eddie, trying to concentrate on opening a can of peaches from Mr. J's food storage. "Besides, he will let those kids play with it. And when he does, we will take it from them," he muttered through a mouth full of food.

"How?" asked Earl. "I don't want to get caught and go back to jail."

"We are just going to have to be careful," said Eddie. "Let's go get the map," he said, as he moved slowly toward the stairs.

Earl watched as Eddie started down the stairs. Then he remembered they both were still in their beautiful orange coveralls.

"Wait, Eddie," demanded Earl.

Eddie, afraid he might miss information about the map, turned to Earl and angrily asked, "What?"

Earl stood up and said, "We should find a change of clothes before we go out, don't you think?" as he shook the orange material on his chest.

Eddie looked down and said, "Oh yeah, I forgot. Good catch."

"What are we gonna do?" asked Earl.

"Let's just put on some of this old guy's clothes from the closet. They should work until we can steal something else to wear."

The duo quickly changed from their prison uniforms into Mr. Jensen's old suits.

"What generation do you think these clothes are from?" asked Earl.

"I don't know, but anything is better than prison uniforms."

When they were dressed Eddie again peered down the stairs to see if he could see the Team and the map.

Downstairs, the Team had started taking out the trash. There was a lot of it! They placed all the books on the shelf, sorted and piled the boxes full of miscellaneous stuff, and straightened all the furniture. They were so excited about the treasure map that the work went quickly.

"Do you guys realize what we can do with this treasure?" asked Bubba, lost in contemplation.

"What if we really found it?" asked KP. "What would we really do with it?"

"I know what I would do," said Bean.

"What?" asked Stick.

Bean, excitedly answered the question and said, "I would help the poor. No, I would start some homeless shelters or I would do lots of *Sub for Santa* stuff and help kids. Or… I could think of lots of things to do with it," she said. "If it is money."

"Oh, not me," said Stick. "I'd buy everything I don't have. I think I would build a swimming pool. Maybe, I would have a slide from my bedroom window that went straight into it."

"Come on, guys. Quit dreaming and let's finish so that we can see if there really is a treasure," said Hero.

The Team, still daydreaming about treasure, finished cleaning long before Mr. Jensen expected. Everyone was happy with the finished job.

As Hero walked down the hall to find Mr. Jensen, the smell of canning corn drifted in from the kitchen

"Mr. Jensen?" Hero called.

Excited and anxious to show him the map, the Team waited impatiently. A moment later, Mr. Jensen appeared in the doorway, wiping his hands on a towel.

"Yes?"

"We are done," said Hero.

Mr. Jensen was obviously shocked by the look on his face. He walked quickly down the hall to the Team.

"So, how did it go, Team?" he asked, smiling. "You finished very quickly. I am extremely impressed!"

"Everything is down from upstairs. The attic is all cleaned, swept and dusted," Hero said. "We have sorted everything and have taken out the trash," he said pointing to all of the piles outside.

"Everything else is in organized piles, just like you asked," added Bean.

"Great, Team. Thank You. I appreciate all of your help," Mr. Jensen replied. "Now I am sure you have exciting plans to get to."

Runt nudged Stick and whispered, "Ask him."

"Ask me what?" Did you find something you could use for the Treehouse?" asked Mr. Jensen.

Stick quietly said, "Well, Mr. Jensen, while we were cleaning the attic, we found a secret compartment. And in it, we found this box." He pointed to the small leather chest on the floor.

"Inside of it we found this," Hero said, reaching his arm out and handing Mr. Jensen the map.

Mr. Jensen went white and sat down quickly in an old rocker. He quietly took the map from Hero and studied the leather for a moment. "My goodness," he said, "I remember this from when I was a little boy."

Standing up from the rocker, he walked over to the chest and said, "This chest belonged to my great-grandfather Ole. Where did you find it?"

"It was in a secret compartment in the attic," explained Bubba. "I tripped over a wire that opened a hole in the wall. The chest was hidden inside.

Still studying the map, Mr. Jensen said, "This was my great-grandfather's treasure hunting map. My family thought it had been stolen when I was very young. What an unbelievable discovery! How exciting."

Walking back to the old rocker, Mr. Jensen spent several minutes in silent reflection. He finally said, "You know, there is a very mysterious legend surrounding this map."

Stick perked up and listened intently. "What is it?"

"This map leads to a great treasure left in this valley by the Nephite people. The map was handed down from generation to generation, until it reached my great-grandfather, Ole," he replied.

"Do you know if the treasure had any real value?" asked Stick.

"Well," Mr. Jensen replied. "This treasure was said to be more valuable than anything on the face of the earth."

"How did your family get a Nephite map?" asked Bubba suspiciously. "Could something like that really exist?"

"My grandfather told me it was given to one of my forefathers by a great and noble soldier. The soldier told him to protect this map from those who would seek to destroy or misuse its treasure," he replied.

"Did your family ever try to find the treasure?" asked Runt.

"Yes," replied Mr. Jensen.

"Did they ever find it?" asked Butch, intrigued.

"If they did, I never heard about it," Mr. Jensen replied. "As far as I know, my forefathers kept this map safe until my great-grandfather disappeared seventy-five years ago. I remember, as a little boy, that he always seemed to be going on grand adventures. I always wanted to go with him, but he would never let me. He was very secretive about his trips. I always figured he was out searching for the treasure. One day, he became very suspicious. From then on, he was always looking over his shoulder for someone. He never knew for sure, but he was convinced he was being followed. A few months later, when I was still very young, my great-grandfather disappeared under very mysterious circumstances. We believed he died while trying to keep this map safe," he said, holding up the map, "although we never found his body."

"My father looked for my great-grandfather and this map for fifty years. He died feeling he had missed out on his turn to protect this great treasure. Although my father will not be able to protect the map, I will. You have restored my family's honor. How can I truly thank you, Team?"

The Team looked at each other. It seemed their adventure was over before it had even begun.

"Well, Mr. Jensen. If the map was never stolen and it has been protected all along, then do you think the treasure was ever found?" asked Red.

"Nope, I guess not," replied Mr. Jensen. "No one ever knew what the treasure was for sure, except those that protected it. My great-grandfather would never tell us what he was protecting, other than the map. And no one knew where the map was — until now. As far as I know, this treasure has not been touched since my great-grandfather disappeared over seventy-five years ago."

"Do you think we could use the map to find the treasure?" asked Bubba.

"Well," said Mr. Jensen, "I'm not sure you are old enough to go searching for buried treasure — especially this treasure. My grandfather said it took great knowledge of the gospel and scriptures — especially The Book of Mormon. And you would have to protect this map at all costs — even with your own lives."

He paused and looked sternly at them and then he continued, "You would have to be very, very careful. I have heard that this map has very treacherous obstacles in place to safeguard the treasure. Besides, I'm not sure your parents would appreciate me if I gave you the responsibility of this map."

"We can do it, Mr. Jensen!" shouted the Team.

"I don't know," Mr. Jensen said warily. "This map has been in my family for many generations. I wish that my children lived close by so that they could protect the map. My family has successfully kept this treasure away from those who would seek to destroy it. There are still people out there today who would come after the map if they knew it had been found. How do I know that I can trust you to do what is right with this map?"

"We will be very careful, and we won't tell anyone about the map or the treasure. We will do the right thing. Besides, those people who wanted this map years ago believe that it no longer exists," said Bean. "They wouldn't even know we have it."

"We are all trustworthy," said Hero.

"I never knew exactly what the treasure was, only that a lot of good could be done with it," said Mr. Jensen. "I really don't know if it is gold and riches, or something else of greater value and importance than worldly treasures. If you find the treasure, whatever it is, you must all promise that it would only be used for good."

"We will! We promise!" shouted the Team.

"If we find one," countered Red.

"Well then," said Mr. Jensen, "I hope the map leads to a big treasure — one that can be used to help build the Kingdom of God. Work together as a Team like you did here today, and I am sure you will not have any problems locating the treasure."

He handed Hero the map.

"We won't disappoint you," said Bubba, as the Team raced out of the house, excitedly anticipating the adventure to come.

Being the last out of the house Tater yelled, "Thanks, Mr. Jensen! We will let you know what we find."

The Team ran out into the pouring rain, grabbed their bikes, and raced toward the Treehouse. Mr. Jensen watched from his porch and whispered, "Watch over and protect them, Ole."

Eddie and Earl watched through the tiny attic window as the Team rode up the dirt road and disappeared. Earl cautiously followed Eddie down out of the attic, tiptoeing and maneuvering through the house, carefully watching to make sure Mr. Jensen did not notice them.

"Why don't we climb back out of the attic window to follow those kids?" asked Earl, afraid of being seen.

"'Cuz, I'm hungry," snapped Eddie. "I've got to eat something before we follow them, or I'm gonna pass out from starvation."

"We should be able to follow their tracks in the mud, right?" asked Earl.

"As long as they stay on the shoulder of the road,"

said Eddie. "We need to hurry. I don't want to lose them."

Eddie and Earl slithered slowly into the kitchen, grabbing a loaf of bread and the peanut butter on the counter. They slipped out the back door, ready to find the Team and steal the map.

"How do we avoid the cops?" asked Earl, as he stuffed a piece of bread into his mouth.

"We'll stay in the trees and bushes," replied Eddie. "Hurry. I don't want to lose that map. It's our ticket to treasure."

Carefully sneaking through the trees, the duo remained hidden while they searched for the Team's bicycle tracks. Listening for helicopters and police cars, the duo hurried to catch up to the Team. Eddie was determined to get the treasure — no matter what.

Earl followed as usual, expecting at any minute to be captured again.

Chapter Four

As the Team rode in the rain back to the Treehouse, the wind started to blow the leaves in the trees above them. The noise was almost frightening. They peddled faster as the wind blew stronger. The Team felt as though they were never going to make it home.

Tater screamed into the wind, "I'm peddling so hard, I'm not sure if I'm soaked from the rain or my sweat!"

Nervous about the strength of the storm, Hero pointed to a small barn at Mr. Cahoon's farm and the Team gratefully followed him to the safety of the shelter.

Exhausted from the treacherous ride, they quickly got off their bikes and sat down.

"How scary," said Bean, "I've never seen rain like this."

"Scary nothing. You guys, I am really hungry. I reckon I'm going to starve to death," said Tater.

Hero replied, "Tater, don't you have all the snacks in your backpack?"

Tater frowned. "I already ate them all."

"What?" said KP. "I was hoping for a snack."

Everyone chuckled. "I have a granola bar, Tater," said Bubba. "Will that work?"

Tater grinned and nodded. He carefully broke the granola bar into two pieces and handed one to KP.

As they ate, the rest of the Team talked about the treasure they might find. Ten minutes passed before the rain calmed down enough that the Team could head for home.

Frantically looking for bike tracks, Eddie and Earl crept through the streets of town. Earl was lying in the wet, muddy weeds on the side of the road when he noticed the Team coming out of the barn.

"There they are," he said, smacking Eddie on the shoulder.

"Where?" barked Eddie.

"There," Earl pointed. Do you see them?" he asked.

Eddie spotted them and smiled. "Oh boy! We are back in the money again!" he exclaimed.

As the Team reached the Treehouse, they jumped off their bikes and raced toward the privacy of their club.

Tater, being the strongest, held the ladder so that it did

not sway. One by one, the Team carefully climbed up to the main room of the Treehouse. Tater climbed up last. When he reached the top, he pulled the ladder up so no one could sneak in on them. The map was definitely top secret and the Team wanted to keep it that way. Hero's little sister, Squeaks, was notorious for somehow learning exactly what the Team was doing. She always knew their plans.

"I want no surprises this time," Tater thought.

Not worrying about their soaked clothes, they quickly found their seats at the table. Hero cautiously pulled the map from his front coat pocket, where he had placed it for safety. His chest was the only part of his body that had not been soaked from the rain. He opened the map carefully and laid it on the table. The Team hovered over the table, straining to see if they recognized anything.

The top of the map was titled, "Moroni's Treasure Map". Those were the only words on the map written in English. They had been written in blue ink. Just below and to the left of the title sat mountain cliffs. A small stream meandered slowly around the curves of the cliffs from east to west. However, a section of the stream seemed to be missing. On the right side of the map were three distinct lines, which seemed to cut into the foothills of the mountain. An enormous tree was centered on the map. The tree was the most prominent feature.

As they scanned further down to the bottom of the map, the Team saw several large boulders that formed a ridge. Beyond and to the left of the ridge was a large wooded area with small lakes or ponds scattered throughout. Criss-crossing the map were faint blue, dotted lines running north to south and east to west, written in the same hand as the title. On several parts of the map were small diamond shapes with hieroglyphs inside each one. Each symbol inside the diamond faced a different direction, as if to look at or point to something. Just to the right of the tree were dozens of small domes, which resembled beehives. And at the bottom right corner was a small legend that had a few recognizable symbols — dashes for trails, triangles that signified the mountainous areas and a pale yellow line that represented some sort of route. The rest of the legend was written in strange symbols the Team had never before seen.

As they turned the map over, the Team saw two paragraphs of writing, which they hoped were clues. But they were also written in strange symbols.

Red ruffled his fingers through his hair and said, "How are we going to find the treasure if we can't even read the writing? It looks like something from an Egyptian Pyramid."

"Don't worry, Red. I'm sure we can figure it out," replied Bean.

The Team studied the map longer, hoping for more clues. Maybe they would recognize something from the area. But nothing seemed to fit.

Frustrated, KP picked up the map off the table to have a closer look. "I wonder if these two holes mean anything," he said. Several minutes later, he had an idea.

"Look, I think if you fold down the top left corner of the map, the markings on the back complete the stream on the front. That stream looks like the one that flows past the church and into Kimball Creek. It looks to be about the length of the creek that runs by the cliffs."

"Hey, I think you are right," replied Red. "We have walked that stream many times, but I don't remember a treasure over there anywhere."

"Well, the treasure wouldn't just be lying out in the open where you could find it easily," replied KP.

"I wonder if we have ever seen it and just missed it?" questioned Runt.

"Let's go see if we can find it ya'll!" squeaked Tater, ready for an adventure.

"Hang on. We don't even know where we are going. We have to figure out a way to translate these words so that we know we are heading in the right direction," said Hero. "We don't want to get ahead of ourselves."

"You're right," replied Bubba, mirroring Hero's worried look. "Let's make sure we start at the right spot."

"We don't even know if this map has anything to do with this area," said Butch.

"Mr. Jensen thought that the map's treasure was around here somewhere," said KP.

"Well, it only makes sense that the map is an ancient drawing of this area," declared Hero. "Otherwise Mr. Jensen never would have known about his great-grandfather's adventures."

"I think we should assume that we are in the right area, and start to search for the treasure," insisted Bubba.

"We possibly found the creek by the cliffs. Are there any more landmarks we recognize that work together with the creek?" asked Bean, still excited.

"Lay that map back down here, KP," said Red. "I want to figure this out."

KP placed the map back on the table with the corner folded in so the Team could continue to study the details. They stared at the map for along time, but they found no additional clues. The Team was so intent on finding another clue that no one even noticed the torrential rain outside.

As they were studying the map, Butch asked, "Are there any old Nephite maps in The Book of Mormon that might give us some more clues to this map?"

Hero shrugged his shoulders and said, "I don't think so. Bubba, go grab your scriptures. Let's check it out."

Suddenly, a loud buzz made everyone jump. Bubba, in fact, was so surprised by the noise, that he fell right off his chair. The Team laughed as they watched him stand up and dust off his pants.

"You're always good for a laugh, Bubba," chuckled Hero.

He answered the Team's walkie-talkie, still laughing at Bubba. "What's up, Mom?"

"Mom said to tell you dinner is ready," Hero's little sister, Squeaks, giggled.

"Great!" yelled Tater, "I'm starved."

"When aren't you starved, Tater?" asked Bean.

Tater just shrugged and smiled like a big teddy bear.

"We might have better luck finding more clues on the map if our stomachs stopped growling," said Bean.

"I reckon we might be able to think better, too," said Tater, holding his stomach.

"Tell Mom we will be right down," replied Hero into the walkie-talkie.

Runt tucked the map inside his shirt and covered it

with his hand to keep it dry.

Still laughing at Bubba, they climbed down the ladder. They headed inside, running quickly through the pouring rain. The Team grabbed sloppy joes and chips and sat around the kitchen table. Runt placed the map in the middle of the table and was about to take a big bite.

"AHEM," Mom said. "A prayer would be appropriate first."

Runt quickly took the sloppy joe out of his mouth and said, "Sorry, I almost ate some."

Squeaks, as always, raised her hand high in the air, shaking it back and forth anxiously because she wanted to say the prayer. The Team, excited for her to say it fast, quickly got ready.

Squeaks said what must have been the longest prayer she had ever offered, and finally ended with, "Help the Team to find Moroni's Treasure, and have them take me, too."

Hero's eyes shot a dagger at Squeaks. "How in the world does she keep finding out about our secrets?" he whispered to Bubba.

The rest of the Team sat there with their mouths hanging open. How did she always seem to know about their secrets?

KP asked Tater, "You pulled up the ladder, didn't you?"

Tater, looking baffled as well, replied through a mouth full of food, "I did pull up the ladder. I promise I did!"

The Team all looked at Squeaks. She had sauce dripping down her grinning face. She quietly went on eating her sloppy joe. The Team, hoping Mom had not heard her, ate as though they did not hear what she had said. They finished eating while they continued to stare at the map.

After several long, quiet minutes, Hero's mom asked, "So, what are you looking at? Is this the 'Moroni's Treasure Map' Squeaks told me about?"

Hero replied, "Mom, how is Squeaks getting up into the Treehouse? We had the ladder pulled up and everything?" he added, hoping to avoid her question about the map.

"Don't worry about her; she can't do much harm. Now tell me about this map, Team," insisted Mom.

"Oh, it's just an old treasure map that Mr. Jensen gave us. We think it has something to do with The Book of Mormon back in ancient times. We are going to go treasure hunting tomorrow. Is that okay with you?" Hero rambled as he handed her the map.

Hero's mom looked at the map for a minute. "Mr. Jensen gave this to you?"

The Team all nodded.

"Are you sure?" she questioned.

"Yes, we can have it." Bubba replied. "He told us all about his family and everything. We just have to take care of it and keep it safe."

"What does it have to do with the Book of Mormon?" asked Mom.

"We don't know for sure yet. That's what we are going to try and figure out," replied Hero.

"Yeah, but it's kinda hard 'cause we can't read any of the writing," interjected Bubba. "You don't happen to know any Egyptian, do ya, Mom?"

"No, I sure don't. Sorry," Mom replied.

"Do you think it would be okay, Mrs. M, if we go on a search for treasure?" asked Runt.

"Well, I guess it would be all right – with, of course, a few restrictions," said Mom smiling.

"What restrictions, Mom?" asked Hero.

"Don't leave town without talking to me first. Be careful not to go anywhere that might be dangerous. Stay together, and no scary stuff. Is that clear?" Mom said firmly. "I don't want anyone getting hurt."

She set the map back down in the middle of the table and continued, "Make sure everyone gets parents' permission before you go. And keep your walkie-talkie with you at all times in case of emergency. I always want to be able to get a hold of you. Okay?"

The Team nodded in agreement to her restrictions.

Bubba asked, "Mom, do you recognize anything on this map? It is supposed to be an old map of this area."

Mom again picked up the map and said, "I'll bet the boulders on the map are from the ridge."

The Team looked up at her inquisitively and Hero asked, "Where, Mom?"

"Ghoul's Gulch," she answered. "You know, where you always go for Scouts?"

"I know that area," replied Runt. "I'll bet you're right."

"There are tons of big rocks over there," said Stick.

"I think they are just about the same shape," Mom said, as she pointed to the map.

"Yeah, and they are over next to the mountains by Mr. Cahoon's farm. Right?" asked Bean.

"Yep. That is the ridge, or Ghoul's Gulch as you know it." Mom replied. "And Bubba, I am not as old as that map," said Mom with a grin.

Bubba smiled at Mom.

"Mr. Cahoon's farm — you mean the police officer?" asked Butch.

"No," replied Mom. "I mean the police officer's dad."

"Where that old barn is?" asked Red.

"Yes, that's the one. Now remember what I said, Team — everyone get permission, and be extremely careful. Old maps can be fun, but they can also be very dangerous. Do you all understand?"

The Team again nodded as Mom set down the map and walked into the kitchen.

"Can anyone figure out what those lines are?" Hero asked.

"It could be some sort of ladder to the top of the mountain," said Stick.

"Yeah, but it looks like it goes straight through the mountain," said Tater.

"Well, it couldn't be train tracks," said Butch. "There aren't any trains around here!"

"How old do you think this map is?" asked Bean.

Everyone thought a minute. Then Bubba answered, "Well, if it's been handed down for generations, it has to be hundreds of years old, right?"

"That makes sense to me!" stated Red nodding.

"There are clues written on the map, too. If we could only read what they say, I bet we could figure out how to find the treasure," said KP.

"Yeah, but they look like ancient Egyptian," said Runt.

"Do we know anyone who can read ancient Egyptian?" asked Butch.

The Team pondered for a moment, trying to remember if any of their Primary teachers or Sunday School teachers might know how. But no one could think of anyone.

"Do you think the library would have any old maps of town?" asked Butch.

"Or maybe even a book on how to read Egyptian?" suggested Hero.

"Maybe we should go there and see if we can find anything that might help!" said Bean excitedly.

"Great idea. Maybe if we find a book, we can decipher the writing ourselves," said Hero. "Everyone grab your bikes and let's go. Hurry, the library closes in about an hour."

"Mom, is that okay?" asked Bubba.

Mom smiled and said, "Only if you clear your plates."

The Team hurried back to the table, cleared their plates and yelled, "Thanks, Mrs. M."

Tater, who was half way through his second sloppy joe, moaned. "I'm not done eatin'. Can't we go in a few minutes?"

The Team ignored him and ran out the front door, excited to find more clues. Tater grabbed another roll, stuffed it into his pocket, and yelled, "Wait for me!"

The library was only a few blocks away, down the main street of town. They had taken this route to the library hundreds of times. This time with their minds on treasure, they did not notice the wind blowing or Eddie and Earl following closely behind them.

They headed north into town, waving at everyone in the retirement home on the west side of the street as they always did. They passed the post office, flower shop, cemetery, Timber Creek City Hall, theatre, Glenview Feed and Supply, the neighborhood mercantile store on the east side of the street and finally reached the library.

The library had previously been an elementary school building, and then City Hall, before it became the library many years ago. The building was so old, its bricks had started to crumble and the exterior looked very run down. The date "1902" was engraved on the cement just outside the front door.

The library was surprisingly large, with a small room in front and several larger rooms off either side of the hallway. It usually smelled of mildew, and it was always cold. The Team felt damp, sticky and sweaty every time they visited, but the library always seemed to have exactly what they needed.

As the Team swiftly pulled up to the bike rack, they parked their bikes, locked them up, and ran to the door. Tater, shoving his last bite of sloppy joe in his mouth, was just pulling up as the rest of the Team ran inside.

The Team found the librarian, Cheri, at the information desk.

"Good evening, Team," she said. "What can I do for you today?" She was about seventy years old with long, silvery white hair worn up in a bun. She had weathered, olive skin and pale hazel eyes. Hero thought she looked like a skinny, loveable Mrs. Santa Claus.

"Cheri, where can we find the oldest known maps of

the area?" asked Hero.

Cheri looked over the top of her glasses, studied them intently, and took a deep breath. Puckering her lips and thinking for a moment, she said, "Let me see what I can do. Give me a minute."

She smiled, emphasizing her rosy, red checks, turned and quietly hushed the panting Tater who had just caught up with the Team. Then she disappeared down one of the aisles. The Team waited anxiously for nearly fifteen minutes.

"I wonder if she's gotten lost?" Red whispered.

"No, she's forgotten what she is doing," said Bubba.

They all laughed. Then Bean said, "Relax. Give her a few more minutes."

"She asked for one!" said Butch, impatiently.

After another five minutes passed, Cheri poked her head around the corner of the mystery aisle and said, "Follow me, Team. I think I found what you are looking for."

Eagerly, the Team followed her to a private area in the back of the library where a map lay on a long narrow banquet table.

"This is the only map of this kind," she said, smiling. "I believe this is the oldest map of the town. Be very careful with it. If you need anything else, please don't hesitate to ask. And please don't forget to check the map in at the front desk before you leave."

The Team thanked Cheri and sat down around the table. Remembering Mr. Jensen's cautions, Hero asked Tater and KP to stand guard and watch for anything suspicious. Then he set the treasure map to the right of the town map and the maps from the Book of Mormon to the left.

The Team started to compare the maps. They located what they thought was the big tree, the stream, as well as Ghoul's Gulch, or the ridge that Hero's mom had shown them. And then there it was — on the library map too — the three lines in the mountain.

"Well, those lines are on the treasure map and library map, but not on any of the Book of Mormon maps," stated Stick.

"If you really think about it, nothing will cross over with the maps in the Book of Mormon," stated Bean.

"Why is that?" asked Runt inquisitively.

"Because, the Book of Mormon was written before this map was made. All the Book of Mormon maps and events correlate to events prior to our treasure map," she replied.

"I hadn't thought about that," said Hero. "I'll bet you're right. I guess we better just use the other two maps."

"What do you think those lines are?" asked Butch. "They can't be train tracks, they are on the side of the mountain."

"Besides that, trains didn't exist back then," said Runt.

"Maybe we should ask Cheri," said Tater, no longer providing security, but now intently studying the map.

KP, who was still standing guard asked, "Should I get her?"

"It can't hurt," said Hero, as he hid the treasure map. KP quickly returned with the librarian.

"Do you happen to know what these lines are on the map?" asked Hero, pointing to the town map.

The librarian looked at the lines and smiled, "Yes.

These are the old Native American hieroglyphs up on the Skarpal Mountains. The area used to be a state park and monument. However, the state closed the area years ago due to vandalism. The lines look like a ladder on the mountain because each plateau has been cut into the side of the mountain by an ancient civilization. They are very interesting. If the state ever re-opens the hieroglyphs, I'd bet you would all like them. They were really neat to try to read until the area was closed," Cheri said excitingly.

"Could you tell what the writing said?" asked Bubba inquisitively.

"I tried to read them once before the ruins were closed, but the words seemed to be written in some form of ancient Egyptian. I was not familiar with that exact dialect."

"How did you learn to read it?" interrupted Red.

"I was the Egyptology professor of comparative ancient history of the Timber Creek Archaeological Institute for several years," Cheri replied.

"What does that mean?" asked Runt, completely bewildered at her response.

"Well, in short, I studied the history, language and culture of ancient Egypt for a while," Cheri said.

"Cool. Did you ever find any mummies?" asked Bubba, intrigued at her previous job.

"I was in Egypt when several mummies were excavated," Cheri replied. "I was the expert they called in to translate the writings on the tombs."

"You have got to be kidding," blurted Butch. "I think that is so great."

"Do you know a lot about Egyptian writing then?" quizzed Bubba curiously.

"I sure do. But I'm not as good at it now as I used to be," replied Cheri. "I can generally decipher enough to get the meaning of most writings, but I was never exactly sure what the writings at the state park said. I believe some of the writing talked about a treasure and some of danger, but I can't really remember anymore. I am getting older and my memory just isn't what it used to be."

Bubba, now convinced that she might be able to help them decipher the clues on the map, hastily looked at the Team and said, "We can trust her!"

Hero looked at Bubba with eyes as big as golf balls, cleared his throat and then turned to the Team and said, "Well?"

The Team nodded nervously. So Hero apprehensively pulled out the map,

"Do you think you could translate these writings for us?" he asked, as he laid the map on the table.

The librarian, instantly intrigued, sat down at the table. She pulled her glasses down from the top of her head, put them on and asked in an inquisitive voice, "So, what do we have here?"

"The Team is on a treasure hunt," explained Hero, "but we can't read the writings on the map."

"The map is top secret," warned Red, covering it with his hands. "So you wouldn't be able to tell anyone about it."

Cheri smiled, put her hand across her heart and said, "On my honor, I won't tell a soul. I promise."

Satisfied, Red slowly pulled his hands away.

Again the librarian carefully picked up the map and started to translate the first clue. KP grabbed paper and a pen, ready to write down every word she said.

The librarian quietly looked over the map and mumbled under her breath. She glanced up several times with a very puzzled expression. Then she would look down again, keeping the Team on pins and needles. She finally looked up and curiously asked, "Is this a real Book of Mormon map?"

Hero, surprised that she knew about The Book of Mormon, took the map from her and said, "Yes. We have been told this map relates directly to the Book of Mormon, but we really haven't figured out how yet," he replied.

Shaking her head, Cheri said, "I can't believe this. Moroni was the last prophet to have The Book of Mormon. I bet he left a great treasure behind," she said, trying to play along with the Team's enthusiasm.

"What does the writing mean? Does it tell us where the treasure is?" asked Butch impatiently.

"Well, the symbols are a clue, and the clue seems to be made up of scriptural references. The scripture must contain a piece of information that helps you to locate the next clue. Without the information from the scriptural reference, this clue is incomplete. But, I can translate most of what is here and help you locate the reference that goes along with it," said Cheri sweetly.

KP, still ready with paper and pen, wrote down every word.

Everyone was so interested in what Cheri was saying that no one even noticed Eddie and Earl hiding behind the book cart. Pretending to look at books, they were only interested in the information Cheri was giving to the Team.

"Can you hear what she is saying?" asked Eddie.

"Not really," replied Earl.

"Then how are we gonna get there before those kids?" muttered Eddie.

"We could just follow them and take whatever they find," suggested Earl.

As he strained to hear, Eddie said, "We should just follow the Team. They can do all of the work, and we will just take the treasure from them when they find it! What do you think?" he asked with a big smile.

Earl shook his head, "Great idea, Eddie," he said dryly.

The librarian meticulously translated almost every word on the map. Stick was so excited to begin the treasure hunt, he surprised everyone by giving the librarian a quick hug as she finished with the last part of the clue.

She finished just in time; the lights had flashed several times signifying that the library was now closing. The Team thanked Cheri for all of her help. Stick reminded her that she had promised not to tell anyone about the existence of the map. She reassured them with a nod of the head, and then smiled as they raced toward the door.

Nervous and excited, the Team quickly unlocked

their bikes and headed back through town toward the neighborhood.

Once back at the Treehouse, Hero said, "Everyone needs to head for home and get a good night's sleep."

"Yeah, We need to be ready for a full day of treasure hunting tomorrow!" said Stick.

"Okay, here are your assignments for tomorrow: KP, bring a rope; each of you bring a flashlight; Stick, bring a first aid and snake bite kit; Butch, bring extra water; Bubba, bring copies of all the maps of the area; Red and Runt, bring collapsible shovels; Bean, bring a Swiss army knife and compass; and Tater, you be in charge of the snacks for the Team. I will bring my Book of Mormon and hold the treasure map for safekeeping. Also, be careful not to tell anyone about the map or what we have already discovered," finished Hero.

Everyone left, excited for the adventure that lay ahead.

Chapter Five

The next morning, the Team met back at the Treehouse with permission from their parents for a fun-filled day of treasure hunting.

Eddie and Earl listened intently from their new hiding place at the top of the Treehouse. The Treehouse was a great place to hide. Not only did the Team not notice them, but the leaves and branches hid the fugitives and had offered shelter from the rain during the night. The Treehouse even provided food for them. While Eddie searched for the map, he ran across Tater's secret snack stash. The duo had enough food to last them three days. Had it not been for the howling wind, the fugitives would have had a great night's sleep.

The Team gathered around the table in the Treehouse, and Hero pulled out the notes KP had written from the librarian's translation the night before.

Tater quickly checked that Squeaks was not hiding anywhere inside. "I think all is clear," he said. "But you never know for sure with that girl."

"Come on. Let's start anyway. Everyone listen," Hero said. "According to Cheri, this first part was not the clue — maybe just important instructions," he said.

Then he began reading:

> "'They who go forth with the will of the Lord,
> Take only one plain key with no reason for more.
> If you follow Him with His will on your mind,
> Your reward will be His treasure, you won't
> fall behind.'"

Hero continued, "Now here is what the librarian said was the first clue,

> "'Clue number one:
>
> Enos, chapter one, verse fifteen.
> Heading down rocky trails isn't all fun.
> The water runs warm in the hot summer sun.
> Dig up the sand and also the rocks.
> Do it where the X marks the spot.'"

"What in the world does that mean? The clue doesn't even rhyme. Aren't clues supposed to rhyme?" asked Red.

"It doesn't rhyme because one of the lines in the clue is replaced with a scripture reference and because it's a translation," said Hero.

"So then, how do we find the clue?" asked Red.

Bean looked at Red, shook her head and said, "Red, we have to find what is missing out of the clue in the scripture reference! Then we will be able to find it."

"Well, in the clue, what do we know for sure?" asked Bubba.

"We know for sure where the water is, and we know the area must be rocky," said Hero. "Look at the map. The stream is west, right?"

"Yes, but where on the stream?" asked Bean. "It's a long stream."

"We need to look up the reference in The Book of Mormon. That will help us," concluded Runt.

Hero pulled out his Book of Mormon and turned to Enos 1:15. He read, "'Wherefore, I knowing that the Lord God was able to preserve our records, I cried unto him continually, for he said unto me: Whatsoever thing ye shall ask in faith, believing that ye shall receive in the name of Christ, ye shall receive it.'"

"How could that fill in the blank? I have no idea how that refers to the clue," protested Tater. "This is not going to be as easy as I thought."

"We need to carefully review the scripture's meaning. That's what will help us," said Bean. "Did you think this would be a cake walk?"

The Team read the clue and scripture reference again.

"Well," said KP, ready to get moving, "instead of reading it over and over, let's get started and head toward water! At least we will be on our way to a clue. We can figure out what to do on our way."

The Team carried their supplies down out of the Treehouse and loaded up their bikes with their backpacks full of treasure hunting gear. Then they told Hero's mom they were on their way to find Moroni's treasure.

"Be home by six o'clock. Don't lose your walkie-talkie, and don't forget to check in every few hours. Have fun! Hope you find a great treasure," Mom said. "Oh, and be careful," she hollered as the Team jumped on their bikes and set off on their journey. "There was a prison escape a few days ago, so don't talk to any strangers," she yelled after them.

But, before they had even made their way down the driveway, Tater hollered, "STOP! Wait a minute ya'll! I forgot something. I'll be right back."

He jumped off his bike and ran back to the Treehouse. Eddie and Earl were nearly to the ladder when Tater began climbing.

"Hide, Earl. Hide!" whispered Eddie frantically.

Both men scrambled back up the tree to hide in the branches. Tater quickly grabbed a bag from the table and shoved it into his backpack. Then he ran to his secret hiding spot for his stash of snacks, but they were nowhere to be found.

"I am really going to get Squeaks this time!" muttered Tater. "She's got to be hiding them somewhere in here."

Unable to find his snacks, he took a quick look around the Treehouse, thinking he had heard voices.

"Where are you, Squeaks?" he whispered. With no response he said, "I'm going to find your hiding spot." Still there was no reply. He shook his head, shrugged his shoulders and swiftly returned to his bike and the waiting Team.

"Ready," he said, as he picked up his blue Schwinn bike with its yellow banana-seat.

"What did you forget?" questioned Red.

"Only the most important stuff — the food!" he replied seriously. "But I think Squeaks got the good snacks. I couldn't find my secret stash anywhere."

Everyone laughed, and KP said, "Let's go!"

Peddling down the street, everyone considered what the clue and scripture reference might mean. Bean was stuck on the scripture reference, trying to figure out what it really meant. She knew that it had to be the solution. She continued to ponder how it might help as Butch and KP discussed the rest of the clue.

They were still heading toward the stream when Butch said, "Everything could have changed in the valley since that map was drawn. How do we even know that we are headed to the right area of water?"

"Everything could be changed," said KP. "But what kind of adventure will we have if we don't try? You are always the one who keeps the Team excited, Butch. Come on. We can do this."

"Besides, this was written in olden days. We must know more than they did," concluded Red. "We do live in the twenty-first century."

They were only a few blocks away from the stream

when Bubba, who had been very quiet during the bike ride said, "Hey! I have an idea. The rocky trail in the clue could be the cliffs over by the church. They are steep and rocky and lead down to the sandy part of the stream."

"Yeah, I bet you're right. I forgot about the cliffs," said KP.

"And the trails to the water," said Butch. "Let's try there."

The Team changed their direction and peddled faster toward the church and the cliffs.

"What a great idea!" yelled Hero, who had taken the lead and pulled ahead of the Team. He really wanted to find the first clue.

As the Team reached the cliffs, Hero got out the map and said, "Well, where to from here?"

Bean studied the map carefully and asked, "What are all those dashes — almost faint lines?"

"Those are longitude and latitude lines," replied Hero, abruptly.

"Who would have put those on the map?" Bean asked.

"I don't know, but I bet it was Ole. The lines are faint, but they are definitely blue," replied Hero holding the map close to his face and squinting his eyes to focus.

"Well then, what would Timber Creek's numbers be on the map?" she asked.

Hero and KP studied the numbers for a minute and then in unison replied, "About one hundred fifteen."

"Come on already! Let's get going!" Red yelled.

"Everyone, grab your packs and leave your bikes. Be very careful; these cliffs are extremely dangerous," warned Hero.

Carefully, everyone started down the side of the mountain called The Cliffs. The terrain was rocky and covered with dense scrub oak. Five-foot tall weeds between the scrub oak trees made it difficult to see what lay ahead.

Everyone was doing great until Stick spotted a snake on the trail. He instantly froze with fear and squealed at the top of his lungs, startling everyone. The snake paused, lifted his head to see where the noise came from, and quickly coiled.

"Stick, are you okay? What's wrong?" yelled Bubba.

"There's a snake! There's a ten-foot long snake!" yelled Stick, pointing frantically toward the ground.

Runt, the neighborhood snake expert, walked toward Stick and said, "Well, it looks like a garter snake. Let's not mess with that one, Stick," Runt chuckled as he turned around, now laughing out loud. "Even Squeaks knows that garter snakes are not dangerous," he said.

"Stick," said Bubba; "just slowly move off the trail a couple of steps and walk around the snake."

"I can't do it. What if the snake comes after me?" Stick asked, his voice trembling.

"Come on, Stick. You can do it. Just carefully move around the snake," reassured Bubba.

Stick listened to Bubba and cautiously took several baby steps off the trail, shuffling his feet as he moved quickly and quietly. As soon as he passed the tail of the snake, he ran as fast as he could, screaming and waving his arms wildly.

He ran right into Runt, who was not expecting the collision. Runt started to slip on the rocks, and instinctively grabbed Stick's shirt. Both boys fell backwards down the mountain, sliding on the slippery, wet, small shale rocks. The boys tried desperately to catch their footing before they slid off the edge of the cliffs.

They slid directly into Bubba and Bean who were just ahead of them on the trail, which caused all of them to start sliding. Bean slid off to the left of the path, losing her footing enough to fall on her backside. The other three were lucky enough to collide with Tater, who held his ground and stopped them from continuing on a deadly course to the bottom of the cliffs.

"Careful," Tater said. "I reckon those jagged rocks down at the bottom will hurt you if you hit them."

"Good catch," said Bean, as she dusted herself off and checked for tears in her clothes.

"Thanks, man," mumbled Bubba, Runt and Stick as the Team continued down the hill.

When they reached the bottom, Bean, the Team's mother-hen asked, "Everyone make it down safe?"

"Thanks to Tater and his strength," said Runt, glaring at Stick.

The Team headed down stream about three hundred yards. No one even noticed Eddie and Earl crawling on their hands and knees through the weeds and shrubs, watching the Team.

Eddie leaned over to Earl and whispered, "This is going to be easier than I thought. Let's let those kids do all the work!"

"Good idea," replied Earl. "Let's just take the treasure away from them after they find it!"

"No one, not even the cops will know that it was us. They all think we are long gone by now!" said Eddie.

"The Warden wouldn't even think that we headed toward town," said Earl reassuringly.

The Team continued to follow the path a few yards further. The stream meandered back and forth, and then flowed into a small pond filled with rocks and sand, before continuing on further around the mountain. They followed the path down from the cliffs, crossed the pond on round, rock stepping-stones and continued on to the west.

As the Team reached the pond, Hero pulled out his Book of Mormon and said, "Before we can go any further, we have to decide which way to go."

"Let's read the clue again. I can't remember the exact words," said Butch.

Bubba pulled out the paper and read:

"'Enos 1:15.
Heading down rocky trails isn't all fun.
The water runs warm in the hot summer sun.
Dig up the sand and also the rocks.
Do it where the X marks the spot.'"

The Team listened for anything that might give them a clue. Again, Enos chapter one, verse fifteen did not seem to give them any direction.

Red picked up his shovel. He decided on a good spot and started digging. The rest of the Team sat on the shore contemplating their next move, content to watch Red dig while they tried to find the actual location of the next clue.

Bean again asked, "What do those lines do? I've never had to use them before."

KP answered, "They give specific information as to location on the earth, okay?"

Somewhat appeased, but still not quite satisfied, Bean kept thinking. Everyone else sat motionless, looking at the map and reading the verse over and over.

Close to thirty minutes had passed when Runt said, "Maybe this is just too hard. Look, Red has dug three holes already and all he's found are tin cans and rocks!"

"At least he is doing something," replied Butch sharply.

"Come on, Team," Hero said. "We have just barely started. We wouldn't give up on a game this quickly. There are nine innings in the game and we're not even to the bottom of the first yet. We can do it. Let's concentrate on finding the answer to the clue."

"I don't think Mr. Jensen would have given us this map if he thought we would give up this easy," added Bubba.

"What would our current location be on the map if we used the lines?" asked Bean.

"Are you still fixed on those lines?" asked Stick. "How could they possibly help us?"

Bubba, knowing Bean well, could see that she had an idea. "What is it Bean?" he asked curiously.

"What would our location be on the map? Is it possible that we are at one, fifteen?" she asked, not knowing exactly how to read the lines.

Hero and KP took the map and located their position. Hero then told her they were approximately at longitude line one hundred fifteen, not one, fifteen.

Bubba, convinced that Bean might be on to something asked, "What is the scriptural reference again?"

Runt replied, "Enos, chapter one, verse fifteen."

As Bubba pondered what Runt had just said, a light came on in his head. He said, "Bean, I think you might have figured it out."

Bean replied, "Are you thinking what I'm thinking?"

"Well, I think so," answered Bubba.

Runt, annoyed, said, "Kindly let us in on your little secret!"

"Hero, can I see the map?" asked Bean. She told the Team, including Red, who was now on his sixth hole, to watch. She laid the map on the ground, located the longitude line that crossed through the area they were searching and said, "Here is line one hundred fifteen. It runs right across the cliffs and then directly crosses the stream. Where the line crosses the stream an X forms, leaving us with a location to dig for treasure."

"That is a good idea, except for one thing," replied Tater in a snooty voice. "Nowhere in the clue does it tell us to follow the longitude line down across the stream."

"Yes, but the scripture reference does," Bean replied.

"Where?" asked Runt, while he furiously re-read the scripture.

Bean took the scriptures and pointed. "See, we are looking at chapter one, verse fifteen and the numbers: one, one, five."

The Team stared in awe, and Butch said, "We have been searching the words, and all along we only needed the numbers."

"Ole also left a clue when he drew the lines on the map," said Bean.

"You are so smart, Bean," said Hero.

"Let's dig up the treasure," said Red, still excited to dig, even after his six holes.

Butch took the map and calculated on the stream where he thought the Team should start digging.

"According to the map, longitude line one hundred fifteen is right here," said Butch, pointing to a line on the map.

Red picked up the small shovel and said, "Where do you think I should start digging?"

Hero pointed to the edge of the stream where most of the sand and rocks were located and said, "That looks like a good spot. Let's start there."

Hero, Runt and KP moved the rocks out of the way and Red, Tater and Bean started digging. They were about three feet deep when Runt said, "Do you think we have the right spot?"

"It could be anywhere along here," said Bean. "We just have to search."

"How can we pick the right location?" asked KP. "Especially since the map is so old."

"Let's try to narrow down the search if we can. Where is the map?" questioned Hero.

Bubba pulled out the map from his pocket and handed it to Hero. As Hero and Bean looked over the map, Bubba and Butch crossed the stream and looked on the other side. Butch located a small shallow pond covered with water lilies. To the side of the pond was a small, very rounded tree that resembled a magnolia. It had small, fragrant white flowers covered with beautiful diamond-shaped leaves. Grass came to the edge of the water. Smooth, golf-ball sized rocks and white sand glimmered just under the waterline beside the stream.

"What about over here, Bubba?" asked Butch.

Bubba looked around for a minute and then replied, "I'll bet this water is warm, and it is full of sand and rocks — just like the clue says." He turned to Hero and yelled, "What about over here?"

The Team was still looking at the map when Bubba yelled. They looked up to see him pointing to the small pond.

Red yelled, "Looks good! Let's try it."

He grabbed his shovel and headed for the pond. The Team followed closely. With just two shovels, everyone took turns digging. Once again, the hole was getting deeper and deeper with no sign of the treasure.

Just as Runt was about to question the location, Tater yelled, "I hit something!"

Everyone gathered closer to the hole, excited to see what Tater had found.

"Keep digging, Tater!" shouted Bean.

They watched anxiously. Bubba, who was hanging off the edge of the pond, finally jumped in to help. He saw the edge of what looked like a box. The two boys threw their shovels up out of the hole and continued digging with their hands, scraping away the dirt, rocks and water until they uncovered a small stone box.

Fighting the weight of the stone and water, Tater and Bubba removed the box from its resting place and headed to the shore. Suddenly Bubba jumped screaming.

"OWWIE! A stream monster," he shouted, crazily jumping around in the water.

The Team all started laughing.

Bubba yelled, "What's so funny? It really hurts. Get it off! Get it off!"

They all pointed to the crab still hanging on to Bubba's shorts and pinching his backside.

Bubba yelled, "Would someone please help me?"

Hero, still laughing, helped him remove the crab and revealed a small hole in his shorts. As Bubba rubbed his backside, Hero grabbed the box with Tater and carried it to the edge of the sand.

A very old rope was wrapped completely around the box and appeared to hold the box closed. No one had ever seen anything resembling the rope or box. Puzzled about how to open the box, everyone looked to Bean.

"Don't look at me," she said. "I opened the last one."

The box was just a little larger than a shoebox. It had no visible openings or locks.

Bubba wiggled the dark-brown, leather rope back and forth until it slid off the box. He inspected the box and shook it vigorously, trying to see if it would open. Nothing moved on the outside, but the Team could hear something rattling around inside the box.

"Maybe we should take the entire box back to the

Treehouse," Red suggested.

"We can't," said Hero. "Remember the directions from the clue? There must be a few things in there. The clue said 'take only one'."

Everyone on the Team took a turn. They tried to twist the top sideways, pull the lid directly up, and push every side watching for movement. But after several attempts, they were no closer to finding the clue. They sat down on the grass by the shady magnolia tree to consider what to do and how to open the box.

KP sat and played with the box, searching for anything — a button, a latch, maybe even just a small hole. As the Team sat there, everyone became more and more frustrated. They could not continue until they found the treasure.

After several anxious minutes and many failed attempts to open the box, Hero finally said, "Let's all try to open it together. Everyone take hold of the box from the top. Maybe with some force, the lid will give way. I will count to three, and everybody pull together. KP can you bring the box over?"

"Well, it couldn't hurt," replied KP. He leaned his hand on the box to stand up. Something clicked. "Hey, something happened," KP said nervously.

The Team moved in closer. To their astonishment, KP had leaned on something that allowed the box to open. KP removed the lid, and the Team looked at the contents in awe.

"Keys?" Red said. "Where's all the money, jewels and good stuff?"

Everyone was puzzled. Not sure what to do next,

Bean said, "Look! There are five different keys, and an inscription on every key. The words are written in the same language as the clue. So how do we know which one to take?"

"Okay," Hero said. "Let's figure this out. What kind of metal do you think Moroni would have had then?"

KP said, "I think they would have had brass."

Butch said, "I think they would have had gold. That's what the Book of Mormon was written on."

"Yes, but what about copper?" asked Runt. "Didn't they use that back then?"

"I'm not sure what they used," said KP.

"Any other ideas?" asked Bubba.

No one said anything, so Hero suggested, "I think we should take the key that is made out of the material that was most common at that time. Maybe we should take one that looks plain, like the clue says. 'Take only one plain key with no reason for more.' We need to decide which one matches that description. I see keys made of brass, silver, iron, copper and gold."

Bean, who had been examining the keys said, "Each key has a different inscription on it. So, it probably does matter that we get the right one."

"Well, which is it?" asked Butch, a little anxious.

"Why don't we take them all?" asked Red.

"We can't," said Stick. "The clue said, 'take only one'."

Hero thought for a minute. "To be fair," he said, "maybe we should take a vote. Everyone ready?"

Hero held up the gold key and said, "Any votes?" Butch started to raise his hand and then hesitated. Hero, held up the silver and iron keys and asked, "Any votes?" Not one. He held up the copper key and asked, "Any votes?" Runt, knowing that he had read that copper was used a lot back then, raised his hand and said, "I do."

"Okay, one vote copper," said Hero.

He held up the brass key and said, "Any votes?" The rest of the Team raised their hands.

So Hero replied, "Brass it is."

Hero handed the brass key to Bean for safe keeping. Hero, Bubba and Butch shut the heavy stone box and replaced the rope. They moved slowly as they placed it back in the hole. Then they covered the hole with sand and replaced the rocks.

"This way, no one will know we have been here," said Bubba. "Besides, if we picked the wrong key, we will be able to come back and get the right one."

Bean placed the key in a small pocket inside her backpack and excitedly asked, "Ready to find clue number two?"

Everyone hurried back up the cliffs as fast as they dared go over the slippery, wet rocks. Eddie and Earl lay quietly in the brush. The Team was so excited they did not even notice the two men lying just to the side of the trail. Eddie and Earl watched the Team get to the top of the cliffs before they moved an inch.

"What do you think?" asked Eddie. "Should we follow them, or get the treasure box?"

"I don't want to lose them. Besides, there is nothing in that box except worthless keys. Let's go get the good stuff," replied Earl.

Chapter Six

Thrilled about finding the first clue, the Team raced back toward town and the library.

Butch asked, "Do you guys think the clues will really lead us to a Book of Mormon treasure?"

"I think the map will," replied Bean. "Why?"

"Well, did anyone besides me notice all the hieroglyphs engraved on the stone box we pulled out of the stream?" Butch questioned.

Bean replied, "I sure did. I think this map must really be from Moroni's time. Did you notice that some of the engravings on the map are the same as on the key?"

"I didn't. Cool! Are you sure?" asked KP.

Bean, excited to have noticed something that KP had not, confidently nodded. "Yes," she said.

"I hope so," said Stick. "I don't want to be doing all this work for nothing."

"I wish I knew what Moroni meant on some of these clues. Finding them would sure be easier!" said Runt.

"And faster," said Bubba.

"Yeah, this clue was pretty hard," said Tater, cramming a potato roll into his mouth. "It would be a bummer if we never found anything. I hope this map really leads to something," he said, mumbling through a mouth full of bread.

"I hope the next clue is easier!" said Red.

"Easier? Are you serious?" questioned Bean. "They are only gonna get harder. This is probably the easiest clue we will have."

Red shrugged, "Well, I was just hoping for the best."

"Do you think Cheri, the librarian, will be willing to help us with this next clue?" asked Bubba nervously.

"I'm sure she will," responded KP. "She said to let her know if we needed more help."

"I am so excited, I can hardly think about anything else," said Stick.

"With any luck, the search will only get more and more exciting," responded Runt.

The weather this summer had not been typical. In addition to heavy rain, it was misty and cold, which was so unusual for the summer time. The rain created an air of mystery floating off every road, everywhere the clouds descended. Finally the chill in the air was almost more than Bubba could bear.

"Everyone, stop. I'm freezing," he said.

The Team pulled over to see what Bubba needed. The break gave him just a minute to catch his breath. He quickly rummaged through his backpack and found his gray San Diego Padres sweatshirt. It was his favorite. The Padres did not have a winning season very often, but they were still his favorite Team. As he frantically pulled the sweat shirt over his head, he thought he heard voices coming from the grass. He quickly poked his head out and looked around.

"Did you hear that?" he asked.

"Hear what?" questioned Runt.

"Voices and noise?" responded Bubba.

"I didn't hear anything," said Bean. Looking at the Team she asked, "Did you?"

The Team shrugged as if to say no.

Bubba shrugged. He hoped the wind and his imagination were just playing tricks on him. He zipped up his backpack and hollered to the Team, "Sorry, guys. I'm ready. Let's get moving."

As the Team continued on their way Bubba said, "I think this map is playing tricks with my mind."

"Why? What's the matter?" asked Hero.

"Nothing really. I just thought I was hearing voices back there," Bubba replied.

"Really?" asked Tater.

"Yep," Bubba said. "I must be going crazy."

"Well, back at the Treehouse, I thought I heard voices too," said Tater.

"That's funny. So did I," interjected Bean. "Back at Mr.

Jensen's house, I could swear I heard voices in the attic."

Hero looked worried. "Hopefully it's nothing," he said. "But everyone keep an eye out for anything out of the ordinary. Okay?"

The Team agreed.

A few minutes later, they arrived at the library and raced to find the librarian. She softly put her finger to her lips to quiet the excited Team.

"What can I do for you, Team?" she whispered, as she leaned over the check-in counter.

"Sorry for the noise," Hero quickly said, "We need your help." Without another word he grabbed her hand and whisked her to the back room, so they would not be overheard.

"Would you translate our second clue, please?" asked Red anxiously.

Excited, she pulled up a chair and asked, "So you found another clue?"

"We sure did," exclaimed Tater proudly.

"You used the scriptures to find a real treasure map clue? I can't believe it." She laid the key on the table and pulled her glasses down from the top of her head. She handed KP paper and a pencil, saying, "You did so well last time, would you please write the translation down again?"

KP agreed, taking the pencil and paper.

Curious, she picked up the old key. It had three teeth along the bottom, a long round shaft in the middle, with a round handle at the top. Engraved on the top was a sun burst of rays. The key was about six inches long. Though it appeared old, the key had been preserved in wonderful condition, making the inscription surprisingly easy to read. Cheri looked it over carefully and then started translating from the round top of the key handle, moving from right to left.

> "'Head south by southeast to a place that is old.
> You'll find tracks in 1 Nephi 17:7, built by prophets of old.'"

She paused a moment, scratched her head and then continued,

> "'When you get to that place, you will know what to do.
> You will find that your 1 Nephi 16:33 goes all the way through.'"

"Oh, this is not going to be easy," complained Runt. "Two scriptural references."

"Did you think that they would get easier as we moved from clue to clue?" asked Butch.

"I was hoping," replied Runt.

"I told you they would get harder," said Bean, almost arrogantly.

The Team all thanked Cheri for her help.

"I need to get back to the front desk," said Cheri, "but I'm excited for you. I can't wait to translate the next clue. I'm positive you will be able to find it."

Hero quickly took charge. "Bubba, pull out the map and see what part is south by southeast. Runt, find the scriptures and read the references to us. Tater, check the perimeter and make sure no one is listening. Let's get started," he said, as he sat down at the table.

Bean suggested they move two tables together so the Team could form a small circle. "That should help us have some privacy," she said, as she pulled the tables together and moved the chairs around them.

Quickly, the Team sat around the tables and formed a tight circle. Bubba hastily placed the map in the center of the table.

As he looked at the map, Bubba said, "There is nothing to the south except the mountains and those three lines. I think the librarian said they symbolized the ruins where we could find ancient hieroglyphs."

Hero asked, "Runt, did you find those scriptures yet?"

Runt quickly responded, "I did. Are you ready for the first one?"

Hero nodded, and Runt quietly read, "1 Nephi 17:7, 'And it came to pass that after I, Nephi, had been in the land of Bountiful for the space of many days, the voice of the Lord came unto me, saying: Arise, and get thee into the mountain. And it came to pass that I arose and went up into the mountain, and cried unto the Lord.'"

"Do you think it could just be the numbers again this time?" asked Butch, hopefully.

"Did you guys listen to the scripture? It said go to the mountain," replied Runt.

"We have a location this time," said Bubba excitedly.

"The location has to be the ancient Native American hieroglyphs Cheri was talking about," said Red.

"Besides, the mountains are south by southeast, and the scripture says to go to the mountain," said Tater. "Let's get started. We can finish with the second half of the clue when we get there."

As the excited Team stood to leave the library, Stick hollered to Cheri, "We figured out the location. We'll be back to see you with the next clue."

Tater grabbed Stick, hissing, "Would you be QUIET?"

Cheri smiled and waved as the Team filed outside.

Once outside, Tater pulled out his compass and verified that Red was right. The Team jumped on their bikes and headed straight south by southeast toward the base of the mountains.

Excitedly, Red hollered, "Off to the mountains!"

The mountains were only about three miles from the library as the crow flies. However, riding bikes would require the Team to travel about five miles. Not caring about the distance, the Team headed back toward the main street in town. Unaware, they passed Eddie and Earl.

"They have no idea we are here," muttered Earl, as the Team rode by.

"This is almost too fun," replied Eddie.

"I am tired of going back and forth down this street," said Earl.

"Yeah, but what else can we do?" said Eddie.

Eddie and Earl watched as the Team rode toward the mountains.

Earl asked, "Should we follow them?"

"Well, thanks to that kid, we know they are heading south to the mountains. The police are still looking for us.

Let's just take our time, stay in the fields, and work our way to the mountains. That route will take longer, but we should make it safely. Maybe by the time we get there, they will have found the next clue," replied Eddie.

"Whatever you say," said Earl.

The two set out moving covertly through backyards and down side streets.

As the Team reached the base of the mountains, they parked their bikes, grabbed their backpacks and headed up toward the hieroglyphs. The ruins were only about two hundred yards up the mountain, but the area had been fenced off years ago.

"We'll have to jump the fence," said Runt.

"We will be breaking the law," said Bean, nervously looking through the fence.

"We might be, if we were planning to draw any graffiti or do any destruction," said Red.

"Since we are just looking at it as a state park, we should be okay," reassured KP.

Once they had all safely climbed the fence, the old trail was easy to follow. The weeds had grown four to five feet tall on both sides, but the trail was still visible through the shorter weeds. Tater led the way up the mountain. Stomping the weeds as he went, he made the path easier for the Team to follow.

When he reached the ruins, he patiently waited for everyone else before inspecting the drawings. No one was sure where to go from here or even what to look for. As they stood around the base of the mountain, the thunder blasted the loudest boom the Team had ever heard.

"I hate this kind of weather," said Stick. "It makes me kinda nervous."

"May I have the map and the translation?" Runt asked. He began reading the clue again, "'Head south by south-east to a place that is old.'"

"Okay, we did that," said Red confidently.

Runt continued, " 'You'll find tracks in 1 Nephi 17:7 built by prophets of old.' "

"Okay, we are there," pressed Red.

"'When you get to that place, you will know what to do. You will find that your 1 Nephi 16:33 goes all the way through,'" finished Runt.

"Well, I don't know what that means!" complained Red. "Where to from here?"

Hero pondered their options. They did have two scriptural references this time. He pulled out his scriptures and said, "We know the first scripture refers to the mountain. Let's start with the second scripture."

He turned to 1 Nephi 16:33 and read, " 'And it came to pass that we did again take our journey, traveling nearly the same course as in the beginning; and after we had traveled for the space of many days we did pitch our tents again, that we might tarry for the space of a time.' "

"What do you think that means?" asked Bean.

"Well, I'm not sure. Let's try every word and see what fits," suggested KP.

The Team used every word to fill in the blank and decided that only two words, *traveling or journey,* really fit into the sentence.

"We have to find a way to journey or travel through

the mountain," said Runt. "What do you think? Could that be right?" he asked.

"I think so. Where do we start?" asked Tater.

"How do we travel through something," asked Bubba.

Hero, lost in thought and entranced by the drawings on the mountain, finally replied, "Stick, take Tater, Runt and Bean with you and head north and search all the drawings. Use your flashlights to look in every hole, small tunnel or cutout. Look for anything that might lead to a passage. Bubba, Butch, Red and KP, you stay with me. We will head south down the mountain and look for the same. Don't try to explore anything by yourselves; we will do that as a Team. Meet back here in ten minutes. Look for anything that resembles an opening or anything that we might be able to journey through," he reminded everyone.

The two groups started searching their assigned areas. Both groups searched for anything that might be a passage, a door, a marking or even a hole. Without finding anything, they met back at the hieroglyphs ten minutes later.

"Nothing to the north," reported Runt.

"Nothing to the south either," stated Hero.

"Where to from here?" asked Bean.

The Team sat down by the front of the hieroglyphs to study the map and clue again. They were definitely stumped.

Suddenly KP said, "We are looking for tracks, not a passage or hole. Did anyone see tracks?"

"What kind of tracks?" asked Red.

"Anything that might show or point a direction," replied KP.

With renewed excitement, Tater yelled, "Let's search again."

The Team quickly set out again, looking for anything that might resemble tracks. This time everyone fanned out and started searching the walls of hieroglyphs.

A few minutes later, Bubba yelled, "Hey Team, I found something! Come look."

Everyone came running.

"Look! Tracks," Bubba said, as he pointed toward deer-like tracks carved into the mountain. "What do you think?" he asked.

Red, sighed, "Bubba, those don't lead anywhere. They just head up toward the top of the mountain. They're just deer tracks!"

Bubba hung his head, "Sorry, guys. I thought they might be what we are looking for."

Everyone turned to continue looking. Bean, who had been intently studying the tracks, suddenly said, "Wait! Look carefully. If you follow the tracks up the mountain, they lead to the next level cut in the mountain. There might be a passage up there. Let's go look."

Bubba excitedly asked, "How do we get up there?"

Hero looked around for anything to help them climb. Finding nothing he said, "Tater and Red, break down some willow branches and gather any sticks you can find. Let's try to make a ladder."

Everyone immediately helped. They braided together willow branches that grew all over the area, hoping their creation would be strong enough to hold everyone as they tried to climb to the upper level of the cave. After almost an hour, they had finally fashioned something that resembled a ladder.

Hero carefully leaned the ladder against the mountain and asked Bubba to hold it steady. Then he said, "I will go first and check to see if it is strong enough to hold us."

He inched his way up the ladder, moving very cautiously. Hero nervously listened to every creak and snap of the branches. He breathed a sigh of relief as he reached the top. He stuck his head over the ledge and called down to the Team.

"It's a little nerve racking. Go slowly, and I will steady the ladder from up here."

As fast as they dared, the Team followed Hero. Bean first, then Red, Butch, Bubba, KP, Runt, Stick and finally Tater. Everyone was relieved when Tater reached the top. KP quickly pulled up the ladder behind them.

Bean continued to follow the tracks in the hieroglyphs. They again moved up to an even higher level. The Team situated the ladder and worked their way up the mountain to the third and final level of the ruins.

"There has to be something here," said Bubba, as he and Bean closely followed the tracks.

"They seem to end abruptly," said Butch.

"They run right into this carving that looks like a waterfall," said Hero.

"What now?" asked Stick.

Everyone thought for a minute. Bean started following the tracks over again, this time feeling them with her hands. They led her back to the waterfall carving. Again, she found nothing.

"This is no good!" said Red, looking at the waterfall. "There has to be something else here," he yelled, as he hit his hands on the center of the waterfall.

He dropped his head in frustration. Suddenly, a hole in the hieroglyphs opened and Red fell forward, straight into the mountain. Just as suddenly, the hieroglyphs closed again, leaving no sign of Red.

"Oh, man! What happened? Where did he go?" asked Hero.

"I have no idea," replied Runt.

"He was right here!" said Bubba nervously.

"I don't want anyone getting hurt," said Hero.

"He found a passage," said KP.

"I guess that could be possible," said Bubba. "Either that or he has pulled off a super prank."

"Well, let's all give it a try," said Bean, following Red's example. "We have nothing to lose." She hit her hands on the waterfall. Suddenly, she too disappeared into the mountain.

"All right! It works," said Hero excitedly. "Maybe he's not hurt after all."

Quickly, the Team took turns following the same procedure. One by one, they all disappeared through the opening by hitting the waterfall engraving on the mountain. Hero, having pulled the ladder up to the top level for safekeeping, checked again to make sure they were not being followed. Everything seemed okay, so he followed his friends into the mountain.

When Hero got to the other side, he was surprised to

find everyone patiently waiting for him. He had entered a magnificent, jungle-like scene. The Team sat on shimmering, white sand, soaking their feet in a steaming natural spring. The warmth felt wonderful, especially to Stick, whose feet were always aching.

The warm water meandered fifteen feet, falling softly over a ledge to a picturesque, crystal-clear lake. The bubbling pool of water was a stunning blue, with visibility easily reaching thirty feet. The valley was filled with lush, green trees and long, hanging vines. The muggy air made breathing more labored for the tired teammates, the air was almost too warm.

"Wow! This is so great! How did the hot springs get here?" Stick asked. "I have never heard of this before."

"Me neither," said Bean.

"I bet I could swing from vine to vine like Tarzan," said Tater, as he grabbed one of the vines. He flexed the muscles in his bulging arms for everyone to see. Then he grabbed a hold of the vines and said, "Watch ya'll."

Just as Tater started to swing Hero grabbed the vine and said, "Next time Tater, we have a treasure to find."

"I bet we are in a dormant, ancient volcano," said Hero. "This hot spring must be the waterfall the tracks on the mountainside led to. I bet the waterfall and jungle have been hidden here for hundreds of years," he reasoned.

"I can't believe we have found a way inside the mountain," said Runt. "We are amazing!"

"If we can do that, we can definitely find the next clue, right?" asked Butch.

"I sure hope so," said KP.

Stick looked around nervously. "Let's find the clue and get out of here. There might be snakes and big ancient bugs down here."

"Not to mention a volcano that could erupt at anytime! Look the water is bubbling. It might be erupting now!" Red threw in, just to scare Stick.

Frantic, Stick glanced over at the bubbling water. "Oh great," he said. "Are we safe in here?"

"Relax, Stick. It's not erupting," said Hero, as he patted Stick on the shoulder.

Tater pulled out the map and said, "Where to now?"

"We need to look for a passage that might take us all the way through the mountain," suggested Bean.

"Any idea where to start?" asked Butch.

The Team took a look around the area. Everyone's eyes wandered different directions around the lake, looking for engravings or anything that might give a hint toward the next clue.

Runt walked along a narrow path toward the stream that fed into the lake. Excited, he called to the Team.

"Hey, everybody! Come look over here. I think I might have found something," he shouted.

As the Team ran toward him, he pointed to the trail and said, "I bet if we follow this path it will lead us somewhere — maybe to the next clue or a way out of the mountain."

"Great idea, Runt," said Bean. "Good find."

"This gives us a good direction to start," said Hero. "Everyone grab your stuff. Let's get moving."

"The path is a great place for our next journey to start," said Butch.

The Team agreed. They started climbing cautiously up a small ledge where the stream flowed down to the lake. Tater, being the biggest and strongest, followed everyone — just to make sure there were no accidents.

They had barely begun the climb when Bean let out a blood-curdling scream. She slipped and started sliding backwards down the ledge. Frantically, she grabbed for anything that might stop her fall. Just before she slipped into the water, Tater reached out and grabbed her arm. He pulled with all his strength and helped her regain a solid footing.

"These rocks are slippery and wet, we need to move slowly and be very careful," Tater warned, helping Bean move past the rocks.

"Thanks, Tater," she said. "I thought for sure I was going for a swim."

Tater smiled and the Team cautiously continued to climb, searching for the next clue.

Suddenly Bubba, who was first in line, yelled, "Oh man! Someone please help me quick! I can't hold on much longer."

Hero yelled sarcastically, "Oh, what's the matter now? Is there another crab?"

Bubba yelled back hysterically in a scared, shaky voice — one Hero had never heard before. "I'm sliding down the rocks. I can't get my footing and there is LAVA down here! Help!"

KP quickly opened his backpack, pulled out the rope and threw it over the crest of the trail. It went taut as Bubba grabbed it and ended his frightening slide toward the lava below. Relieved, he looked around trying to locate a safe place to climb down.

"Move the rope south off the trail," Bubba hollered. "I see a safe place to get down."

KP quickly slid the rope off the south ledge, and then yelled, "Is that far enough?"

Bubba replied, "Yes, tie it off and have everyone slide down. I can see hieroglyphs and a small hut down here. The air is unbelievably hot, and it's hard to breathe. Be really careful," he added.

KP quickly tied the rope to the biggest rock he could find. Everyone cautiously slid down the rope to meet Bubba. Everyone, that is, except Stick.

"It's a little too dangerous down there," he yelled. Maybe we should choose a different area."

The Team ignored Stick. They were excited about the ancient ruins.

"This has to be a hut that people from the Book of Mormon lived in," stated Hero assuredly.

"I bet you're right," said Red. "This is sweet down here."

"Look. It has a bedroom, a larger room, one that looks like a washroom, and even a kitchen that has a steam oven," said Bean.

Stick called down, "How does the steam get into the kitchen?"

KP replied, "The heat looks like it was piped in from the steam off the volcano."

"Is it neat?" Stick asked curiously.

"It's really awesome, Stick. You need to come check this out," replied Red.

They found dishes in the kitchen, animal furs apparently used for blankets, and a few pieces of clothing. They also saw several drawings, which someone had engraved into the stone walls of the cave.

"I wonder what happened to these people," said Runt.

"Could they have just disappeared?" asked Tater.

"That's a possibility," replied Butch.

"Maybe they died off," said Red.

"Maybe the volcano had a small eruption and the lava came up enough to get them," Stick said frantically. He peered over the edge at the lava below, checking to make sure it was not getting ready to erupt.

"Come on, Stick. Everything in here, including the blankets and clothes, would be charred ash. Nothing would be here at all if that had happened!" said Red.

Bean suddenly started screaming. "Everyone come quickly and see what I found!"

The Team looked around and found her sitting at the top of a slick rock chute. The slide seemed to travel even deeper into a tunnel in the mountain.

"Let's go try it out!" Bean said excitedly, as she got ready to push off for a ride.

"Wait, Bean," said Hero. "Let's not move on until we are sure the clue is not in this area. Everyone fan out and search."

"What are we looking for?" asked Butch.

"Another key, or something that looks like it might have a clue written on it," Hero replied.

"Before you guys get too spread out and maybe get lost, how about I stay here and keep watch here," offered

Stick, who still had not climbed down the rope.

"I guess you could, but what about the dangerous volcano and poisonous snakes and maybe even the giant ancient bugs up there?" asked Runt.

"Do you think there could be big bugs in here?" asked Stick apprehensively.

"There very well could be, Stick," stated Hero.

"All right, I guess I will go. Wait for me," Stick replied. "Don't let me fall in the lava." He quickly climbed down the rope to catch up with the rest of the Team.

"Hey everybody. Come here," Bubba called.

"What is it, Bub?" asked Red.

"The keys," he said, pointing just above the slide where Bean was sitting. "I found the keys!"

Hero glanced above the keys and saw a diamond-shaped symbol. It had been meticulously carved in the rock. Encased inside the diamond were five keys.

Bean, who was closest asked, "Hero, which one should I take?"

"Take the brass key," Hero said.

Bean reached up and with some force pulled the key from its spot on the wall. She held it up for everyone to see, zipped it into her bright green backpack and took off sliding down the rocks as fast as she could go. She squealed in delight all the way to the bottom. Not wanting her to get too far ahead, everyone on the Team jumped on the slide and followed. Even Stick, who had finally climbed down the rope, jumped on the slide to catch up with the rest of the Team.

Bean landed in an open area at the end of the slide.

This time, instead of a hut, she saw a path leading toward a bright light. More hieroglyphs covered the canyon walls.

As the rest of the Team reached the bottom of the slide, Stick also noticed some engravings. He ran toward one and yelled, "Hey everyone, look! Another diamond-shaped pattern!"

"I bet there must be a lot of jewels in the treasure that we're looking for," said Bean, as a soft smile spread across her face.

Red ran his fingers along the wall. "I bet there are tons of treasures inside the walls," he said.

Hero and Bubba were the last teammates to reach the bottom on the slide. They saw the engravings and ran to feel the hieroglyphs for themselves.

"What an awesome feeling," said Hero, completely overwhelmed by the surroundings.

"I wish I understood their meanings," said Bubba.

"I wonder if these engravings are warnings of things to come, like the prophets of old wrote about in The Book of Mormon," said Hero.

His thoughts were interrupted by Tater.

"Man, this is so cool. My Mom would love this stuff," Tater said.

"The trail here looks like it leads to the end of the passage. Maybe it will show a way out. Come on. Let's go," said Red, pointing to the bright light. "We have a key to translate. We can always come back here later, now that we know about this place."

"Wait," said Butch. "Where is the key?"

Bean pulled out the second key and held it up for the

Team to see. "Safe and sound in my backpack, right next to the other one."

Satisfied, the Team was finally ready to have the next clue translated. They started walking toward the light. Jagged rocks lined the walls, and the path switched back and forth like a maze. As they moved closer toward the light, they could see that every piece of rock was covered in hieroglyphs.

Hero studied each rock that he passed. Every picture seemed to tell a story. How he wished he knew how to read Egyptian. He would love to know what the ancient people had written. After several yards of multiple cutbacks in and out through the rocks, they arrived at a small, basketball-sized opening.

"I'm never gonna get out of that hole," said Tater.

"I can," said Stick smugly, as he wiggled his body through the opening.

"Don't worry, Tater. If we have to, we can dig around the opening to make it bigger," said Hero.

As the teammates squeezed through the hole on their stomachs, Stick helped pull them through on the other side.

Finally, it was Tater's turn. With a few shovels of dirt removed, he could slide out as well.

As Butch exited, he realized that they were in a clearing only one hundred fifty yards south of where they had entered the mountain. Once everyone had made it out, he insisted that their discoveries inside the mountain would remain their secret. Tater was the first to agree. He rolled a large rock over the opening, keeping their new passageway hidden. They could come enjoy the hot springs later without anyone else knowing. Everyone was astonished at the marvels in the mountain and amazed that they were able to find another key.

"What a great secret," remarked Hero.

"I can't wait to come back," stated KP.

After a few minutes, they made it back to the hieroglyphs and headed down toward their bikes. Eddie and Earl had been sitting by the Team's bikes for hours. They were startled as the Team climbed back over the fence to retrieve their bikes. The convicts barely had enough time to lunge forward onto their stomachs and into the tall weeds before the Team could reach their bikes.

"We need to hear where they are going," whispered Earl.

"Quiet," Eddie whispered back. "We know where they are going."

"We do?" asked Earl.

"Back to the library. I'm sure they need help to get the next clue translated," Eddie said arrogantly.

"Oh," replied Earl, as he watched the Team quickly grab their bikes and start walking down the mountain.

The teammates were still talking about the volcano, the ruins and the drawings as they walked by the two men. Struggling to hear the Team's conversation, Eddie and Earl were excited to learn the kids had found another key. They knew this had to be good news.

Tater, who was lagging behind and trying to catch his breath, suddenly heard Eddie laughing.

"This is so easy. All we have to do is follow the little brats," said Eddie.

"What are we going to do with the treasure when they find it?" Earl asked, snickering softly.

Tater gasped in shock. "Mr. Jensen was right; he knew we might be in danger," he whispered to himself. Tater quietly sat down in the weeds and waited for Eddie and Earl to move ahead of him. Scared to death for the safety of the Team, Tater's heart began to beat faster and faster.

"So much for catching my breath," he said to himself. "I have to tell the Team, and quick, before someone gets hurt."

Chapter Seven

After Eddie and Earl silently disappeared into the brush on the mountain, Tater grabbed his bike and rode frantically to catch up with the Team. He breathed a long sigh of relief as he saw the Team contently riding toward the library. He had to get the Team out of the area as fast as he could. Not knowing what else he could do, he rode past the Team at top speed, and yelled, "I'm gonna beat ya'll to Fort Street!"

The Team loved a challenge. Everyone took off chasing Tater, including Bean and Hero, who would risk life and limb to win. Tater was doing all he could to just stay a few feet ahead. The competition was fierce. Bean would move a few inches ahead, and then Hero would make his move. They raced full speed down Skarpal Mountain and barely made the sharp turn onto Kimball Trail.

The trail was the safest bike route in town. It was about ten feet wide and was paved in most areas. This trail provided one of the best places in town for bike races. The Team rode the three, flat miles toward town, trading leads the entire way.

As they neared Fort Street, Tater pedaled with all his might. With sweat dripping off his chin, he took one more deep breath and pedaled like crazy. Usually content to just watch the race unfold, his determination to save the Team had consumed his every thought. He had to win. After all, he was the one the Team looked to for protection. He had to get the Team as far away from Eddie and Earl as he could.

As the rest of the Team watched, Hero, Bean and Tater took hold of their front handlebars, leaned forward, put their heads down and raced toward Fort Street. At about twenty-five feet away, Tater finally took the lead for good and won the race. Hero, Bean and Tater, breathing heavily, waited for the rest of the Team to catch up with them.

As they arrived, Red shrieked, "Way to go Tater! Dude! I have never seen you move that fast!"

"That was amazing," added Runt.

"Impressive, Tater! Congratulations on your first win," said KP.

Tater beamed proudly with his accomplishment. He had never experienced the feeling of winning a bike race until now, and he liked it. Tater enjoyed his glory for only a moment. Then he stopped, cautiously looked around, and motioned the Team into a huddle.

"Ya'll remember how we were talking about hearing voices?" asked Tater, still panting.

"You heard them, too?" asked Bean. "Then I'm not crazy!"

"Yes," replied Tater. Not only did I hear them, but I saw where they came from."

"What do you mean?" asked Hero, alarmed at Tater's tone.

"You know how I stopped behind ya'll up on the mountain? Well, I saw two men and heard them talking," he explained to the Team.

"What two men?" asked Hero.

"I don't know who," replied Tater.

"No way, Tater. Are you sure?" asked Butch.

"Yes," he answered. "They laughed about how easy taking the treasure from a bunch of little kids would be for them."

Butch, feisty as ever said, "Give me the treasure. They will never get it!"

Bean, still panting from the race said, "I would like to see them get these away from me." She held up her backpack containing the two keys.

Tater continued, "They're fixin' to take the treasure from us after we find it. They are following us around from clue to clue, letting us do all the work."

"How did they find out we are searching for treasure?" asked Bean, looking shocked.

"Who are these men?" asked Bubba.

Tater just shrugged. "I don't know how they know anything or who they might be. I just know that we need to be careful!"

"Do you think Cheri would have told anyone?" asked Runt.

"Not a chance!" snapped Hero.

"How they found out is not the worry," said Tater. "We need to focus on not lettin' them get the treasure."

As the Team continued toward the library, Tater kept a close eye out for the villains. He was very distraught, knowing that the duo could be watching the Team from afar or be hidden close by.

Hero asked, "Does anyone want to quit searching for the treasure? I am worried that this hunt is too dangerous. I don't want to end up like Mr. Jensen's great-grandfather, Ole."

"After the cool stuff we just saw?" questioned Red. "Are you crazy? No way!"

"No one is going to scare us off this easy," said Bubba assuredly.

No one wanted to quit.

"Okay," said Tater. "Ya'll know what this means, right? We will have to keep careful watch at all times. We will have to hide each clue we find, and the clues can no longer be discussed openly in public. All of us will have to be extra cautious. Agreed?" he asked.

"Now I can't wait to find the treasure — just to hide it from them," said Butch.

"We will be careful, Tater," said Bean.

"Tater, since you are the only one who saw these guys, you need to watch for them. If you see any sign of them, let us know immediately," said Hero.

"Tater should be head of security for us," said Butch.

"Great idea," replied Hero.

With his adrenalin pumping, KP said, "I want to help with security. I want to catch these guys."

Tater agreed.

As the Team reached Main Street and the library, Eddie and Earl had just made it to the base of the mountain.

"Where are those dumb kids?" yelled Eddie, scanning the area frantically. "We should have moved faster."

"We don't know for sure where the pack is going this time," said Earl.

"Yes we do! We know they will go to the library first," stated Eddie angrily. "I just wanted to keep up with them," he said.

"After they go in the library, how will we keep an eye on them? How will we get our treasure?" questioned Earl. "Should we go to the library and find out what is next?"

Eddie replied sternly, "No, I guess we really don't need to know where they're going. We know where their hideout is. We can go back to the Treehouse and wait for them there."

"What if they don't find all the clues?" asked Earl. "They are just dumb little kids."

"They will! And when they do, we will take the treasure from them. Come on. Let's move," commanded Eddie. "We don't want to be seen by the cops."

Eddie and Earl disappeared into the weeds. They were still very aware that the police were hunting for them. The two men were only about a mile from the Treehouse when Earl spotted a police car through the field.

"Duck!!" he squealed, as he pushed Eddie down.

Eddie, unaware of the patrol car, jumped up with fists drawn, ready to pop Earl for pushing him down.

"What the heck is your problem? What are you doing, Earl?" he yelled. Then he noticed the patrol car heading straight for them. "I hope they didn't see us," he told Earl, falling to his knees in a panic.

Through the weeds, they watched the patrol car pull up along side the road and stop. Two policemen stepped out. Eddie's heart began to race, pounding so loud that he was afraid the officers would hear.

Officer Cahoon, positive that he had seen something, retrieved his binoculars and scanned the field for any movement. Meanwhile, Officer Nelson, still bothered that the duo had escaped right under their noses, moved slowly and stood at the edge of the weeds. Officers Cahoon and Nelson stood motionless, searching the field for more than fifteen minutes.

Afraid to move a muscle, Eddie and Earl held as still as possible. One small move would send them back to the jail. And they knew that Warden Willard would certainly inflict severe punishment on them if they returned. As the two officers climbed into their patrol car and drove away, Eddie and Earl finally breathed. Cautiously, they moved toward the Treehouse. At least they could find safety in the tree.

Meanwhile, Officers Cahoon and Nelson began a house-to-house search, acting on the orders of Warden Willard. They still wanted to be the heroes who returned the escaped convicts.

The Team entered the library. Tater immediately set up a perimeter, found a secluded table where the Team could inspect the key, and waited patiently until the librarian finished helping the other patrons.

Excited to see the Team, Cheri headed for the table. "I am so proud of all of you!" she said, "Let's see your third clue."

Bean pulled out the key, but hesitated before handing it to her.

"Uh oh. What's the matter?" Cheri asked, seeing the hesitation in Bean's hand.

Bean told her about the two men following them, and then explained their plan to steal the treasure.

Cheri, looking concerned asked, "Is the treasure hunt too dangerous for you, Team? You are very young to be searching on your own for this treasure," she said.

"We'll be careful and protect each other," Hero promised.

"They could be those two escaped prison inmates,"

she stated firmly. "I am not sure if I should translate any more clues. The danger may be too great."

"We have a security plan already set up. We promise to watch out for each other. Please help us," KP pleaded. "Without your help, we will never finish."

"I'm fixin' to keep everyone safe," chimed in Tater. "Ya'll can trust me."

"We will all work together to be safe," said Bubba. "We promise. Right, Team?" he asked.

Everyone nodded.

Cheri still looked apprehensive. "Stay together and be very careful. This news has made me a little nervous," she said.

Then Cheri slowly handed KP a piece of paper. She reluctantly asked him to write the next clue. She then reached for her glasses, but they were not on her head. Irritated, she looked around but did not see them anywhere.

"I can't translate the key without my glasses," she stated.

Runt quickly ran to the check-in table, hoping to locate the glasses. They were sitting on the book she had been reading. He brought them back to her in less than a minute.

"Thanks," she said. "I can't read anything without these. You must be excited for this next clue. Let's see what we have."

Cheri again started to translate the clue, reading the strange symbols from right to left.

> "You could finish the job if you had the right key.
> Head back to the mountain, to get clue number three.

Each time that you choose, just pick a new one.
You'll need all four clues before you are done.'"

"What does that mean?" asked Stick.

"We got the wrong key!" exclaimed Red.

"How did we do that?" asked Bubba.

"The clue said to get the plain key. We did that when we picked the brass key," said Bean. "Didn't we?"

KP pulled out the previous translation and read:

"'They who go forth with the will of the Lord,
Take only one plain key with no reason for more.
If you follow Him with His will on your mind,
Your reward will be His treasure; you won't fall behind.'"

"Didn't we do that?" Butch asked, obviously puzzled.

"Bean, pull out the other key please. Let's take a look at it," said Hero.

Bean set her backpack on the table, unzipped the inner pocket and pulled out the first brass key. That key was mostly smooth. The only rough texture was the writing engraved on the handle. The Team could plainly see that the second key was beautifully decorated with ornate lettering and pictures. It was a little larger, and the teeth on the key were longer. The Team had no difficulty seeing the difference between the two keys. They had definitely chosen the wrong key.

"We should have paid a little closer attention," admitted Hero.

"Maybe we shouldn't have been so confident," said Runt.

"What do we do now?" asked Stick.

"We head back to the mountain and the hieroglyphs to find the right key," responded Hero.

"I can't believe we did this," Butch said regretfully.

"We have to pay closer attention," said Bean.

The Team, disappointed with themselves, collected their gear. They thanked Cheri for her help and headed back toward the hieroglyphs. Cheri quietly watched as the Team learned a valuable lesson.

"Remember to rely on the Spirit of the Lord. He will guide you if you only ask for his help," she whispered, as the Team filed out of the library.

Deflated, the Team climbed on their bikes and slowly headed back to the mountain. As they passed the park, Tater, whose stomach was starting to think for him, had a great idea.

"Ya'll, STOP!" Tater shouted, scaring the Team half to death.

"Will you please stop doing that?" cautioned Butch. "Next time, I might think you have spotted the bad guys and just start punching."

Hero, laughing at the bugged expression on Butch's face, said, "What's up, Tater?"

"I know why we missed that last clue," said Tater.

"Why is that?" asked Runt.

"'Cause we didn't pay attention," said Red sarcastically.

"No! It's because we haven't eaten since breakfast and it's already two o'clock. We need nourishment to think straight, and we need to make a new plan. This is the perfect place," said Tater, pointing to the park.

Laughing at Tater's determination to eat, the Team readily agreed. They pushed their bikes over to a picnic table and hastily pulled the sack lunches from their backpacks. As they ate, Hero made some suggestions.

"We really need to work together. Everyone helps with every part of the clue, and everyone agrees on which key to choose," he suggested.

"As a Team, right?" asked Stick, while looking around for the crooks.

"Yes," responded Hero. "And Tater watches out for the safety of the Team. We will have to work together, or we will never make it. Does everyone agree?"

Everyone nodded. The Team stopped talking and finished eating lunch.

Bean, who had been sitting quietly, nervously asked, "Would it be too embarrassing to say a prayer and ask Heavenly Father for help and guidance?"

The Team sat in silence, contemplating Bean's suggestion.

KP finally said, "That works for me. If we're going to make a commitment to serve him no matter what, I think it must be okay if we ask for his help!"

"I agree," said Bubba. "Who will say the prayer?"

Again, the Team remained silent for several moments. Hero finally said, "If everyone is okay with it, I will say a prayer."

The Team approved and Hero humbly said a prayer. He thanked Heavenly Father for the wonderful adventure, the exciting new challenges and the amazing map they had discovered. He also asked for protection from anyone wanting to cause them harm and for direction in finding the treasure.

Hero closed the prayer and said to the Team, "We have a treasure to find. Let's move."

Excited again, the Team repacked their backpacks and headed toward the mountain. When they arrived this time, they knew just what to do. They scurried over the fence and headed to the foot of the hieroglyphs, remembering as they reached them that Hero had pulled the ladder to the third level.

"Man, why didn't I throw that ladder down," Hero said.

"Because we didn't want any company," reassured Tater, starting again to pull branches from the surrounding willows.

Hero rapidly wove them together to make a ladder. This ladder, was not quite as good as the first one, but seemed adequate.

"I'll go first," Hero volunteered again.

Moving slowly, he listened to the cracks and creaks of each limb as he stepped from branch to branch. Everyone gasped each time a branch cracked. About three-quarters of the way to the top, a step snapped beneath his feet and left him hanging. Hero held on by gripping the sides of the ladder. Nervously, the Team watched, encouraging him to pull himself up to the next branch.

Worried about his brother, Bubba stood at the bottom of the ladder, ready to catch him if he slipped. But after a few moments, Hero regained his composure. He slid his left hand a few inches higher on the ladder, followed by his right and then his left. He finally reached the first level.

Still a little shaky, he leaned over and said, "I guess we should have built that ladder a little stronger."

After a minute, Hero finally breathed normally again. He took hold of the ladder and pulled what remained of it to the second level. He quickly rewrapped the branches to make the ladder as sturdy as he could. Then he inched his way to the third level, moving slowly as the branches creaked and cracked beneath his weight. The Team held their breath.

When he reached the top, Hero grabbed the good ladder. He set it over the side and climbed back down to the second level. Then he lowered it to the waiting Team. Eagerly, the Team climbed up to meet Hero. Together, they moved up to the third level.

At the top, Red said, "Hey, I know what to do here." He promptly beat his fists on the wall and disappeared. Everyone followed in turn, with Hero again pulling the ladder to the top and then moving through the mountain.

Once inside, the Team waited impatiently for Hero. Bubba was anxious to get back to the keys. He located the rope they had left anchored to the large rock. KP checked to make sure the line was still secure. He nodded, and Bubba slid over the crest of the rocks, down toward the bubbling lava. Once Bubba landed, the rest of the Team was on the move, sliding down to meet him. As the Team reached the bottom, they moved straight to the keys. This time they looked for the plain key — just like the one from the first clue.

Butch quickly located a perfectly plain key. It had no engraved pictures, only lettering. With the Team's approval, he pulled the key down from above the slide.

"I think we have it," Butch said in his gruff voice. "I knew we could do it."

Bean quickly placed the incorrect key back into its place. Then the Team rode the long, slippery rock chute back to the bottom of the mountain. Even Stick, this time knowing for sure there were no snakes or spiders on the slide, enjoyed the ride.

They quickly ran through the maze of rock ledges toward the pale light, glowing softly through the opening. Tater sat at the hole and pushed the rock away, allowing the Team to crawl out of the mountain. Once out, Tater replaced the rock. The Team climbed the fence, ran to their bikes and retraced their route to the library.

Chapter Eight

"Where do you think this clue will be hidden, Hero?" asked Bean.

"Well, let me think," replied Hero, rubbing his chin. "So far we have been to the cliffs and seen the hieroglyphs." He paused looking as though he was in deep thought and said, "I'm not quite sure where we might have to go next. Does anyone have any good ideas?"

"I think maybe the woods," answered KP.

"The woods? I hope not," said Bean. "I really don't like them."

"I wondered if we might end up at the lake?" said Bubba.

"I could go to the lake. I do like it there," Bean said.

"I can't wait to find out," added Tater.

"I'm just ready to move to the next clue," said Stick. "We have been on this one way too long."

"We still need to watch out for those escaped prisoners," added Butch.

"Yeah," declared Runt. "I bet they are still planning to take our treasure."

"Not if I have anything to say about it," said Tater.

"Come on, Team. Let's hurry and find Cheri. I want her to take a look at our clue," said Hero.

The Team, peddled into the parking lot of the library, for the third time today. They jumped off their bikes, locked them up and headed in to see Cheri. Everyone, that is, except Tater.

Tater scanned the surrounding area, looking for any sign of the two criminals. As far as he could tell, they were nowhere in sight. So, he turned and followed the rest of the Team into the library.

They entered the musty smelling library. Red did not even hold his nose or make a face, although the smell had become more intense with the increased humidity and continuous rainfall over the past eight days.

The Team moved quickly to the front desk, hoping to find Cheri. With no sign of her, they spread out and moved into action. KP, Bean and Runt searched the aisles, while Hero, Bubba and Red raced back to the reading rooms trying to locate her. Stick, Tater and Butch stayed at the front desk for two reasons: first, they needed to be available if Cheri returned, and second, they wanted to make sure the library was safe from the crooks. Several minutes passed. Cheri was nowhere to be found, and the Team was starting to get nervous.

"What if she has gone home?" asked Red.

"We find out where she lives," replied Hero, trying to be calm.

"We don't even know her last name. How would we find her?" asked Bubba.

"We will find her. Relax," replied Hero. "She can't be too far away. Especially if she lives in town."

"I don't think she would have gone home. She knew we were coming back with the next clue," replied Bean, trying to sound positive.

"Let's just keep looking. She's got to be here somewhere," said Bubba.

KP was still checking each aisle in the library, when he noticed a figure sitting on the floor. He quietly whispered, "Cheri, is that you?"

She startled him as she jumped up from her seat on the floor and asked, "Did you find the right key?"

Surprised, he jumped back. His heart raced from the shock of how fast Cheri could move. He finally composed himself.

"Oh, it is you!" he remarked, instantly relieved.

"I'm sorry, KP. Did I scare you?" Cheri asked timidly.

Not wanting to admit a little old lady could startle him, KP replied, "No, no. I'm not scared. I'm fine."

"Well, did you find the next clue?" she excitedly asked.

"Yes!" said KP, with an enormous smile.

"Let's go have a look at it," Cheri said, as she walked toward the back room.

"Wait," said KP, as he quickly climbed up onto a chair. Waving his arms in the air, he signaled the Team to come.

The Team hurried over to show Cheri the new key. In a rush, they started telling her all about their return to the ancient hieroglyphs.

Concerned about security, Tater placed his finger on his lips and whispered, "Everyone, please, SHHHHH!" Looking around to see if anyone was watching them, he hurried everyone to an isolated table.

Once there, Tater said, "Now you can go ahead and talk."

Cheri again asked, "Well, did you find the right key, Team?"

Bean quickly opened her backpack, unzipped the inner pocket and retrieved the newest key. She handed it to Cheri, and everyone nervously waited for the translation.

After several tense minutes, Cheri finally said, "I think you have found the right clue this time, Team."

Stick let out a loud sigh of relief.

Then Cheri continued, "This clue is much harder. The hints are scarce and the clue contains many more scriptural references."

She handed a pen to KP. Then she asked, "Team, are you ready?"

Seeing a quick nod of Hero's head, she started translating the clue.

"'The 3 Nephi 18:12 in this valley are treacherous, it's true.
But with Moroni 10:4, you will know what to do.'"

Cheri paused for a moment, looked up at the Team and said, "Thank you, Team, for allowing me to be a part of your adventure."

Red, impatiently said, "Oh, come on Cheri, no gooshy stuff. We just want to find the treasure."

Cheri looked over to Red and said, "I'm excited for you to find it too." She turned back to the key and continued.

"'Each stone holds a number, engraved just for you.
Look eastward to find the Egyptian number twenty-two.
The Helaman 5:12 is sure; it stands with great might.
Climb to the top and look for the 3 Nephi 12:16.'"

"This is the most difficult clue yet. Are you sure you are up for the challenge?" asked Cheri.

Hero firmly replied, "We are a Team. We can do it! Right?" he asked, looking at everyone.

"You bet we can," responded Bean, before anyone else could answer.

"Well, I think you may need to find the answers on this one before you leave," Cheri stated. "Pay close attention to the references."

As she stood up, she pushed back her chair and turned to leave. Then she paused for a moment and said, "Rely on the Lord for help, and His Spirit will guide you."

As she started to walk away, Hero said, "Thank you, Cheri. Will you be here when we bring back the next clue?"

With flushed cheeks, Cheri smiled and replied, "I wouldn't miss it for the world."

Hero nodded and turned back to the Team. He scooted his chair up close to the table, dug his scriptures out of his backpack, and firmly said, "We have a lot of work to do on this one. We better get started."

"Where do you think this clue is?" asked Red.

"Where is the map?" asked Bean. "Let's take a look and see if we can figure it out."

Bubba jumped up, grabbed his backpack, unzipped the front pocket and retrieved the map. "Here it is. I have it," he said.

"Lay it over here on the table," said Red, pointing to the center.

Bubba laid the map down and said, "Hero, we can all see the map now. Would you please read the clue again?"

Hero cautiously looked around for anyone suspicious in the room. Satisfied no one was watching, he quietly read the clue to the Team.

"'The 3 Nephi 18:12 in this valley are treacherous, it's true.
But with Moroni 10:4, you will know what to do.
Each stone holds a number engraved just for you.

> Look eastward to find the Egyptian number twenty-two.
> The Helaman 5:12 is sure. It stands with great might.
> Climb to the top and look for the 3 Nephi 12:16.'"

The Team sat motionless at the table for several minutes. Momentarily stumped, everyone tried to picture where this clue might be leading them.

Not more that three minutes passed before Runt said, "We are going to have to start with the scripture references, Hero. Try reading 3 Nephi 18:12. We don't have time to guess!"

"If we are lucky, the scripture will tell us where to go," said Red.

"Fat chance of that," replied Stick. "None of the clues have been easy so far. Why would this one be?"

Hero, opened his scriptures and said, "Stop! Be quiet, and I will read the scripture. 3 Nephi 18:12 'And I give unto you a commandment that ye shall do these things. And if ye shall always do these things blessed are ye, for ye are built upon my rock.' "

"Hey, this one shouldn't be too bad," said Stick.

"Only a few words might fit into that sentence," said Bean.

"Read the first line of the clue again, will you Bubba?" asked Red.

"'The 'blank' in this valley are treacherous, it's true'," read Bubba. "It has got to be '*rock*'," said Hero.

"None of the other words in the scripture really

fit into the sentence," said Runt.

"Well, fill that word in Bubba. Will it work?" asked Hero.

"'The rocks in this valley are treacherous, it's true'," Bubba read.

"That's it," said KP. "That has to be it."

"I agree," said Butch. "That is it."

"Now read the second line, Bubba," urged Stick.

"'But with Moroni 10:4, you will know what to do'," Bubba continued.

"Hero, now read Moroni 10:4," demanded Tater.

Everyone listened intently to the verse and Hero started reading again.

"Moroni 10:4, 'And when ye shall receive these things, I would exhort you that ye would ask God, the Eternal Father, in the name of Christ, if these things are not true; and if ye shall ask with a sincere heart, with real intent, having faith in Christ, he will manifest the truth of it unto you, by the power of the Holy Ghost.'"

"Oh man, I don't have a clue with this one," said Red.

"Let's just try to fill in the blank," said KP. "Bubba, will you read the second sentence of the clue?"

Bubba again read from the clue, "But with 'blank', you shall know what to do."

"Okay," said Runt. "We can get this. What are some of the nouns or phrases in the scripture?"

"Well, some are 'God, the Eternal Father' and 'Christ'. Do either of those work?" asked Bean.

"Both of those kinda work," replied Tater. "Do any of

the others phrases sound like they fit better?" he asked.

"The other phrases I can see in this scripture reference are: 'with a sincere heart', 'faith in Christ' and 'power of Holy Ghost'," said Hero.

"Do any of these sound like they fit better?" asked Runt.

"Everyone listen, and I will read the clue to you," said Bean. She read the clue over and over, filling in the 'blank' with each phrase. They listened attentively to every sentence that Bean read.

Tater was the first to chime in with, "I think that the 'blank' sounds best filled in with, 'with a sincere heart, you will know what to do'. What do you guys think?" he asked.

KP replied, "I'm not sure if that is right. I think it might be 'with faith in Christ, you will know what to do.'"

"Why do each of you think the phrase you chose fits more than any other?" asked Hero.

Tater replied, "I just thought maybe the clue was about being honest and sincere when we find the treasure."

KP replied, "I thought maybe if we believe in what we are doing and have faith, the Lord will bless us."

Hero shrugged his shoulders and said, "I bet you are both right. All these phrases seem to fit pretty well. I wonder if all of the phrases will work on this part of the clue."

"Maybe we should read the clue to the next scripture reference and work on that one?" Bubba suggested.

"I think that is a good idea," responded Tater. "Bubba, will you please continue reading the clue?"

Bubba nodded then read,

"'The rocks in this valley are treacherous, it's true.
But with faith in Christ, you will know what to do.
Each stone holds a number, engraved just for you.
Look eastward to find the Egyptian number twenty-two.
The Helaman 5:12 is sure, it stands with great might.'"

"Hey, how do we know what an Egyptian number twenty-two looks like?" asked Stick.

"I guess we better find a picture," replied KP.

"I will go find one," said Tater, already headed for the foreign language section of the library. "Work on the rest of the clue. Ya'll are better at filling in the blanks than I am anyway," he said, smiling back at them.

"Funny, Tater," responded Bubba. "You just don't want to have to figure it out."

Tater continued to smile as he disappeared around the romance aisle, on his way to find a book about the Egyptian language. The rest of the Team continued to work on the next scripture reference.

"Come on. Let's get this finished," said Runt.

"I agree. Read that next one to us, will you Hero?" asked Bean.

"Sure," replied Hero, as he grabbed his scriptures and turned to Helaman 5:12.

" 'And now, my sons, remember, remember that it is upon the rock of our Redeemer, who is Christ, the Son of

God, that ye must build your foundation; that when the devil shall send forth his mighty winds, yea, his shafts in the whirlwind, yea, when all his hail and his mighty storm shall beat upon you, it shall have no power over you to drag you down to the gulf of misery and endless wo, because of the rock upon which ye are built, which is a sure foundation, a foundation whereon if men build they cannot fall'," read Hero.

"Boy, they keep getting longer and longer, don't they?" asked Red. "Why couldn't they be short and easy like the first one!"

"Harder and harder, you mean," stated Butch.

"I wouldn't say so," responded Bean. "I think they are easier and easier," she said with a smirk.

"What do you mean, Bean?" asked Hero.

"Well guys, if you listened, two words were repeated several times. Can any of you remember them?"

Bean looked around at the Team, but no one had an answer.

"What were they, Bean?" asked Butch.

"Come on. We all know that you are smart. What were they?" pressed Runt.

Bean gloated a little, paused, and then said, "Well, the first one was *foundation.*"

"And the second?" asked Bubba impatiently.

"The second was *rock,*" she replied.

"Do either of those two words fit the sentence?" asked Stick.

Bubba read the clue, filling in the blank with the

words that Bean had suggested. To the Team's surprise, one actually fit.

"Bean, how did you know?" asked Red. "I don't know how you do this!"

She smiled and said, "Just glad I can help."

Excited to go on to the last scripture reference, Bubba read the entire translated clue this time.

> "'The rocks in this valley are treacherous, it's true.
> But with faith in Christ, you will know what to do.
> Each stone holds a number, engraved just for you.
> Look eastward to find the Egyptian number twenty-two.
> The foundation is sure, it stands with great might.
> Climb to the top and look for the 3 Nephi 12:16.'"

"All right. We are almost there," said Stick.

"Hero, hurry and read the last scripture reference, please," pleaded Runt.

"Everyone ready?" Hero asked, as he hastily flipped through the pages of his Book of Mormon.

"3 Nephi 12:16, 'Therefore let your light so shine before this people, that they may see your good works and glorify your Father who is in heaven.'"

"This one actually is easy," said Red. "I think that I know the answer," he boasted.

"Okay, Red. What is the answer?" asked Butch.

"The clue reads, 'Climb to the top and look for the 'blank'. I think the blank is the word *light,*" said Red.

"That sounds right, but how did you come up with it?"

asked Hero.

"If you think about it, light is the only thing you can really look for in that scripture," Red replied.

"Way to go, Red. I think we have the clue just about figured out," said Butch.

"We are only missing the Egyptian numbers and what they look like," said Bean.

"Has anyone seen Tater?" asked KP.

Tater was nowhere to be found.

Anxious to get moving, Bubba said, "Hang on just a minute. I will go find him." He swiftly moved through the library aisles searching for Tater, softly calling his name.

Bubba spotted Tater sprawled out on the library floor. He walked up to him and asked, "Tater, what in the world are you doing? Get up."

Tater looked back over his shoulder, surprised to see Bubba. He whispered, "Quick, get down here and be quiet."

"Um, okay." Bubba dropped down on the floor next to Tater and whispered, "What are you doing, and what am I suppose to do now?"

"We have company," Tater replied, not wanting to take his eyes off of something. He motioned for Bubba to look at the library reading room.

"What do you mean, 'we have company'?" Bubba asked.

Tater pointed to the farthest east side of the library and softly asked, "You see those two guys over there in the corner? The men with the funny, old suits."

"Yes, what about them?" Bubba asked.

"Those are the two crooks that are gonna try to take our treasure."

Bubba jumped up and moved back behind the shelf. "How long have they been here?" he asked anxiously.

"Not very long," Tater replied. "I watched them walk in the library just a few minutes ago."

"Do you think they know anything about the clue?"

"No, I don't think so. They haven't seen any of us yet, as far as I can tell, and I haven't taken my eyes off them since they arrived," said Tater. Still not looking up at Bubba, Tater handed him a book on Egyptian letters and numbers. "We should be able to find the Egyptian number twenty-two in this book. Take it back to the Team. Finish working on the clue, and I will keep an eye on these two," Tater said.

"Let us know if they get close," said Bubba, very concerned.

"Okay," said Tater. "Go quick. Get the clue finished. I don't want them to know we are here."

Bubba agreed and frantically hurried back to the rest of the Team. He rounded the aisle and reached the table. He handed Bean the book and said, "Tater has spotted the two crooks. Bean, hurry and find the number twenty-two. Let's finish the clue and get out of here quick. Tater is keeping an eye on them until we are ready to go."

"They are here? Are you serious?" asked Butch, walking toward the romance aisle.

"Wait, Butch," said Bubba. "Tater wants us to finish and get out of here as quick as we can."

"That's a good idea, Butch," Hero said. "Tater's good

at this stuff. Let him do the security. Come on. We need to hurry."

Hero turned to Bubba and asked, "Are we in any danger?"

Bubba replied, "Tater said he will warn us if they get close. He doesn't think they know we are here."

Bean rapidly searched through the book Tater found. "I have them. Let's go," she said, as she quickly wrote them down.

"What do they look like," asked Butch.

Bean showed him the symbols , which looked like legs, squiggly lines and birds. She quickly stuffed the paper in her backpack.

As Bean left to return the book to the shelf, she thought, "I wonder if we might need these symbols for something else?" She headed for the counter, checked out the book and carefully placed it in her backpack. Then she quickly joined the rest of the Team.

Everyone helped gather up the clues, scriptures and map. Then Hero turned to Bubba and said, "Hurry, go get Tater. Meet us at the front door. Let's get out of here before they see us."

Bubba nodded in agreement, turned quickly and disappeared down the aisle.

The Team quietly headed for the exit. As they reached the door, Cheri called out, "Good luck on finding the next clue, Team."

Hero cringed, but politely responded, "We'll be back again soon."

Cheri smiled and waved.

Tater was the last member of the Team to leave the library. As he walked out, he said, "I reckon these two are gonna try to cause us a lot of trouble."

"What do you think we should do?" asked Butch.

"I think we need to go find the next clue and forget about them," said Stick.

"I think you are right, Stick," responded Hero. "But we need to think of safety also."

Tater watched the library door for the two men. Then he said, "So, where do we need to go for this clue?"

"Straight to Ghoul's Gulch and all the rocks, right?" asked Bubba.

"That is what I was thinking," said KP.

"Me too," said Runt.

"Well then, I guess we are all thinking along the same lines. We are heading for Ghoul's Gulch," stated Hero, as he unchained his bike. He jumped on his bike, and as he sped south down Fort Street he screamed, "Follow me!"

Quickly, the Team followed his lead. They were all heading straight toward the next key, unaware of the dangers that lay ahead.

Chapter Nine

Midway through town, Bubba called to Hero and asked, "Hey, have you called Mom to check in yet?"

Hero looked down at his watch and panicked. "Oh man! I am going to be in trouble," he moaned, as he rummaged nervously through his backpack, searching with one hand for the walkie-talkie. After several moments of searching, he found it and quickly called home.

"Anyone there?" he asked, hoping no one would answer. Maybe he would get lucky and Mom would be out shopping or something.

Seconds later, Squeaks sang out, "You're late, Hero. You're gonna get in trouble."

"Funny, Squeaks. Get Mom, will you?" asked Hero.

"Did you find your treasure yet?" Squeaks asked.

"No, get Mom now!" demanded Hero.

Hero heard Squeaks telling Mom, "It's Hero, Mom, and he's late."

Mom said, "You're late, Hero. Where have you been?"

"I know, Mom," said Hero.

"I expect you to be more responsible than this, Hero," said Mom, "or your treasure hunting fun will have to end."

"I know," Hero replied.

"So, did you find the treasure yet?" asked Mom.

"Squeaks just asked me the same question, Mom," replied Hero.

"So, did you find it? Is that why you were late to check in?" Mom asked, as if hoping for a reason not to get upset.

Hero scrunched up his face as he replied, "Sorry, Mom. We got caught up in the last clue, and I forgot until just a minute ago."

"Hero, did you find anything yet?" she asked insistently.

"We have a few clues, but no treasure yet. We are still looking," Hero answered.

"That's all right. I don't want you to get your hopes up too high. You know a lot of these old treasure maps are just for fun," she said.

"Okay, Mom. We are having fun," Hero insisted.

"Good," said Mom. "Now where are you?" she asked.

"We just had the last key translated by Cheri at the library, and we are heading to find the next clue," answered Hero, "Is that all right?"

"And where might that be," Mom asked, a little worried.

"We think it is somewhere in Ghoul's Gulch," Hero replied, hoping she would be okay with the distance.

"All the way out there? You guys had better be careful," she warned, sounding extremely concerned. Then she hollered into the walkie-talkie, "Team, can you all hear me?"

She waited for their reply.

Hero held up the walkie-talkie and answered, "Yes, Mom. We can all hear you."

"Good. I hope you are all having a great time. But remember, you all need to be back to our house by seven p.m. sharp. The Team's parents are all going out to dinner and a movie tonight, and you *can't be late*."

Hero moaned, "Mom, we are on a really serious treasure hunt here."

"I mean it, Hero. Be home on time. That only gives you a few more hours, so make the most of them. And remember, not one minute past seven o'clock," Mom said sternly. "We will miss our reservations if you are late."

"All right, Mom. Everyone heard you," replied Hero. Taking a deep breath he continued, "See you in a few hours."

"See you at seven o'clock sharp, Team," said Mom reminding them again.

Hero returned the walkie-talkie to his backpack.

"I guess we only have a few hours, Team," he said dejectedly.

"That will have to be okay," said Tater. "We can still do it."

"We will need to hurry with this clue," stated Bean, as she started peddling faster.

Knowing they were now under a deadline, the Team peddled quickly toward Ghoul's Gulch.

As they reached the popular park, they looked out across miles of red rock and red sand. The red sandstone rocks in the area had been carved by the wind over time, and now they resembled a field of mushrooms. Each carved rock stood from two feet to twenty-five feet tall, and several looked like goblins growing out of the sand.

Hero asked, "So guys, what do you think? Do we start looking on all the rocks for the engraved numbers?"

"Why don't we read the clue to have it fresh in our minds, then split up and start searching?" asked Red.

"Great idea," said Butch.

"It shouldn't take us too long. The park isn't really that big," said Runt, with a big grin.

"Who has the clue?" asked Butch.

"Hang on a second. I've got it here somewhere," Bubba replied. He hastily searched every pocket in his jacket for the clue. Then he looked up at Hero, who was getting a little anxious, and said, "I know it's here somewhere. Just give me a minute."

Red said, "Why don't you check your pants pocket? You put everything in there."

Bubba smiled and said, "Great idea."

He reached in his pants pocket and quickly started pulling out everything. He had a fruit roll, a spare pair of socks, ten smarties' wrappers, several Tootsie Rolls, three small rocks and a crumpled piece of paper.

"Oh, here it is," said Bubba, as he looked up, obviously relieved.

The clouds moved lower to the ground, and they instantly started to drizzle. The wind whipping around the rocks quickly intensified. Above their heads, the clouds let out a booming warning of lightning and thunder. The Team, not wanting to get soaked again, pulled up the hoods on their windbreakers.

"That was way too close," said Stick, nervously looking toward the sky. "Let's just find this clue quickly and get back indoors."

Bean agreed. "Yeah, let's see how fast we can find this one. I'm tired of being wet and cold. I would love to be indoors for a while," she said.

"If we can get this key quickly, maybe we will still have time to hurry back to the library and have Cheri translate for us," added KP.

"That way we don't have to wait for the library to open tomorrow. We could decipher the next scripture references while our parents are out tonight," said Butch.

"Well then, we better get moving," said Hero. "Bubba, are you ready with that clue yet?" he asked.

"I sure am," Bubba said as he finished straightening out the paper. He read the clue.

> "'The rocks in this valley are treacherous, it's true.
> But with faith in Christ, you will know what to do.
> Each stone holds a number, engraved just for you.
> Look eastward to find the Egyptian number twenty-two.

> The foundation is sure; it stands with great might.
> Climb to the top and look for the light.'"

As he finished, Butch asked, "Where are those pictures of the Egyptian number twenty-two?"

"I have them," chimed in Bean, as she pulled them from her backpack.

"Let's see what they look like," said Tater. He pulled the paper from her hands.

"Well, Tater, what do they look like?" asked Butch.

Tater realized he was not allowing anyone else to see the picture. He quickly held out the picture and said, "Sorry ya'll. They kinda look like lots of stuff."

"Wow," replied KP. "The numbers have legs, squiggly lines, a bird and I'm not sure on the last thing."

"So, we are heading east and looking for a picture engraved on the rocks that looks like a little of everything, right?" asked Red, obviously tired of waiting.

"I guess so," replied Hero.

"That and a bird," said Runt, trying to be funny.

"Well, it shouldn't be too hard with only about a thousand rocks out here," added Red sarcastically.

"I guess we better get started, then," said Hero, as he picked up his backpack and parked his bike.

"Especially if we plan to meet our deadline for getting home on time," said Bean.

"Hey, everybody. We better be careful out here. These rocks might be cool to look at, but we could really get hurt if we are not careful. Especially you, Stick," said

Bubba, patting him on the back.

"And if someone gets hurt, our treasure hunting fun is over for sure!" stated Runt.

"Where to from here, Hero?" asked Bean.

"Let's separate into three groups: Bubba, Tater and Red as one, KP, Bean and me as another, and Stick, Butch and Runt as the last," he said, pausing to take a breath. "Everybody stay together in your groups and meet back at the front gate in thirty minutes. Search for anything that resembles Egyptian writing or markings, and stay to the east side," instructed Hero.

Red took off running with Bubba and Tater. He yelled back to the others, "I bet we can find it before you guys do!" Then they disappeared into the rock formations.

"Let's go," said Butch to his group.

Hero and his group decided to make a plan.

"Instead of searching all the formations, we should start as far east as we can and move in about twenty-five feet. Then we can search from the south end of the valley to the north end," said Bean with confidence.

"Great idea, Bean. Let's go," replied KP.

They raced in and out through the red and orange rock formations.

"This would be a great place for a game of fugitive," said Hero. He did not really take time to look closely at the rocks and their shapes, but quickly scanned for anything that looked similar to the ancient pictures of the number twenty-two.

"I'm not finding much on any of these rocks," said KP.

"Me neither," said Hero.

"Do you think we could be in the wrong place?" asked Bean.

"We have only been looking for fifteen minutes," said Hero. "There are lots of rocks out here. Let's keep looking."

"The others may have found something already," said KP hopefully.

The others had indeed found something. Not wanting to waste time, Bubba stopped his group and asked the park ranger if he had ever heard about or seen any hieroglyphs in the park.

The ranger thought for a minute and said, "Actually, yes. I think I have seen a few formations which have writing on them."

"Could you show us where they are?" asked Bubba, with a huge grin.

"Sure boys. Follow me," said the ranger. "Do you have a school report?" he asked.

"No, we are interested in hieroglyphs and hoped there were some here," replied KP.

As they followed the ranger deeper into the formations, he told them many legends about the park. He explained why the area was called Ghoul's Gulch and where the ridge was in the park. He also told them about a mysterious ancient map that supposedly existed and illustrated the valley and the rocks.

"Really? A real map?" Tater asked the ranger. "A treasure map, maybe?"

"As far as I have heard," replied the ranger. "Old timers around here said that this map led to great treasure."

"Have you ever seen the map?" asked Red.

"Nope," replied the ranger. "But my grandfather knew of a man years ago who came to Ghoul's Gulch looking for treasure."

"Did the man ever find it?" asked Tater.

"I don't think so. At least I have never heard that anyone found a treasure in this valley," replied the ranger. "My grandfather tried to buy the map, but the owner would never sell it to him."

"It sure would be fun to see something like that," said Red, trying to keep a straight face.

"Fun to search for it, too," said the ranger. "I wouldn't mind having a map that could make me rich."

"Me neither," said Tater firmly.

Several more minutes passed before the ranger finally stopped and said, "Okay, here is the first one. I don't know what it is or what it means, but it is really cool to look at. Unfortunately, it has almost been washed away completely."

"From the weather?" interrupted Bubba, worried that the engraving could have been destroyed.

"Yes," answered the ranger. "The wind blows hard off the mountain, and it carries dirt and debris. Every time it blows across here, we lose a little more of these pictures."

"Are there a lot more of these writings out here?" asked Bubba.

"A few. One is just a few rocks east and another is a few hundred yards beyond that," said the ranger, pointing as he received a call on his radio. "Sorry, guys I have to go. Someone has slipped and is hurt. There might be a few other formations with hieroglyphs engraved on them besides those I told you about. They are scattered throughout the east side of the park, and I'm not sure where they all are located. They are not in any other part of the park that I am aware of. You will have to look hard to find them. Some of the writings have been covered with sand and dirt over time. Good luck," he yelled, as he lifted his hat and ran back toward the entrance of the park.

"Can you believe that?" asked Tater, as he brushed the dirt away from the writing.

"Believe what?" asked Red.

"That the ranger knew about the map?" replied Tater.

"No, I can't. And we better be careful. Don't say anything. I think Mr. Jensen was right. If anyone knew we had the map, we could be in a lot of danger," said Bubba.

"Can you tell what number that says?" asked Red, as he turned his head sideways, trying to get a better look.

"I have the Egyptian book that Bean checked out of the library," said Tater. "Let's look and see."

He quickly pulled the book from his backpack, opened to the picture of Egyptian numbers and said, "The number one in the book looks like a cell phone followed by a rectangle with a circle above it. The number two looks like a leg, squiggly line, bird and two-legged triangle above three horizontal lines. The number three looks like an eagle."

"That one was easy," stated Bubba.

"Keep going," pressed Red. "Let's get this figured out."

Tater continued, "The number four looks like a flamingo with a lady sitting behind it."

Bubba chuckled at Tater's descriptions.

"The number five looks like a...," Tater paused and looked over to Bubba. "Man, I don't even have a clue how to describe this one."

"Just try, Tater," Bubba urged.

"Well," said Tater, releasing a long slow breath, "how about just odd shaped lines in a vertical row?" he smiled and continued. "Six is easy; it is a fish, a zigzag line and a rectangle. Seven looks like a foot, followed by a zigzag line with circles above and below it. Eight looks like a teepee, bird, and two flag poles followed by a guppy above three lines."

After every description, Red laughed harder and harder, until finally Tater asked, "Do you want me to stop, Red?"

Trying to be serious, which was really hard for him, Red shook his head and said, "Sorry, Tater. I think the guppy just pushed me over the edge."

Tater, who was also trying to keep a straight face, continued. "Okay, the number nine looks like two oval pools, and finally the zero looks like the an arrow followed by a large bird and then four small, circular figures."

"So what would you say this is?" asked Bubba, pointing to the first character.

"Well, that looks like the number four followed by the number one," said Tater, holding up the diagram of the Egyptian numbers next to the rock.

"Forty-one. Okay, now all we need to look for is twenty-two," said Bubba, moving to the next rock.

"Thirty minutes have passed. Don't you think we better meet up with the rest of the Team?" asked Tater. "We don't want them to worry."

"Sure we do!" said Red sarcastically. "I want them to worry."

"No, you're right. We don't want everybody to worry. Why don't you two hurry back and get the rest of the Team. I will stay here so that we don't lose our find," suggested Bubba.

"Yeah, good one Bubba. You just want to stay here and look," said Red.

"No reason to waste time," said Bubba, smiling from ear to ear.

"Stay right here," said Tater. "We will be right back with the rest of the Team."

"Don't go anywhere," warned Red.

Bubba smiled and said, "Hurry. Time's a wastin'."

KP and Tater knew they would never get Bubba to leave, so they started back. As they ran toward the entrance, they called out for the rest of the Team.

Hero was the first to hear them calling and answered, "Tater, Red, we are over here."

Within just a few minutes, Tater and Red found the rest of the Team waiting. Red excitedly explained, "We found some rocks with writings on them. Now all we have to do is find the right number."

"Way to go," said Bean excitedly. "We're getting closer to the next clue for sure."

"Come on, ya'll. Let's go. Bubba is waiting back at the

writings for us," said Tater. "And you know, Bubba won't sit still for long."

Eagerly, the Team followed Tater and Red back toward Bubba, the rock and the writings.

"Look," said Tater, pointing toward the rock formation. "This symbol means forty-one according to the book from the library."

"Have you found any other writings?" asked Butch.

"Not yet," said Red. "Bubba was going to keep looking for more."

"Where is Bubba?" asked Hero, walking around the rock looking for him.

"Is he gone?" asked Tater, a little surprised. "He was suppose to wait here for us."

"I knew we shouldn't have left him here alone," said Red.

"He can't be too far. Don't worry, guys," said Hero, scanning the area and calling Bubba's name.

Several minutes passed with no response to the Team's continuous calling. Tater asked, "Should I go get the ranger?"

Hero said, "Let's wait a few more minutes. He's probably close. He most likely can't hear us calling. Don't worry. I'm sure he's okay."

"Quiet! I think I hear something," said Bean, waving her hands in the air.

The Team listened, but they could only hear the wind.

"He's not here," said Stick, sounding worried.

"Quiet, I'm sure I heard him," said Bean emphatically.

Intently, the Team listened again. "There, can you hear it now?" asked Bean.

"I can't hear anything," said Butch.

"Hear what?" asked Runt. "I can't hear anything but wind and rain."

"Yeah, what are we listening for?" asked Stick.

"Bubba!" replied Bean. "I think I can hear him," she said angrily.

"I can't hear anything," said Butch again.

"That's because you won't be quiet," snapped Bean. "Just listen for a minute," she said, as she held her hand to her ear.

To their surprise, the Team could hear a faint sound in the wind.

"Is that him?" asked Tater, relieved to finally hear something.

"I don't know. Let's go look, Team," said Hero.

The Team moved slowly toward the sound, stopping every few feet to listen again.

"What is that noise?" asked Red.

"It almost sounds like singing," said KP.

"Singing? Do you think Bubba would sing out here?" asked Tater.

"Sure he would," said Red. "Bubba loves to sing."

Slowly, the Team moved closer to the sound. They traveled through three hundred feet of switchback paths, up and over mounds, and in and out of rock underpasses.

Finally, Hero peered over a ledge into a small, bath-tub-shaped opening to find Bubba crawling around the base of an enormous rock. Bubba was singing the *Singles*

Ward rock version of "Popcorn Popping on the Apricot Tree" as he searched for the symbols carved into the rock.

"Hey Bubba, where are you?" asked Tater mockingly.

Bubba looked up, surprised, and answered, "Glad to see you guys. I just thought I would keep looking for the right rock."

"Bubba, we were worried about you. You should have waited for us," replied Red angrily.

"Sorry, everyone. I was just trying to find the clue for us as quick as I could," Bubba replied.

As he was about to climb back up to the Team, Bubba noticed the tops of some hieroglyphics engraved into the rock.

"Hey, everybody! Get down here quick. I think I just found another set of numbers," said Bubba, excitedly brushing the sand and mud away from the rock.

Everyone jumped down around the base of the rock.

"Well, do both of the pictures look about the same?" Bean asked, trying to see for herself.

Lying on the ground, Bubba held the library book next to the engraved writing on the rock.

"I think that's the right number," said Hero excitedly.

Stick jumped up and down and yelled, "Are you sure? Wahooo."

"It looks about right to me," answered Butch.

"One step closer to the treasure," said Stick excitedly.

"Where to from here?" asked Runt.

"The clue said, 'Climb to the top and look for the light'," replied Butch.

"Who wants to climb to the top?" asked Hero, as he

leaned back trying to see the top of the rock through the misty rain.

"I will," replied Bubba.

"So will I," added Runt, Butch and Stick.

"Who's the best climber?" asked Bean.

"We all know the answer to that," replied Tater, with a smile aimed toward Bubba.

Everyone agreed. Bubba was definitely the best climber on the Team. No one could scurry up a tree as fast as he could.

Bubba took a few steps back, looked up toward the top of the rock, then walked around the entire base of the rock surveying the area. He picked the area with the best terrain for climbing and quickly started up the steep, rock wall. The rain made the climb treacherous, and each new handhold seemed slicker than the last. Bubba cautiously inched his way toward the top. Time ticked by slowly as the Team watched Bubba meticulously choose each move.

As Bubba reached about the half-way point, Butch bellowed from below, "Come on, Bubba. If you don't hurry, we're gonna be late getting home."

When Bubba looked down to answer Butch, he noticed the distance he had climbed and froze. Bubba really did not like heights — good climber or not. He clung to the wall, closed his eyes and tried to regain his composure.

Seeing this, Hero yelled, "Take your time, Bubba. We're in no hurry. If we have to, we can come back tomorrow."

Bean quickly called to Bubba, "It might even be better to try and climb the rock tomorrow. Maybe the rain will have stopped by then."

Bubba opened his eyes, looked up, let out a heavy breath and replied, "I'm fine. No worries. Besides, we are already here. I don't want to have to come back. I'm almost there." Trying to change the focus away from his fear of heights, Bubba asked, "Now what am I looking for when I get to the top? Some sort of light, right?"

"That's what the clue says," replied Bean loudly.

As Bubba continued the climb, Bean reread the clue, trying to help keep his mind off of the long climb to the top.

After a long time, Bubba finally pulled himself over the crest of the rock. Hero was relieved that Bubba had made it safely.

"Let's climb back up to the ledge surrounding the rock. I'm sure we will have a better view from up there," Hero suggested.

The Team climbed back to the ledge and waited for any word from Bubba as he searched for the light. More than five minutes passed with no response from Bubba.

Stick started to call Bubba's name. When Bubba finally poked his head over the top, he called, "I think I have found something."

"What is it?" asked Stick. "What is it?"

"There is a diamond-shaped cut in the very center of the rock. From inside, the rock glows with a bright light. I have been trying to see what is inside, but the reflection is too bright. I can't see anything," Bubba responded. "What do you want me to do?"

"Hey, try throwing a rock or stick or something inside

and see if you can hit anything down there," Butch answered.

"Just reach in and feel for the key," suggested KP. "The hole can't be that big."

"No way, KP. You don't reach your hand into some hole that has been here for thousands of years. I could get my arm bit off," Bubba defensively replied.

Hero thought for a minute and then said, "Does anyone remember the movie *Indiana Jones and the Last Crusade?"*

Some of the Team nodded, wondering where Hero was heading.

Hero continued, "In that movie, Indiana Jones had to do three things before he could enter the temple. What were they? Does anyone remember?"

Runt was the first to respond. "That's my favorite movie. The first thing he had to do was enter on his knees."

"Wasn't the second that he had to step off the ledge with nothing under his feet?" asked Butch.

"Yeah, I think so," said Tater.

"No," said Runt. "The second is when he spelled the name of 'God' and almost fell through the stones."

"Oh, yeah. You're right," said Tater.

"Does anyone remember the third?" asked Hero.

"Wasn't that a choice of faith?" asked Bean.

"Yep. That is where he had to choose the cup, based on his prior knowledge," replied KP.

"No," said Runt. "The third is when he has to step off the ledge. He has to have faith that something will be there to stop him from falling to his death. Then he chooses a cup."

"I was fixin' to say that," said Tater smiling.

"Why?" asked Bubba.

Hero excitedly said, "Can't you see? This is a leap of faith, Bubba. You are going to have to reach into the hole and have faith that you will find the box, even though you can't see it."

"Are you kidding?" Bubba asked. "I am not reaching my hand in there! Do you know what could be down there?"

"I'm with you, Bubba. I wouldn't put my hand in there either," said Stick.

"Come on, Bubba. You can do it," said KP.

"You gotta do this Bubba. We have to get that key," said Bean.

Hesitantly, Bubba shook his head. Then with a long heavy sigh, he said, "Guys, you're killing me up here. I think you would make me jump the forty feet down off this rock if you thought we might find the key faster! I've already been pinched by a crab and almost fell into hot lava. What's next?"

"Come on, Bubba. We're all in this together. I will come up if that will help," said Hero, ready to climb.

Bubba quickly stood up, turned back toward the center of the rock and said, "All right. I'm going, I'm going. I'll figure out something."

As Bubba disappeared, the Team waited anxiously. Several minutes passed before Bubba's head again appeared over the edge of the rock.

With an exasperated look, he hollered down to the Team. "I think I have found something, but I need some help to reach it."

"Why, what's wrong?" asked Butch.

"The opening is to small for me to get inside. I'm sure something is there, but the hole is tiny, making it impossible for me to see for sure," Bubba replied.

"Impossible for you?" Butch questioned.

"I will go. I can help," said KP.

"I can, too," sounded Tater.

"Wait, wait!" Bubba quickly responded.

"What's up, Bubba?" asked Hero.

"I think I'm gonna need Stick's help on this one," he replied.

"Stick's help? What are you talking about?" asked Runt. "If it's really scary, he's not going to be a lot of help."

"I'm not as afraid as Stick is about this kind of stuff, Bubba," said Bean. "Do you want me to come up there and help?" she asked.

"No guys, I need Stick on this one," Bubba replied. "Come on, Stick. I need your help up here now."

"He's awfully afraid of stuff like this, Bubba," replied Hero. "Is he actually going to be able to help you?"

"I think he is going to be the only one who will be able to," said Bubba confidently. As he looked down toward Stick, he lifted his eyebrows, smiled, and said, "Stick, you da' man on this one. Get up here and help me out, will ya?"

Reluctantly, Stick looked up to Bubba and asked, "Are you sure you really need me? I think Bean might be better help."

"Seriously, Stick, I need you," Bubba answered. "Get up here. Hey Team, help him start the climb," Bubba insisted.

Nervous at how hard the climb was for Bubba, Stick slowly started climbing up the rock, moving slowly from one handhold to the next. As the Team watched, they were sure he was purposely moving as slowly as possible.

"Move it, Stick. We're gonna be late getting back, and I don't want to get into trouble tonight," said Tater.

"We can't afford to be late. Our treasure hunting fun will be over if we are!" reminded KP.

"I'm going, you guys. Just give me a minute," replied Stick.

Stick continued on his slow and steady pace. As he reached the top, everyone cheered, whistled and clapped.

Stick twisted his head around and bowed to the Team saying, "Thank you, thank you. Now leave me alone."

Bubba grabbed Stick's arm and said, "Quit messing around. We've got a key to find. Let's go."

As the Team watched from the ledge, the two boys disappeared.

Bubba quickly ushered Stick to the small, diamond-shaped opening in the rock.

"Stick, I can't fit into the opening, but I think you might be able to," said Bubba, as he pointed to the rock.

"I really don't want to wiggle down in there," said Stick. "What if something is down there, and then I can't get back out? Oh, why did you have to pick me?" he asked.

"Because you're small, and can fit, and because I am strong enough to hold your weight. I don't think anything bad is in there," replied Bubba. "When I stuck my head into the opening, everything was alright. The light was bright, but if felt warm inside. All of the walls are white. Even the small box, that I hope holds the key, is white," said Bubba. As he pointed toward the opening, he said, "Look for yourself."

Stick bent down on one knee and hesitantly inched his head toward the small, diamond-shaped opening. As he reached it, he slowly opened his eyes and peered inside. He scanned the small room. To his surprise, he felt warm and comforted. He saw the beautiful, soft white walls and felt very peaceful.

"Do you think you can fit inside?" asked Bubba, interrupting Stick's solace.

Intrigued, Stick sat up and asked, "Did you see that there are no bugs or crawly things inside?"

"No way, are you sure?" asked Bubba.

"Yep," Stick replied. "And no rain. It is warm and beautiful in there."

"That's cool. Are you sure?" Bubba asked, wondering if he should have tried to wiggle inside.

"Yes, and boy will it be nice to climb in and get out of the rain," Stick answered.

Stick, laying flat on his stomach, said, "Bubba, hold on to my feet. Don't let me go, and I will try to maneuver myself inside."

"That works for me. How far do you think it is to the floor?" asked Bubba. "Can you see?"

"It's hard to tell with everything being the same color," replied Stick. "So don't let go of me. I don't want to fall if it is twenty feet to the bottom."

He slid his head, right arm and shoulder, then his left arm and shoulder slowly into the opening in the rock. Using his arms to push, he wiggled left and right, inching his body further and further through the opening. Stick was moving along fine until his belt reached the opening. He continued trying to pull himself through the hole, but his belt wedged tighter and tighter into the rock. With a small stone box in sight, Stick stretched out as far as he could. But as hard as he stretched, the handle was just out of reach.

Frustrated, he called to Bubba, "Pull me back up a little, will you?"

Bubba pulled, but Stick wouldn't budge. Knowing he could lift Stick easily, Bubba slapped his hands together. He grabbed Stick's ankles and pulled with every ounce of his strength. Finally with a loud pop, Stick's belt came free from the rock. Stick pulled off his belt and wiggled back inside. Bubba barely had time to stand back up and grab Stick's ankles again before he slid back down inside the opening.

"Hold on," he called. "Wait a minute before you get hurt. I don't have hold of you yet."

Stick was already within inches of reaching the stone box. As he maneuvered his hips past the opening, gravity pulled the rest of his body through. Once inside the rock, Stick hit the soft, white sand with a thud.

"Hey, what happened to holding on to me?" he called, as he picked himself up and dusted off his pants.

"I told you I didn't have you yet," replied Bubba. "Are you okay?" he asked anxiously.

"Yep, I'm fine," replied Stick, brushing off the sand.

"Is the key in that stone box?" Bubba asked excitedly.

"I'm not sure. I'm just getting to it," Stick replied. He bent down to pick up the stone box. After several attempts, Stick still had not moved it an inch.

"Bubba!" shouted Stick. "This box is stuck."

"Stuck where," asked Bubba.

"Partly in the wall," Stick answered.

"Can you push the box on its side?" Bubba asked.

"Let me try," replied Stick. He pushed it with his hands. "It won't move at all," he said.

"Come on, Stick. You can do it. I have faith in you," encouraged Bubba. "Try one more time. Push with everything you've got," he said.

Stick inspected the stone box. It was about eight inches square. It was set into the wall about three inches deep. He thought for a minute Then he sat down as close as he could to the wall of the small cave. With his feet on the side of the box and his back to the cave wall, Stick started pushing. His entire body strained under the pressure. His veins began to bulge and make ridges in his face and neck, but still he struggled with all his might to move the stone box.

As Stick was about to give up, the box moved slightly. Feeling a surge of adrenalin in his small body, he again pushed with as much mighty force as he had. Within seconds, the square box tipped on its side, teetered on its edge and finally fell out of the wall. As it did, the lid slid forward from the top just enough for Stick to reach his small hands through the opening.

Inside the box was the usual set of keys. But this

time, Stick also found a rock engraved with an Egyptian drawing.

Stick screamed, "Bubba! Bubba!"

"What? Did you get the box open?" Bubba asked, poking his head back through the opening. "Did you find the keys?" he asked excitedly.

"Not only did I find the keys, but look at the picture on this rock," Stick said, as he held the rock up toward the opening for Bubba to see.

"Cool," replied Bubba. "Should we take it?"

"I don't know. I wonder what it means?" questioned Stick, as he gazed at the rock.

"Bring it, and grab the key. We are never going to make it back home on time," said Bubba, looking at his watch.

Stick glanced at his watch and jumped when he saw that the Team had only twenty-five minutes to get back home. He hastily ran back to the stone box and looked at the five keys. None of the keys seem to be the most plain. Stick again called to Bubba.

"I'm not sure which one to take. They all look plain. What do you think?" he asked, holding up the keys for Bubba to see.

"You are the only one who can really see them, Stick. Which one looks plain?" asked Bubba.

"They all do," replied Stick. "I don't want to choose the wrong key."

"Well, it's in your capable hands, Stick. But please, pick the right one. I don't want to have to come back here again," said Bubba.

Stick looked up at Bubba and shrugged. He gazed back down at the box and keys. Then noticed on the box a small, carved picture of a man and an eye. He thought for a minute and wondered if the picture might represent Moroni. He again studied each key. He prayed in his heart for help to choose the right key. As he did, he noticed one of the keys had the same carved picture of a man and an eye.

"This has to be the right one," he thought. He carefully placed the key inside his pants pocket and pushed the lid back on the stone box. Then he tried to set the box back up straight.

"You can do it, Stick," Bubba cheered.

Stick again strained every muscle as he attempted to stand the box up straight. After teetering on its edge, Stick gave the box one final push, and it stood upright once again.

"Bubba," called Stick. "Pull me up. Let's get home quick."

Stick moved as close to the opening as he could. Bubba leaned inside, reached down, took hold of Stick's hand and pulled with all his might. Stick tried to help by walking up the interior walls of the cave.

"Pull! Pull hard," yelled Stick. "I am almost there."

Bubba's face was red and his cheeks puffed out from holding his breath. With one more hard tug, Stick was through the opening and on the top of the rock with Bubba.

"Come on. We've got to hurry," said Stick.

Bubba crawled over to the edge of the rock, closed his eyes and hollered down to the Team. "We have the key. Watch out. We are coming down," he said. Then he turned to Stick and asked, "Ready?"

Stick replied, "Going down will be the easy part."

Bubba opened his backpack and pulled out his rope. He tied one end of the rope around Stick, and then he tied the other around his waist. Without a word, Stick moved to the edge of the rock and started rappelling down toward the Team. Within minutes, he had reached the bottom.

He untied the rope and bellowed to Bubba, "You're next. Hurry! We're going to be late."

Bubba pulled the rope back to the top, placed it in his backpack, and slowly dropped his legs over the edge. He carefully maneuvered down the rock, jumping as he neared about ten feet from the ground. Without a word the Team rushed to the main entrance, unlocked their bicycles and raced toward home.

Chapter Ten

As they reached the neighborhood, they could see the street lined with cars — one belonging to the families of every member of the Team.

Hero, prodded the Team, "Come on guys. We're not gonna make it."

They had less than one minute. No one wanted to be grounded for the next day, so they peddled as fast as they could, straight up and over the curb. Dropping their bikes on the front lawn, they ran as fast as they could into the house.

"We're here," yelled Runt, throwing open the front door.

"You're kinda pushing it, Team," said Butch's mom.

"I wasn't sure you were going to get here in time," said Bean's mom.

"Good for you, Team. You might get to go out searching for treasure tomorrow after all," said Runt's dad.

"Just barely in time, Team," commented Tater's mom, as she glanced down at her watch.

"How is your treasure hunting going?" asked Hero's Dad.

"We're still looking," responded Hero. "Nothing yet."

"But we are getting closer," said Red.

"Yes, we could be rich by tomorrow if we are lucky," chimed in Stick.

"That close?" asked KP's mom curiously.

"We sure are," replied KP confidently. "I'm sure we could find the treasure any time now."

The Team smiled, excited at the prospect. The adults chuckled, as if they did not really believe the Team would find any treasure.

"With all that searching, you are probably hungry," said Mom. Pizza is on the counter for everyone. Also, Hero and Bubba, make sure you two watch Squeaks. She is your responsibility tonight," stated Mom sternly. "Take good care of her, and be nice."

"Red, no funny business tonight," warned his mom. "I don't want to come back to any pranks. Is that clear?"

"Don't worry, Mom. I'm focusing on finding treasure right now," Red replied.

"We will be home around ten o'clock. Don't let anyone in the house. We need to be careful with those prison escapees still at large," said Stick's mom.

"We rented a movie for you. It's on the T.V. Have fun, and make sure you all behave," said Hero's dad. "See you in a few hours."

They all turned to leave when Bubba nudged Hero and whispered, "Ask."

"D...D...Dad," stammered Hero. "Do you think we could run to the library really quick? We will take Squeaks with us."

"Not a chance, Hero," said dad. "You are in charge tonight, and I don't want to worry about Squeaks or the Team outside in the rain."

"Especially with those fugitives lurking around town," said Stick's mom. "Just stay home tonight, Team."

"Mom, where is Squeaks?" asked Hero.

"She is in my room watching television. Make sure she eats," said Hero's mom.

They were disappointed, but the Team understood. Eager to look at the new key, they quickly waved good-bye to their parents.

Hero cleaned off the kitchen table. He laid the key and rock down so that everyone could inspect them. Tater, as head of security, checked the house carefully. He had not seen the two men, but he wanted to make sure that the Team had not been followed.

"How are we going to translate the clue on this key?" Stick asked.

"We can't split up and go to the library?" asked Butch.

"Not a chance," said Hero. "We would end up getting caught and be grounded for a week."

"Do you think Cheri could translate the key if we called her on the phone and explained the pictures on it?" asked Runt.

"I don't think so. How would we even know where to start?" asked Bean.

"Well, Bean, we could always try," said KP.

"Otherwise we will not be able to start figuring out the clue until after the library opens tomorrow," said Bubba.

"It's not a bad idea," stated Hero. "We could at least try. Red, hurry and get the phone," he said. "Bubba, please go get the phone book. Let's call her."

Hero picked up the key and tried to decipher some of the writing. Bubba quickly looked up the number, and Red dialed the phone as quickly as Bubba read it to him. As the library phone started to ring, Red handed the receiver to Hero and said, "It's for you."

Before long, Hero had Cheri on the phone.

"Hi, Cheri. This is Hero from the Team. You have been helping us translate some clues?" he said nervously.

"Hello, Hero. How can I help you?" Cheri asked in a cheerful voice.

"We have found the next key," Hero replied.

"Great! Bring it down," said Cheri. "I will be here for about another hour," she said.

"Well, that is why I am calling," said Hero. "We have been ordered to stay home while our parents are out to dinner tonight."

"I will be at the library in the morning," Cheri replied. "But probably not until about eleven thirty."

"We were hoping to get a faster start," said Hero. "That is why I am calling."

"Oh," responded Cheri. "What would you like me to do?"

"If I explained the picture, would you be able to translate the clue over the phone?" Hero asked hesitantly.

Cheri was silent for a minute before she responded. "I'm not sure that would work very well, Hero. If I thought that you described one figure, but it was actually something else, I could send you to the wrong place. If that happened, you could get into trouble, or someone could get hurt."

"Okay," Hero responded dejectedly. "We will just come see you tomorrow."

"Well, could I stop by your house on my way home?" she asked. "I would be willing to do that."

Hero's eyes perked up and a huge smile spread across his face. "We would love that. Is that really all right with you?"

"Not a problem," Cheri responded. "I don't want to hold you back from finding the treasure. Now, tell me where you live."

Hero quickly gave her the address and thanked her again before he hung up the phone. "We are in luck," he said to the Team. "She is going to come over here."

"All right. That is perfect," said Bubba excitedly.

"Hey, we can't let any strangers in," said Squeaks.

"She is not a stranger, Squeaks," said Hero. "Mind your own business anyway."

"Fine, but you are going to get in trouble if you don't ask," she replied.

"She is right, Hero," said Bubba.

"Call Mom on her cell phone and get permission, Bubba," said Hero, scowling at Squeaks.

Bubba called his mom and quickly had permission for Cheri to come by the house.

"Wasn't that easy?" smirked Squeaks. "Beats getting into trouble."

"Great job, Squeaks," said Bean, patting her on the back.

"Good. That's fixed. Let's eat, ya'll," said Tater.

Famished, everyone sat down around the table and grabbed a piece of pizza. Even Squeaks joined the Team, much to Hero's frustration.

"Do we still need to worry about the two men who want to steal our treasure?" asked Bean, between bites of pizza.

"I think we do," responded Tater. "I'm not sure where they are, or how much actual information they have. But I think we do need to be concerned about them."

"What if they know where we live," asked Stick nervously.

"They will never find that out," said Butch. "We would see them following us."

Squeaks started to giggle.

"Yeah, I bet you are right. How could someone follow us and we not notice them?" asked Runt.

"How did they find out about the treasure then? Do you think they overheard us at the library?" asked Bubba.

"That has to be it," replied Hero. "We really haven't talked about it anywhere else except the Treehouse."

Squeaks started shaking her head and laughing.

Finally Hero said, "Squeaks, you can eat with us. But, if you are going to be loud and irritate us, you can leave. All right?"

"Okay," answered Squeaks, still giggling.

"If we stay away from the library, then there would be no way for them to find us," said Runt.

"Then we wouldn't even have to worry about them," said Red.

Squeaks, laughing uncontrollably now, almost fell off her chair.

"That's it, Squeaks. What is so funny?" demanded Hero.

"Look out the sliding door at the Treehouse, and tell me what you see," Squeaks replied.

"What am I looking for?" asked Bubba, gazing out back through the pouring rain at the Treehouse.

"Look at the roof, " she replied.

Bubba looked and looked, but saw nothing.

"Why are you laughing?" asked Hero.

"Just go look and see," said Squeaks, as the doorbell rang.

"Let me see if I can tell," said Tater, looking out the window.

Squeaks ran to open the front door as Tater, Bubba and Butch all looked out at the Treehouse. Squeaks led Cheri back to the kitchen to meet the Team.

Tater said, "Hey, there is something on top of the treehouse. Look," he said, as he pointed towards the tree.

"I can see it, too. What is it?" Bubba asked.

"Something is moving," said Butch, just as Cheri walked in the kitchen door.

"What's moving?" Cheri asked inquisitively.

The three boys spun around instantly.

"Oh, Cheri. Hi," said Bubba. "Sorry, you startled me. I wasn't expecting you for another hour."

"I wanted to have plenty of time to translate the clue correctly, so I left work early. Now, is something out there?" Cheri asked, starting to walk toward Bubba.

"Oh, no. We could see some animal or something moving on the Treehouse, and we were trying to decide what it was," said Tater, matter-of-factly. He was hoping to change the subject as he casually walked over to the kitchen table and sat down.

"Thank you so much for coming over," interjected Hero. "Come look at the new key."

"We were excited to show you the next clue and the picture we found with it," said Stick.

They caught Cheri's attention with the mention of the picture. Curious, she stopped before looking out the window and said, "Picture? That's new. Please show it to me."

Stick retrieved it out of his pocket and said, "Well, it actually is more like a rock engraving."

Cheri was intrigued. She took the baseball-sized rock from Stick and started to inspect it. "I wonder what it has to do with your treasure?" she questioned.

"I wasn't sure, so I thought I would bring it. I hope it might have something to do with the next clue," replied Stick.

"Well, then. Where is the newest key? Let's get this

clue translated," Cheri said, setting the rock down on the kitchen table.

Hero had the key in his hand. He quickly passed it across the table to Cheri.

She quietly studied the writing on the key for several minutes before she pulled her glasses down low on her nose. She peered over the rims toward the Team.

Before she could say anything, Stick asked, "Did I pick the wrong key? I was afraid I chose the wrong one. I had to choose all by myself. I'm sorry, Team. I didn't mean to. I will go back by myself if I need to so that I can get the right key."

As he paused to take a breath, Cheri quickly interjected, "Quiet, quiet. Everything is all right. I think you have the right clue. KP would you please write down the translation again for me?"

KP fumbled around and found paper and pen. He sat down next to Cheri as she started translating.

> "'No 2 Nephi 23:10 is there; enter only if ye dare.
> It opens from the Ether 9:35; then follow the 2 Nephi 21:7.
> Now the key is there inside of the 1 Nephi 4:4.
> Without Alma 47:18 help, none will Jacob 2:18-19 it at all.'"

Wow, Team. I can't believe this. Six references this time. You're going to be working on this one all night," Cheri said.

"We can do it!" said Hero.

"Have you had any further problems with the two men following you?" Cheri questioned.

"No, I think we lost them at the library," said Bubba.

"Good," said Cheri. "Lock the doors and keep a close eye out for them. I don't want any of you to get hurt."

The Team agreed.

Cheri looked at her wristwatch. "I have got to get home."

"Thank you again for coming. We could not have done this without you," said KP.

"Oh, before I leave, I have a thought about the picture engraved on the rock," said Cheri. "I am not sure, but I think it symbolizes an eye that is single to the glory of God. That idea might come in handy at some point. Good luck," she finished, as she walked out the front door and down the sidewalk to her car.

"See you tomorrow with the next clue," said Butch.

"I hope so," Cheri called back to the Team, as she climbed into her car.

The Team quickly returned to the kitchen, knowing they had a lot of work ahead of them.

Hero asked, "Bubba, what was outside that you guys were hiding from Cheri?"

"Something? You mean someone?" responded Bubba. "I think we have visitors in our Treehouse."

"Are you kidding? Who?" Runt asked.

"I think it is the crooks," chimed in Tater, as he walked over to the back door. "It looks like they are fixin' to make themselves a little hiding place up on top of our Treehouse."

"I can't believe this! How did they find us?" asked Bean.

"I have no idea. What are we going to do now?" asked Red.

"Call the police, quick," said Stick, running to grab the phone.

"No. Wait. If you call the police, there goes all of our fun," said Butch.

"Why?" asked Stick, "What are you talking about?"

"Instead of treasure hunting, we will be answering questions and all that police stuff," said Runt.

"Won't the police just take them away?" asked Stick.

"They will probably take us to the police station to fill out reports," replied Bean. "We will be there all night."

"I'm sure they would say something about the map, and then everyone will be after us," said Butch.

"Can you imagine our parents?" asked Bubba. "I can hear them now. 'Treasure hunting is too dangerous. There will be no more of that.'"

"You're right, Bubba. Our treasure hunt will be over for good," said Red.

"Do you think we can handle them for the time being? And after we find the treasure, we can call the police?" asked Butch.

"We could, but we might be taking a big risk," answered Hero. "What do you think, Team?"

"They don't look really dangerous," said Tater, still watching them through the glass door. "Especially in those silly, old suits."

"According to the television news, they are very dangerous," replied Bean fearfully.

"They do want to steal our treasure," said Stick.

"We could just turn them in," said Hero.

"And face all of the questions?" asked Tater.

"And waste all the time?" asked Red.

"Nah, let's have a little fun with them first," said Butch.

"Fun? How?" asked Runt curiously.

"Let's see. We could let them think we don't know anything about them, and that they might have a chance at freedom and the treasure," said Butch.

"We are going to have to act normal," said Hero, sensing some concerns. "Tater, your full focus is keeping an eye on those guys. We don't want any surprises. The rest of us need to translate this clue so we know where we are going tomorrow. Squeaks," continued Hero, "how in the world did you know those guys were up there?"

"I bet you wish you knew." With that, Squeaks turned, flipped her hair, and strutted into the living room.

"Don't worry about that now, Hero," said Bubba. "We will find out later."

As Tater kept peering out the back window, trying to get a good glimpse of the crooks, Hero pulled out his scriptures and said, "Let's get down to business. Bean, would you read the first line of the clue. Let's start solving this."

Bean began to read, "'No 2 Nephi 23:10 is there; enter only if ye dare.' Do you want me to read the scripture reference now?" she asked.

"Yes, please," replied Hero.

Bean started reading, "2 Nephi 23:10, 'For the stars of heaven and the constellations thereof shall not give their light; the sun shall be darkened in his going forth, and the moon shall not cause her light to shine.'"

"The clue says, 'no *blank* is there; enter only if ye dare'," said KP.

"What's not there? Stars?" asked Red.

"That is what we are trying to figure out!" responded Stick, with an infuriated look on his face.

"What else might not be there, according to the scripture?" wondered Runt.

"Well, it says no constellations, no sun, no moon, no stars and no light," remarked Butch.

"That's it!" shouted Bean. "No light is there!"

"That sounds right to me," replied Tater.

"'No light is there; enter only if ye dare. Good job, Bean," said KP.

"I love it when we get an easy one," said Butch. "What's next?"

"Read the second line for us, KP," prompted Bubba.

KP read. "'It opens from the Ether 9:35; then follow the 2 Nephi 21:7.'"

"Butch," said Hero, handing him the scriptures, "read the next two references for us."

Butch grabbed the book, looked up the first reference and read, "Ether 9:35, 'And it came to pass that when they had humbled themselves sufficiently before the Lord he did send rain upon the face of the earth; and the people began to revive again, and there began to be fruit in the north countries, and in all the countries round about. And the Lord did show forth the power unto them in preserving them from famine.'"

"How did it open from that?" asked Bean.

"Do you think we are supposed to humble ourselves?" questioned Stick. "Maybe then these clues would be easier to decipher."

"We have asked for help. Have some faith," replied Butch.

"Let's write down every word that might work to fill in the blank. That might help," suggested KP, already handing Red pen and paper.

Red wrote down every word that might work in the sentence. Then, he crossed the word off the list if it did not make sense.

"The words left are *earth* and *north countries,* and they both work," said Red.

"It is asking us a direction, right?" asked Runt.

"I think so," said Hero.

"I think the answer is north," said Bubba.

"I think you are right," said KP.

"Why?" asked Red.

"Because it is the only direction-giving word in this scripture reference," answered KP.

The Team agreed.

Butch located the second reference and read, "2 Nephi 21:7, 'And the cow and the bear shall feed; their young ones shall lie down together; and the lion shall eat straw like the ox.'"

Bubba knew the clue was difficult. Before anyone could say anything he said, "We can do this. KP, please read the second sentence of the clue again."

KP read, "'It opens from the north; then follow the 2 Nephi 21:7.'"

The Team studied every word. Runt, who had been intently reading every word of each scripture said, "The only words that fit are either *cow* or *bear,* neither of which roam free anywhere in the area."

KP agreed and said, "How could we follow a bear anyway?"

"I don't know for sure, but let's not eliminate either one," suggested Bean. "It may make more sense as we get closer to finding the next clue."

"Read the first two lines please, Bean," requested Bubba.

"'No light is there; enter only if ye dare. It opens from the north; then follow the cow or bear,'" she responded.

"That sounds right," said Red.

"We are doing great," said Stick. "Let's move on to the third line."

Butch read, "'Now the key is there inside of the 1 Nephi 4:4.'"

Hero, already turning to the reference, found it and read, "1 Nephi 4:4, 'Now when I had spoken these words, they were yet wroth, and did still continue to murmur; nevertheless they did follow me up until we came without the walls of Jerusalem.'"

Again, the team systematically tried every word from the reference.

Runt screamed when he reached the word *walls.* "That's it! That's it! The key is inside the *walls.*"

"I think you are right," said Bean.

"That has to be it," said Red. "But how does a key get into a wall?" he questioned.

"I'm not sure, but I bet we can find it," said Tater, who was now paying more attention to the clue than the crooks.

"What is the last sentence of the clue again?" asked Stick.

KP said, "'Without Alma 47:18 help, none will Jacob 2:18-19 it at all.'"

"Butch, would you please read the first reference?" asked Hero, as he handed him the Book of Mormon.

Butch eagerly found the reference and read, "Alma 47 verse 18, 'And it came to pass that Amalickiah caused that one of his servants should administer poison by degrees to Lehonti, that he died."

"Where is this clue leading?" asked Red, with a confused look on his face.

"The clue says without 'blank' help, so it has to be a person right?" asked Butch.

"It sounds like it to me," said Tater.

"Then that only leaves a couple of options," said Runt.

"Who?" asked Hero.

"Well, there are only two names in this scripture — Amalickiah, which I have heard before, and someone named Lehonti. Has anyone heard that name?" asked Runt.

"I haven't," said Bean, "and I have read the Book of Mormon."

"Why don't we just write down both names. We know it will have to be one," said Bubba.

"The second part of the last line is what?" asked Red.

"It is Jacob 2:18-19," said Bean.

"Would you read it for us please?" asked Hero, excited they were already on the last scripture reference.

"Sure," said Bean, as she opened to Jacob. "Verse 18, 'But before ye seek for riches, seek ye for the kingdom of God.' Verse 19, 'And after ye have obtained a hope in Christ ye shall obtain riches, if ye seek them; and ye will seek them for the intent to do good — to clothe the naked, and to feed the hungry, and to liberate the captive, and administer relief to the sick and the afflicted.'"

"Hey, we are gonna be rich. The clue is finally talking about treasure!" said Stick excitedly.

"Yes, but it also says to seek for riches *after* we seek for the kingdom of God," replied Bean.

"I can hardly wait to see what this treasure really is," said Bubba. "Do you think we will get to keep it? Maybe even be millionaires?" he questioned.

"I think you are jumping the gun," replied Hero. "Let's just finish with the clue and decide what to do with those criminals on our Treehouse first," he said.

Tator quickly headed back to the sliding glass door.

"Let's use our system to find the right word again," suggested Runt.

After several minutes, Butch had decided that only two words would fit.

"I think the word that fits has to be either *seek* or *obtain,*" said Butch, confidently. The Team voted and agreed on obtain, so Hero quickly read the sentence aloud to the Team.

"'Without Lehonti's or Amalickiah's help, none will obtain it at all,'" recited Hero.

"Does that sound right?" asked Bubba.

"I think it does. The clue makes sense to me," said Runt, ready to plan where the Team was going next.

"I think so, too," agreed Tater.

"KP will you read the entire clue, please?" requested Hero.

KP picked up the clue and read,

> *"'No light is there; enter only if ye dare.*
> *It opens from the north, then follow the cow or bear.*
> *The key is there inside of the walls.*
> *Without Lehonti's or Amalickiah's help, none will obtain it at all.'"*

"Man, we are so smart!" said Red, strutting around the kitchen.

"Be careful. Last time we thought we had it, but we were wrong," warned Hero.

"I think we have it deciphered correctly. But, where are we going?" questioned Stick.

"I think the location has got to be the caves at Paradise Mountain," said Runt.

"I'm not sure of any cave on the north side of the mountain, but that makes the most sense. They are the only caves around the area," said Tater.

The Team agreed that Paradise Mountain seemed like the right place to start.

"I think we should meet earlier tomorrow so we have enough time to find the clue," suggested KP. "And maybe we will even find the treasure."

"I agree. We should meet at seven a.m. and get an early start," added Hero. "Is everyone okay with that?" he asked.

The Team eagerly agreed. Hero again assigned everyone supplies to bring.

"I'm worried about the map, keys and the clues," Hero said. "I will hold onto the map. Bean should keep the keys, and KP should take the clues. That way, no one person has all the information for the treasure."

Tater, eyes glued to the Treehouse, hastily responded, "I think that is great. We don't want to keep all our eggs in one basket."

Everyone agreed.

"Now, what are we going to do with these criminals?" Stick asked, worried about his chance at the treasure.

As the Team silently pondered exactly what to do with the crooks, Tater finally caught a glimpse of them. He slowly closed the blinds, keeping one slat of the blinds open so that the duo could not see him. After a few minutes, he watched Eddie and Earl make their way down the ladder and out of the Treehouse.

"Everyone, look quick!" whispered Tater. "There they are."

The Team cautiously peeked out the blinds and nervously watched as the duo crept out of the backyard.

"I think we should send them on a wild goose chase," said Butch mischievously.

"I think we should send them back to jail," interjected Squeaks.

"Squeaks," shrieked Hero. "Have you been listening to us this whole time? I thought you were watching cartoons. This isn't your problem. This is the Team's Treasure hunt."

"Well, Mom said I could help tonight. Besides, I already know their names and who they are. They are the escaped bad guys. And I am not going to tell you anything else if you don't let me help," Squeaks said matter-of-factly.

Hero looked at the Team and shrugged his shoulders helplessly.

Tater, still watching the duo said, "Okay, Squeaks. You always seem to know what happens in that Treehouse. What are their plans?"

Squeaks smiled and said, "Do I get to come with you tomorrow?"

"Not a chance," said Red.

"Then I'm not telling you anything," Squeaks retorted.

"Come on, Squeaks. Just tell us. You are too young to go on this treasure hunt," replied Bubba. "You could get hurt."

"If I can't go, then I'm not telling you anything," she said stubbornly.

Hero looked at the Team and asked, "Do you think she really has information we don't already know?"

"Are you kidding? Squeaks, always knows everything. I'm still trying to figure out how she gets all her information," said Runt, amazed at her knowledge.

"Okay, Squeaks. You can help us. Now what are their plans?" inquired Hero.

"Well," she said. "First, their names are Eddie and Earl, and they are the two guys who escaped from the jail. Second, they are going to take your treasure when you bring it up to the Treehouse. They don't know you know anything about them yet. And they found out about the map because they were hiding in a closet in Mr. Jensen's attic. You missed them when you were cleaning it."

"How do you know all of this?" asked Tater, still watching Eddie and Earl.

"I heard them talking about it while they were making their hiding place," Squeaks replied.

"How did you get up there to hear them?" asked Stick, hoping she would give up her secret hiding spot.

"I'm not telling you that," Squeaks answered. "I'm not that dumb."

"I was hoping you weren't paying attention," replied Stick, with a mischievous smile.

"Does Mom know they are hiding up there?" Bubba asked.

"No, not yet," replied Squeaks smugly. "I think you guys are going to have to set them up. Maybe leave the map out and talk about how you couldn't find the last clue. They already know you have two of them," said Squeaks confidently. "Or you will never get rid of them."

"We could use a fake map and hint that they should follow it before we do. Then we could let the police know where they will be," said Butch.

"We will send them on a wild goose chase and lead them right to the cops," said Runt. "Good idea, Squeaks."

As the Team sat around the kitchen table, they

discussed idea after idea about how they could help capture the crooks. Hero thought tracing the map and then changing some of the locations might work. Tater thought using a piece of leather to draw the map on would be good. Butch and Bubba thought holding a meeting in the Treehouse and giving bad information the criminals could overhear might be good, too. Runt was sure that leaving two old chest keys as bait would work. Bean liked the idea of the map leading to the authorities. Stick and KP suggested the Team pretend to just give up. Squeaks, excited to be involved, listened quietly as the Team worked on their plans. The Team carefully planned the next day's events for over an hour. They did not even open the rented movie.

Chapter Eleven

Sleep never came for Hero that night. He tossed and turned, worrying about what the prisoners might try to do.

"Was the risk too great? Was the Team's safety in question?" he wondered. He considered the next day's adventure. He knew he had seen each hour pass on the clock as he planned out in his mind the Team's every move.

The sun had barely climbed over the mountain when Hero slowly wiggled out of bed. Tired of pretending to sleep, he dressed and packed for the day's events. Then he moved quietly into the kitchen, sat down at the table and poured himself a glass of milk. He diligently searched the map, pondering whether the Team's next move was the right one.

"What if the map did lead to treasure?" he considered.

Deep in thought and contemplation, he did not notice Squeaks walk into the kitchen. Bright-eyed and ready to go, she poured herself a bowl of cereal. She carried it to the table, sat down across from Hero and added milk to her bowl. She watched him staring off into space. Several minutes passed, and she finally broke the silence.

"Worried about finding the treasure, Hero?" she asked.

Slowly looking up, Hero seemed surprised to see Squeaks already awake. He hesitantly replied, "No, I am just making sure we are heading to the right place."

Squeaks continued to gobble up her cereal as Hero sat quietly watching her eat. Her swinging feet banged on the chair legs.

"Are you still seriously planning on coming with us?" Hero asked.

"Yep!" Squeaks replied.

"It's going to be dangerous, and you are too small. I really don't think you should try to come," he said, trying to sound concerned for her safety.

"You promised I could go," she replied. "And I did give you all the information."

"Well," said Hero, "did you even ask Mom for permission? She's never gonna let you go."

"I already asked Mom. She said it was fine, as long as you keep a close eye on me," Squeaks replied.

Hero stood up and slammed the kitchen chair under

the table with a loud bang. He grabbed the map and said, "Squeaks, you better not cause any trouble or you are gonna get it," he said, as he stormed out of the kitchen. He stomped all the way down the stairs to his room.

Grinning, Squeaks slowly finished eating breakfast. She walked back to her room and filled her backpack with supplies.

The clouds crawled in over the mountains again, making the valley dark and gloomy. One by one, the teammates arrived at Hero's house. Everyone looked ready and excited to solve the remainder of the mystery.

Stick showed up wearing a safari hat. "Today's the day, Team. We have to be close," he said confidently, showing off his hat.

"Stick, we are not on a safari. What's the deal with the hat?" asked Red mockingly.

"I know, Red. This is my lucky, treasure-hunting hat," replied Stick with a grin.

Red shrugged his shoulders and said, "Whatever works, Stick."

"Do I need to bring my lucky hat?" asked Squeaks.

"Are you going with us?" asked Butch.

"I sure am," she replied.

"Excellent," said Bean, putting her arm on Squeaks' shoulder. "It will be great to have another girl join me on the hunt."

Squeaks beamed with pride.

"Hero, let's get moving. We are wasting time, and there never seems to be enough time in a day to get done all that we need to," said Bean, eager to get started.

"We should have enough time today, as long as she doesn't slow us down," Hero said, pointing toward Squeaks.

The Team watched as Squeaks quietly walked into the garage, pulled out her bike, and placed her purple backpack into the pink flowered basket hanging on the front. She climbed onto her bike, sat down on the seat, placed one foot on the ground and one foot on the pedal. She looked up at the Team with a big, toothy grin and said, "You won't have to wait for me. I am ready to go!" Then she patiently waited for the rest of the Team.

KP hollered, "She's got the right idea. Let's get moving."

Everyone jumped into action, and it was only a few minutes before the Team was prepared and ready to find clue number four.

Bubba yelled, "Mom, we're leaving."

Mom came to the front door. She looked out at the Team, and said, "Oh, I'm sorry, Team. Hero and Bubba have chores to do today. They won't be able to leave for a few hours."

She motioned for the boys to come in and help. As she turned to walk away, Hero's mouth dropped wide open. He jumped off his bike and ran toward the front door.

"Mom, wait. Are you serious?" he yelled. " I did all my chores last night. What are you talking about?"

Bubba just smiled, knowing Mom was teasing.

Before Hero could reach the door, Mom stuck her head out and said, "I'm just kidding Hero."

Hero looked as though he was about to cry. "Mom,

that's not funny," he mumbled through a squeaky voice.

Mom hurried out the door, hugged Hero and kissed him on the cheek. "Have a great day!" she said. "Take care of Squeaks. Remember, she is still a little girl."

"Mom, the guys are here," whispered Hero, as he wiped the kiss off his cheek.

Mom swatted Hero on the backside and yelled to the Team, "The clouds are rolling in. Keep your jackets with you in case the rain starts again. Those prisoners are still on the loose, and I don't want anything to happen to any of you. Take care of each other today, and be careful. Remember, I want all of you to keep an eye on Squeaks! Check in occasionally and...," after a long pause she finished, "have a great time and bring back that treasure today."

She smiled and waved as the Team rode off on their way to Paradise Mountain.

Only six miles from town was Kimball Summit, a large mountain range where the Timber and Skarpal Mountains met, forming a corner. From Kimball Summit, the Team would have a two-mile hike to Paradise Mountain, which was filled with caves, underground streams and waterfalls. The key said the next clue was on the north side, but the Team had never been to, or seen a cave on that side of the mountain.

Peddling as fast as she could, Squeaks was trying desperately to keep up with the Team. Panting for breath, she asked, "Does anyone know of a cave over on the north side of the mountain?"

Tater replied, "I've never heard of one."

"Me neither," said Bean.

"So where do you think we should start looking?" asked Red.

"We should start at the bottom of the mountain and head toward the top," said Stick.

"Well, duh, Stick," said Butch, "That only makes sense."

The Team all laughed, and Stick shrugged and smiled.

As the Team reached Kimball Summit, Butch quickly found a small bush and locked up his bike. Anxious to start the hike toward Paradise Mountain he said, "Come on. Let's get moving. We have a long way to hike."

"Are you sure we can't just ride our bikes to the caves?" asked Squeaks, as the Team all secured their bikes to nearby trees.

"No, Squeaks. But we could take you home really quick if you are too tired to go on the hike," said Hero, sounding excited at the prospect.

"No thanks, Hero," stated Squeaks firmly. "I'm just fine."

Hero said, "You better keep up on the hike."

"She'll be fine," said Bean, as she took Squeak's hand. "I will help her."

Ready to move on, Hero said, "Team, get your gear, and let's get going."

The trail up to the mountain was difficult. The terrain was rough, with only a small path cut through the dense underbrush. One-hundred foot tall trees grew over the trail creating a canopy, which sheltered the Team from the never-ending rain.

"I hope these trees cover the trail all the way to the

mountain," said Bean, grateful for the shelter they provided.

"I hope so, too," said KP. "They sure make this hike a little easier."

"I wonder if anyone from the Book of Mormon has walked this path before us?" Bubba asked.

"I think it's possible," said Bean.

"Why?" asked Butch inquisitively

"Well, don't you remember last year when we all went down to the Pageant?" asked Bean.

"Yes," said Squeaks, wanting to be involved.

"During that play, the actors said that Moroni himself had dedicated that land to be the place where a temple would be built in the future, remember?" asked Bean.

"Do you think that could mean that the Nephites have been in the town of Timber Creek?" asked Stick.

"They would've had to have been here if we really believe that this map is real," said Tater, holding up the map.

"I believe it is real," said Stick, as he adjusted his safari hat back further on his head.

"Okay then. Who has been right here on this spot of the trail?" asked Bubba.

"Moroni has for sure," said Butch.

"Yep, and maybe Helaman and Mormon," said Hero, excited at the prospect.

"What about the two thousand stripling warriors?" asked Red. "Could they have walked along this trail?"

"I bet they could have," said Hero.

"I wonder who else might have walked this path?" asked Bean.

"Or what battles might have been fought in this area?" said Bubba.

"Do you think the Lord might have walked on this trail?" asked Squeaks.

"I guess it's possible," replied Bean. "I have never thought about that until now."

"What do you think, Hero?"

"It most definitely is possible," he replied.

"What do you guys think we should do with the treasure once we find it?" asked Stick, nervous that he was not going to get to keep anything they found.

"Whatever the Lord wants us to do with it," replied Bean.

"Let's figure that out after we actually find the treasure. Okay?" asked Hero.

The Team continued up the trail, pushing forward in silence, contemplating whose steps might have come before theirs on this trail. Suddenly, Squeaks tripped on the rough terrain of the path and crashed into a heap on the ground. Hero rushed to her aid, lifting her up and brushing off her knees.

"Are you all right?" he asked, as he helped her to her feet.

Surprised at his help, Squeaks looked up at him and said, "I think so."

"Good," replied Hero.

"Let's keep moving," she said, as he helped her steady her footing.

Bubba smiled at Hero, knowing that he would never

let anything happen to Squeaks, even if he was occasionally, irritated by her.

The Team continued further up the rugged trail. Loose rocks, slippery moss, treacherous vines and tree roots lined the path. The final hill, before they reached the base of the mountain, was a steep, thirty-foot climb to a plateau. The hill was usually a fairly easy climb, but the torrential rains had made the trail more like a waterfall.

"How are we going to get up the hill?" asked Tater.

"Carefully!" replied Red with a smirk.

"Cute, Red," said Runt. "Real funny."

"What path should we take?" asked Bubba, scooping up and playing with a handful of the mud that flowed freely down the hill.

"I think we need to stay as far to the right as possible," said Bean.

"If we do," said Butch, "we should be able to use the roots from the trees as supports."

"Good idea," said Tater, as he took a hold of a vine and started pulling himself toward the top of the hill.

Everyone followed, using the same technique as Tater, pulling hand over hand. Then Stick saw a snake! He let go of the vine and fell so quickly that he took Runt, Butch and Hero back down to the bottom of the hill with him.

"What's the matter with you, Stick? Are you crazy or something?" asked Butch, picking himself up and trying to scrape some of the mud off the backside of his pants.

"Sorry, guys. There was a snake!" said Stick, frantically looking around. "It was on the vine, and it slithered across my hand," he said, shaking his hand to get rid of the feeling. "It was slimy and gross."

"Come on, Stick. You just about killed us here," said Runt, wiping the mud off his shirt.

"Sorry, guys. I just freaked out when I felt the snake on my hand," said Stick.

"Come on. Let's get going," said Hero, as he picked up his backpack.

Runt, not wanting to be knocked down again, said, "Stick, follow me, and I will make sure no snakes get anywhere near you."

"Thanks," replied Stick.

"But when we get back home, we need to work on this. You shouldn't be so worried about snakes. It's just not healthy. Okay?" asked Runt.

Stick, nervous about continuing the climb, ignored Runt's comments and inched his way up the path. He cautiously, watched every branch and vine around him for movement. He was ecstatic when he finally reached the top.

As the Team rested at the top of the hill, just a few feet from the base of the mountain, they enjoyed the majestic views of a lush, green, flower-covered landscape.

"Wow," said KP. "I have never been on this side of the mountain before."

"I don't think many people have," said Red. "It doesn't have graffiti anywhere. There aren't any broken down cars or trash anywhere. And look," he said, "there are no names carved into the bark of the trees around here."

"I didn't know a place this pretty existed anywhere near Timber Creek," stated Bean, as she scanned the area.

The Team looked around in silence, awed by the beauty. No one said a word until Bubba looked up trying to see the top of the mountain and fell over backwards.

"Bubba," said Hero, laughing, "Are you okay?"

"Yep," he replied. "It's just a long way to the top."

"What were you doing?" asked Butch.

"Trying to see if any caves are up there," replied Bubba.

Butch looked up toward the top of the mountain and said, "Man, that is a long way up. I can't even see the top in all the clouds. Are you sure there is a cave somewhere up there?"

"Well, I guess there's only one way to find out," replied Red, ready to start climbing.

"Let's get movin' ya'll, and quit gawkin' at the mountain," said Tater, as he started moving forward.

Hero hollered, "Tater, wait a minute. I don't want the Team to get separated. Let's make a plan and work together."

Tater paused, turned around to face Hero and said, "How should we start looking?"

Bubba replied, "Let's form a search line."

"A what?" asked Red.

"A search line," Bubba said again.

Bean jumped in and said, "I know, the kind of line a search party makes when they are looking for a missing person, right?"

"Yep, that's the one," said Bubba. "Let's form one long line. Spread out about arm's length apart, and start walking up the mountain."

"Great idea," interjected Runt. "Let's try it."

Everyone quickly spread out across the base of the mountain, which was only about forty-five feet at its widest point. Gradually, they inched their way up the long treacherous climb toward the top.

They were barely twenty feet up the hill when Squeaks asked, "Anybody have any idea what we are looking for, exactly?"

Runt, wondering the same thing said, "Yeah, what am I looking for?"

"I think a cave or at least an opening that leads to a cave," replied Hero.

"That should be easy," said KP. "How can we miss a cave opening in the mountain?"

"I don't know, but it would help if the grasses weren't quite so thick and tall," complained Bean, as she trudged through wet knee-high vegetation.

Stick watched closely for more slithering snakes and creepy, crawly animals as he marched up the hill. He asked, "Do you think more snakes could live up here on the mountain?"

"I think it's too wet, Stick. I wouldn't worry," replied Runt confidently. "They should all be deep down in their holes during this rain."

As Stick continued to carefully place one foot in front of the other, he breathed a cautious sigh of relief.

The Team pushed on, up the slick, muddy mountainside. Bubba broke the silence and asked, "Has anyone found anything yet?

Hero, Tater, Runt, KP, Bean, Butch and Red all shook

their heads.

"Me neither," said Squeaks.

"What about you, Stick? Did you see anything?" asked Bubba.

Stick mumbled, "Nope... nothing except..."

"Except what?" asked Red.

Stick replied, "Well, maybe it could have been a little hole where I'm sure there are snakes, spiders and other creepy things hiding. Besides, it was just a tiny — nothing any of us could really fit down. And it was covered with wood. I don't think it was anything important," Stick responded.

The Team moaned, and KP said, "Stick, come on. Where was it, man?"

"I, I, I really can't remember," said Stick slowly.

"Come on, Stick. We will be careful," said Hero.

"Besides, Stick, we will find it with or without your help," said Red, starting down the mountain.

Then Runt chimed in, "I will watch out for you, Stick. Everything will be okay. I promise."

"The hole was too small for a cave. It's just a small, covered hole," said Stick. "I promise."

"Just show us, Stick. We want to make sure," said Red.

Encouraged by Bubba, Stick reluctantly led the way as the Team carefully slid the forty feet back down the side of the mountain, mostly on their backsides through the muddy grass. The rain was starting to fall harder, making the climb back down even more dangerous. With the Team following closely, Stick moved slowly toward the opening, still unsure whether he should show them where it was.

Red recognized that Stick was not moving very quickly. "Come on, Stick," he said. "Where is it?"

Stick looked pale. "We're almost there," he insisted.

As Stick reached the hole, he pointed to the wood covering and said, "There's no way in, see? I told you it was too small for any of us to fit."

The Team looked at the boards over the small hole. The teammates could see that the boards were very old and weathered, and were filled with termites.

"We can move these," said Tater. He grabbed one board and tried to pull it away. After several hard tugs, Tater was shocked the boards would not budge. Only about two feet long, the boards looked as though they had been undisturbed for many years. Tater stomped the weeds down around them. Still unable to move them by himself, Tater called for Red and KP.

"Come help me. These boards are too wet and muddy. They are not moving anywhere," he said.

The three boys pulled and pulled, but the boards seemed to be anchored to something.

"Everyone should just take hold, and on the count of three, pull," said Bubba. "That might work."

The Team quickly positioned themselves around the perimeter of the boards. Each person grabbed a board as best he or she could.

Bubba counted out, "One, two, three, lift!"

The Team lifted with all their might, but the boards just creaked under the pressure. They seemed to shift slightly, but did not give way.

"I don't think they are going to budge," said Bean,

releasing her grip on the boards.

"Me neither," said Squeaks, as though she had been a lot of help.

"Should we try it again?" asked Bubba.

"They don't seem to be moving at all," said Tater, as he backed away from the boards.

"Does anyone have any other ideas?" asked Butch.

"Not even a clue," said Runt.

"I can't believe they won't move," said Red. "Look how old these boards are. They can't be that strong anymore," he said, kicking at them.

Stick said happily, "Well, it looks like we might have to skip this clue and go on to the next one." He stood on the boards and said, "See I told you. We can't fit in through or move these boards."

"Maybe we need to go back to the Treehouse and get some hammers and a crowbar," said Squeaks, as she joined Stick in jumping on the boards to test their strength.

"We can't really go back to the Treehouse to get tools," said KP.

"I can't think of a better idea," replied Hero, frustrated with the loss of time going back would cause.

"There has to be something else we can do," said Tater.

"Let's see if we can come up with any other ideas before we give up and return to the Treehouse," said Hero.

Everyone sat down on the mountain in the pouring rain. Trying to come up with any idea that would keep them from having to travel all the way back to town for supplies. They thought and thought, but no great ideas came.

"Stick and Squeaks, stop jumping," said Bean.

"It helps us think," giggled Squeaks.

"Yeah," said Stick, having fun jumping on the sturdy boards.

"What if we used our shovels and dug out around the boards?" asked Red, holding his shovel up.

"Good idea, Red," replied KP. "Let's try it."

Red and KP took the shovels and dug a few scoops of dirt from around the wood. Tater grabbed the boards and tried again to remove them. But was not successful, Squeaks and Stick continued jumping.

"This is fun," said Squeaks.

Just then, Stick and Squeaks jumped one too many times. The boards made a horribly loud crack. They creaked, moaned and swayed under the pressure of the two jumpers. Stick froze, holding onto Squeaks. They did not even dare to breath, afraid of what might happen.

"Stick, Squeaks, whatever you do, don't move!" yelled Hero, as he rushed over to help them.

"Hero, what do I do?" asked Squeaks, "I'm scared of falling through."

"Don't worry. Hang on, you two, you'll be fine. I will be right there," replied Hero confidently. Carefully, he braced himself with Tater holding onto the belt of his pants. He reached out to grab their arms.

Again the boards began to creak, making awful noises. Squeaks frantically wrapped her arms around Stick's waist. She was terribly frightened. Hero quickly grabbed Stick's arm and yelled, "Pull, Tater!"

As Tater began pulling, the boards, which had previously been so immoveable, crumbled. Stick and Squeaks screamed as they started falling into the hole.

Tater, who was holding on to Hero's belt pulled with all his might when he saw them falling.

Hero held on to Stick's arm, but he couldn't pull them from the hole.

"Don't let go, Hero," yelled Bean. "Squeaks is gonna fall."

Squeaks' feeble grip around Stick's waist started to give.

"Help me! Help me! I'm falling!" she yelled, as her arms slipped down around Stick's knees.

Watching in horror, the Team was paralyzed. Finally Bubba, not sure what to do, yelled, "How can I help?"

"Help Tater pull us back," yelled Hero frantically. He could not let go of Stick, so he was helpless to reach Squeaks. He knew if he let go of Stick's hand, they would both fall through the hole to the darkness below.

As Bubba and the rest of the Team ran to help Tater, Squeaks' hands slid down to Stick's feet. The rest of her body was hanging through the hole. Hysterically she screamed, "I can't hold on anymore! Help, I'm falling. Hero, help me, don't let me fall!" Suddenly she disappeared, screaming as she fell, into the emptiness below.

As Squeaks' weight left Stick's ankles, Hero and Tater flew backwards. Stick fell across them onto the muddy weeds. Terrified that Squeaks was going to be hurt from the fall, Hero jumped up and ran to the edge of the hole. He listened hopelessly as Squeaks' screams faded. And then — nothing.

"Squeaks!" Hero and Bubba yelled, but they heard no response.

The Team quickly jumped into action. KP pulled off his backpack, unzipped the front pocket and grabbed his rope. He tied one end to a tree and slid the rope down the hole.

"Is it long enough?" he asked.

"It will have to do," replied Bubba, holding on to the rope as he started sliding through the hole.

With no response yet from Squeaks, Bubba continued to call her name as he rappelled down the cave wall toward the bottom. He finally reached the cave floor. Bubba looked for Squeaks, but she was nowhere to be found. Confused, Bubba searched frantically, but he was unable to see much of the cave in the dim light coming from the opening above.

"Someone throw me down a flashlight," yelled Bubba.

"Is she all right?" called Hero.

Ignoring his question Bubba yelled, "Hurry, a flashlight! And get down here. I need your help. I can't find her anywhere."

Butch quickly retrieved a flashlight and handed it to Hero who threw it down to Bubba.

"We're coming down," Hero yelled, as Bubba searched the surrounding area for Squeaks. The Team quickly climbed down to the bottom of the cave. They pulled off their backpacks, found their flashlights and started searching for Squeaks. They continued to call her name, but she never responded.

"Where is she?" asked Bubba, almost in tears.

"I'm sure she's okay," Bean reassured him.

"How could she be okay? We can't even find her," he snapped.

"She's got to be close. We can find her," assured Bean.

The Team was in a small cavern with a high ceiling, approximately twelve feet by twelve feet. Stalagmites in the shape of large cones covered much of the floor. The walls were streaked with watermarks, and a large pile of straw sat directly under the entrance.

As Hero checked the straw for any sign of Squeaks, he hoped that it was thick enough to break her fall. Next to the straw was a narrow walkway to another cavern. The opening was in the center of the wall and looked like a large squirrel hole. As the Team listened for any response from Squeaks, they could hear a noise from the next room. It sounded like a chorus of coins being tossed into a fountain.

Hero quickly took the lead with Tater in the rear. "Team, we need to work together. She doesn't seem to be in this room anymore. Let's move to the next room. Everyone stay between Tater and me, and we'll keep searching until we find her. All right?" he asked.

The search for Squeaks began.

Chapter Twelve

Sticking close together, the Team slowly crawled through the hole in the wall into the next room and deeper into the cave. They searched everywhere for any sign of Squeaks.

"She wouldn't have searched for the treasure without us, would she?" questioned Butch.

"I don't think so," replied Bubba. "She was so afraid, she wouldn't have moved an inch."

"What if something or someone carried her off?" asked Red.

"Don't talk like that," insisted Bubba.

"I'm just trying to help," snapped Red.

"Should I keep an eye out for bears or wolves?" asked Tater nervously.

"Do you think we need to?" asked Bean fearfully.

"Can bears and other big animals get in here?" asked Butch, his voice trembling.

"Probably not, but it's not a bad idea to keep an eye out for animals, Tater," replied Hero. "I hope nothing carried her off," he said nervously.

"Don't worry, Hero. We will find her," replied Bubba.

"I wish I hadn't been so mean to her," Hero whispered to Bubba. "I am going to be in so much trouble."

"I just hope she is alive," stated Red bluntly.

With renewed terror, Hero continued to move faster through the next room yelling, "Everyone try to keep up."

The next room was larger than the last. Hundreds of stalactites hung from the ceiling. Each one dripped continuously into several small pools that covered the floor.

"How old do you think these stalactites are?" asked Runt, curious about their surroundings.

"I'm not sure," said KP. "But, I know that it takes thousands of years to form one that is two or three feet long," he said confidently.

"Some of these are probably twice that long," responded Runt, in awe.

"The noise from all the drips hitting the water is almost deafening," said Butch, covering his ears.

"It actually sounds pretty cool," said Runt. "What do you think, Bubba?" he asked.

"I don't know or care. Squeaks isn't in here, and I need to find her," Bubba abruptly replied.

"Let's move on to the next room," said Hero. "Maybe we will have more luck there."

The Team continued down the primitive path, until Bean surprised everyone by abruptly stopping. She lifted both arms out to her sides and whispered, "STOP! LOOK! What is that?" She pointed to the wall inside the next room.

The Team quickly turned to see her pointing at the outline of a bear.

"Is that really a bear?" asked Stick, dropping his flashlight as he carefully took a few steps backwards.

"I can't see it. Pick up the flashlight, quick," whispered Bean.

"Is it still there?" asked Hero.

Bubba turned on his flashlight, and again the outline appeared on the wall.

"Well, I can't tell if it's a bear or not?" said Butch.

"It looks like one!" replied Runt.

"It's moving," said Bubba. "Should we follow it?"

"I don't want to die in here," said Stick.

"Come on. Let's go before it gets out of sight," said Tater.

"What if it has Squeaks?" asked Butch.

Suddenly, the last clue popped into Bubba's mind. "Hey, doesn't the clue say that we have to follow a bear?" he asked.

"You're right. It does," Bean agreed.

"Come on. We need to find it," said Hero. "Maybe it will lead us to Squeaks and the treasure."

"Do you think we could catch it?" asked Red. "Especially if it is a bear."

"I don't want to catch it," said Hero. "Let's find Squeaks and the treasure."

"What should we do?" asked KP.

"I know what I'm going to do. I'm gonna keep searching for Squeaks," stated Bubba, turning to follow the shadow.

"It could lead us to Squeaks," replied KP. "Come on. Let's go."

"That's true," added Hero, As he turned to the rest of the Team. "Do you want to go back to the opening and climb out to safety while Bubba and I search for Squeaks?"

Hero heard a chorus of, "No way! We're going! We're not leaving now!"

"She was our responsibility, too," said Runt.

"I told her she could hang with me today," said Bean. "I'm not going anywhere without her — bear or not."

"Are you all positive? I don't want any of you to get hurt. She is our responsibility," said Bubba worriedly.

Ignoring his questions, the Team followed Bubba further into the cave, watching carefully for any sign of the bear.

"We've lost the shadow," Red blurted.

"It has to be here somewhere," said Bean.

"Don't worry. I'm sure he will find us," Stick nervously replied.

The Team continued to search, repeatedly calling Squeaks' name, but they heard no response. Hero and Bubba looked worried. Each room they moved into was bigger, with absolutely no sign of Squeaks anywhere.

"We have to find her," said Bubba with a scared, crackly voice.

Red could see that the situation was getting more serious. "Where could she be?" he thought, as he carefully checked every crevasse and corner.

"Don't worry, guys. We will find her," said Tater reassuringly.

They continued on, following the faint trail. They noticed the room slowly start to narrow. It was about ten feet from side to side, and it was twelve feet from ceiling to floor — not quite the size of the first room. As the Team aimed their flashlights into the distance, the end was farther away than anyone could see.

"With the small narrow rooms, we should be able to find her with no problem," said KP confidently.

"Or the bear could find us," replied Stick. "I wonder where it went?"

Bean interrupted, "Can anyone else hear that noise?" she asked.

"What noise?" asked Butch.

"Listen," said Bean.

The Team, anxious to hear what Bean heard, stood motionless. They all strained to hear something.

"What is it Bean?" asked Bubba. "I can't hear anything."

"I don't know for sure," Bean replied. "It sounds like whimpering."

"What do you mean?" Hero asked. "Whimpering? Oh, please don't let that be Squeaks."

"Listen again. It sounds like a hum or a moaning," said Bean.

Listening quietly, and trying to block out the sounds from the rest of the Team, Tater strained to hear. Several restless minutes later, he yelled, "I heard it! I heard something!"

"Me, too," declared KP. "Me, too."

"Could it be Squeaks?" asked Bubba.

"Let's go find out," said Hero, as he turned to run down the passageway of the cave. He called her name over and over, hoping that she would hear him and answer.

The Team ran at least a hundred yards, but found nothing. They did, however, hear the noise get louder and louder.

"Come on, ya'll!" yelled Tater. "We've got to be getting closer. I can hear the sounds more clearly now."

"Is it Squeaks?" Bubba wondered.

The Team raced down the long passageway. Then, unexpectedly, the passageway ended at a stone wall.

Bubba reached it first and said, "Oh, there's a fork in the passageway. Which way now, Hero?"

Hero arrived next, right behind Bubba. He answered, "I don't know. What do you think?"

Bubba shrugged. "Eenie, meenie, miney, mo? Will that work?" he asked with a smile.

"Cute, Bubba. Really funny," replied Hero. "Be serious!"

"Can you hear the humming sound louder to the right or the left side?" asked Bean, who had just reached the Fork.

"Oooh, good idea Bean," said Stick. "Way to think!"

Hero hastily ran ten or so feet to the left fork, while Bubba moved ten or so feet into the right side.

"It's not any louder this way," said Bubba. "Can you hear the sound any louder over there, Hero?" he asked.

"It's tons louder this way," yelled Hero. "Come listen."

"Come on. Let's go," said Red, running past Hero

deeper into the cave.

Everyone followed the left fork, about a quarter of a mile deeper into the belly of the mountain.

Then Runt, who was leading the Team, stopped dead in his tracks. With his eyes as big as golf balls, he turned to the Team and said softly, "Hold it. Watch out Team. There it is. I can see the bear."

"Show me! Show me!" demanded Red.

"Shhhh, quiet, Red," said Hero, "Everyone be very careful. Stay behind this rock. There is enough light in the cave; turn off your flashlights. I don't want the bear to see us."

"Maybe we could sneak up on it and knock it out or something," suggested Bean.

"Maybe we could just check to see if Squeaks is here," said Bubba.

As the Team hid behind the rock, they carefully scanned the surrounding area. About a hundred and fifty feet away was a beautiful waterfall. As the water fell twenty-five feet to the stream below, they could see the turquoise shimmer and sparkle of the crystal clear water.

"It looks like the waterfall is full of emeralds," said Runt.

"Do you think that could be the treasure?" asked Stick.

"I doubt it, Stick. What do emeralds have to do with the will of the Lord?" replied Bean.

The Team also observed a small fire pit. They also saw a low doorway with a covering, which looked like a bearskin, and two other cave openings. The openings led to other passages, which continued further into the mountain.

"Doesn't that look like a campfire pit that you cook on?" asked Butch.

"It does to me," answered Bubba.

"Do you think that bear cooks?" asked Runt.

"Good one, Runt," said Bean. "Really funny."

"Hey, what is that hanging on the wall?" asked Tater.

"Where?" asked Butch.

"By the room," replied Tater. "It looks like a basket with a light in it."

"It couldn't be a light," said Bubba. "There is no electricity down here."

"Could it be a candle?" asked Bean.

"There is no fire flickering," said Hero. "Come to think of it, how is this cave lit at all?"

"Those same baskets and lights are placed all over in the cave," said Tater, pointing to several areas.

"Why would a bear need a light?" asked KP completely bewildered.

"What or who is in here with the bear?" asked Hero nervously.

"Any sign of Squeaks?" asked Bubba.

"No," replied Runt. "But I can't see very well."

"Something could be in that room," said Bean.

"Do you think we could get over there without the bear seeing us?" asked Butch.

"Seeing us? I'm not worried about that," said Hero. "What happens when he gets a whiff of us?"

"I forgot about that," answered Runt.

"What are we going to do?" asked Stick.

Hero thought for a few minutes and then replied,

"Okay, here is the plan. A few of you go back into the passageway of the cave and find some rocks — as big as you can carry on your own. Bring them back here and wait for..."

Bean interrupted Hero, "Over in the small room — Look! I see something moving. What was Squeaks, wearing today?"

Bubba thought for a minute. "What she always wears — her pink pants and her white and pink princess shirt. Why?" he asked curiously.

"I think that might be Squeaks over behind that fur hanging on the wall," she replied excitedly.

Hero, eager to check and see if that could possibly be Squeaks, continued, "Okay, here is the new plan. We are going to have to get rid of that bear. The only way I can think to do that is to hit it over the head and maybe knock it out. If we get rocks and surprise it by hitting it over and over, there is a possibility we could get at least a few minutes to look for Squeaks before it wakes up. Should we try?" he asked.

"It might be our only chance," said Bubba. "And I'm not leaving without Squeaks."

"Let's just try it," chimed in Bean. "We can do it if we all work together. Don't you think?"

"Yeah, let's try it," said Butch.

"And we still need to find the next key. So let's hurry and get this over with," said Stick.

"Well," said Red. "Killing a bear with a few rocks was not on my list today. But, let's go kill us a bear."

Butch, Tater and KP slowly moved back into the passageway of the cave. They quickly searched the floor, found several soccer-ball-sized rocks, which they moved up to where the rest of the Team had assembled.

"We have about twenty-five large rocks and at least two dozen small rocks. Do you think that will be enough, Hero?" asked Tater.

"I hope so," Hero replied. "The rocks won't kill it — possibly stun it for a minute or two. But we're not trying to kill it. Is everyone ready? On the count of three, pick up as many rocks as you can handle. Let's move as close as we can to the bear. Then on my signal, start throwing your rocks as fast as you can."

"Everybody got it?" asked Tater.

"Bean, while we distract the bear, run over to that room and see if Squeaks is there. If she is, and she can be moved, grab her and start heading back toward the entrance as fast as you can," instructed Hero.

Bean agreed, and the Team picked up their rocks and started inching slowly toward the backside of the bear. They were only seven or eight feet away when the bear began to move. Without waiting for Hero's signal, Stick started throwing his rocks. Instantly, the bear rocked forward a little and then slowly moved back.

"Stick, what are you doing?" asked Hero. "Wait."

"He's gonna eat us," said Stick frantically.

Again the bear lurched forward a bit and then slowly sat back on his hind legs.

Stick turned to the Team and shouted, "I got him! I got him!"

"Someone go check it out. See if it is knocked out

or what," said Runt, timidly hiding behind Tater.

Butch was very curious about the bear. Little by little, he shuffled toward the bear, puzzled as to why it had remained still after Stick's direct hit. Suddenly, the bear lunged forward. Frightened, Butch recklessly threw all of his rocks. With direct hits to its head, face and neck, he was sure he had at least stunned the bear.

"Woohoo, guys. I think we've killed ourselves a bear!" said Butch.

"It's still on its feet. Quick, everyone hit it with your rocks," said Runt.

Everyone threw their rocks at the bear as fast as they could. They cheered at full volume when it fell forward and lay sprawled out on the floor.

"No need to hurry, Bean," said Hero. "I think we've got it knocked out for a minute."

Bean called out, "Good job, guys. Way to go!" Then she ran toward the other room.

Tater, wanting to make sure that the Team would not be having any more surprises, walked to the head of the bear. He wanted to see if it was knocked out or maybe not breathing. Something did not look right. He knelt down next to the bear's face and immediately realized what was wrong.

"This is not a bear!" declared Tater.

"What are you taking about?" questioned Stick.

"This is not a bear. Look, check this out. This is just a bearskin rug." He picked up the skin and shook it at the Team.

"Congratulations, guys. We just killed ourselves a rug,"

said Bubba, as he fell to the floor laughing hysterically.

"No wonder it didn't charge us," said KP.

"No wonder it didn't smell us," snickered Bubba.

"Look, Team," said Hero chuckling. "It was propped up on this rack. All we did was knock the rack over."

"I was wondering how a few rocks could stun a bear," said KP, shaking his head. "I figured all we would do was maybe confuse it long enough to get Squeaks out and have enough time to escape ourselves."

"I wasn't sure we would have that much time before the bear came after us," said Tater.

"Well, I hate to be negative, but if this is not the bear, what did we see on the wall?" asked KP, looking worried.

"Bears must be in the cave; otherwise where did this fur and the one hanging on the wall over there come from?" asked Bubba, suddenly regaining his composure.

Suddenly, Hero remembered that he had sent Bean all alone to find Squeaks. Afraid that something else might be in there, he ran toward the small room. Frantically he called, "Bean! Bean! Where are you? Are you all right?"

When there was no response, the entire Team followed Hero toward the room.

As he reached the door, Hero threw back the bear rug.

"Is she there? Is she okay?" asked Bubba, afraid two were now missing.

Hero stopped abruptly, too amazed to react, as the entire Team crashed into the opening behind him. To his utter disbelief, there sat Bean, Squeaks and a strange old, Native American man.

"Squeaks, are you okay?" asked Hero, running to her.

Squeaks beamed from ear to ear. "You came for me. You found me," she said fondly.

"We wouldn't have left without you, Squeaks," replied Bubba, as he threw his arms around her.

"So, Squeaks, what happened? Are you hurt?" asked Hero, as he ruffled her hair. He squeezed her in a big hug and whispered, "I'm glad you're okay. I was really worried."

"Where have you been, and what have you been doing?" asked KP.

"I have been here the entire time," she replied. "I am feeling much better now thanks to Lehonti. I guess I hit my head when I fell and was knocked out for a while. He brought me here and helped me."

"Why didn't he leave you where we could get you and take you back to town?" asked Runt.

"He thought you were chasing me," Squeaks replied. "He was trying to save me. He doesn't know there is a town. He has been living in this cave for centuries," she explained.

"Centuries? Come on, Squeaks. What are you talking about?" asked Red.

"Really. He was left here to protect the final clue. His instructions are to release it to someone who has the real love of Christ in his heart," replied Squeaks.

"He will never age as long as he never leaves these caves," said Bean. "You should hear some of his stories about this old cave and the treasure map."

"The treasure map? What does he know about the treasure map?" asked Stick.

Hero and Bubba, relieved to have found their little sister, refused to leave her side. But the rest of the Team now wanted to focus on finding the treasure.

"Does he speak English?" asked KP.

"A little," replied Squeaks. "A man named Ole taught him what little he knows."

"Tell us what he said about our treasure map," said Butch.

"Why don't you ask him? He is very nice," said Bean.

"So, introduce me then!" said Tater, moving forward with his arm outstretched.

Squeaks proudly introduced the entire Team to her new friend, Lehonti. "Lehonti has been telling me stories about his life and the great treasure," Squeaks said proudly.

"How long have you been down here, Lehonti?" asked Runt.

For the first time, the Team heard Lehonti speak. His voice was strong and bold — a voice that commanded attention. He was a large man, standing more than six feet tall. His powerful body weighed two hundred and fifty pounds or more, he reminded the Team of a body builder — maybe even a professional wrestler.

"Greetings, Team. I am sorry I frightened you," he said with an odd-sounding accent. "I did not know who you were until Squeaks awoke."

"So, was that you — that we thought was a bear?" asked Butch.

"That is correct," Lehonti replied. Looking to Runt he said, "I have been down here many, many years."

"Are there really any bears down here?" asked Stick.

"Not in this part of the mountain," Lehonti responded.

"Lehonti was a great warrior and led a Lamanite group that did not want war with the Nephites," said Bean.

"Why are you here? How are you still alive?" questioned Red.

"Brother Moroni and the Lord called me to protect the key. I will live as long as I am needed," Lehonti replied.

"Is there really a treasure?" asked Red.

"Yes," he responded.

"Have you ever seen it?" asked Hero.

"Only once," replied Lehonti. "Ole showed it to me."

"What is the treasure?" asked Stick.

"I cannot say. You must continue your search. You will find the treasure if it is the Lord's will," Lehonti replied.

"Can you help us find the key to the final clue?" asked Bean.

"Do you have the clue from the last key," asked Lehonti. "If not, I must instruct you to leave the cave."

"We have it," replied Squeaks. "We just had it translated last night."

"Where is it?" asked Butch.

"I've got it. Just a minute," replied KP.

As fast as he could, KP pulled off his backpack, unzipped it and rummaged inside for several seconds before he pulled out Cheri's translation. He held it up and asked, "Do you want me to read it?"

Lehonti nodded.

KP read,

"'No light is there; enter only if ye dare.
It opens from the north; then follow the bear.
The key is there inside of the walls.
Without Lehonti's help, none will obtain it at all.'"

"That is correct," said Lehonti. "Follow me."

"I knew I had heard that name. It is in one of our clues," whispered Red.

"That's right! I was too worried about Squeaks to remember his name," Hero replied.

Lehonti picked up his bearskin and threw it over his shoulder. He grabbed the small basket of light, turned sharply and stepped out of the small room.

"Hey, Lehonti," called Tater.

"Yes," Lehonti replied, poking his head back into the room.

"What is that? How does that light work?" he asked.

Lehonti held up the basket and asked, "This?"

"Yes," answered Tater.

"This is a light stone," Lehonti replied.

"How does it work?" asked Butch.

"By faith," he replied.

"Where did you get it?" asked KP.

"From the Brother of Jared," answered Lehonti.

"From the Book of Mormon?" asked Runt.

"Yes."

"I know that story," said Bean excitedly. "It's the Mahonri Moriancumer story."

Lehonti looked shocked and stepped back into the room asking, "How do you know his name?"

"I read it in the church history," she answered.

"I have heard it also," said Bubba. "The Lord revealed the Brother of Jared's name to Joseph Smith."

Bean glowed with excitement. "The day Joseph Smith had his name revealed to him, he blessed my great, great, great-grandfather with the name the Lord had revealed. He was named after the Brother of Jared."

Lehonti smiled.

"Are these the same stones from the boats he built?" asked Hero.

"Yes," said Lehonti.

"This treasure hunting keeps getting better and better," said Hero. "I never imagined we would ever see stuff from the Book of Mormon."

Lehonti, still smiling said, "Wait for the treasure. Come, we need to leave." He turned and promptly left the cave.

Hero excitedly jumped up. "Come on. The clue said to follow Lehonti. Let's move," he said eagerly. "He's ready to show us the next clue!"

Chapter Thirteen

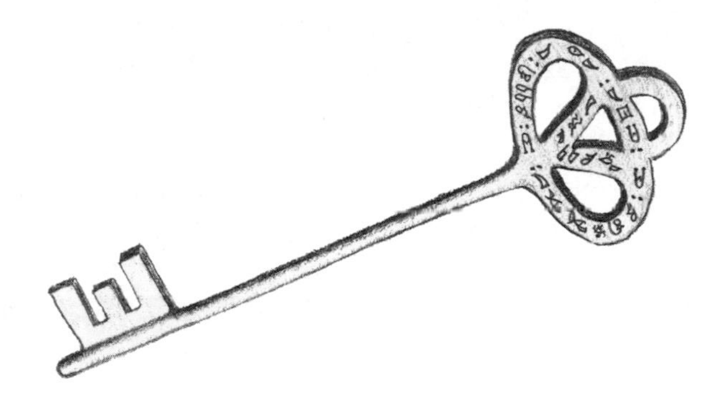

Lehonti walked briskly toward the lake. He followed the eastern shoreline to a secret tunnel hidden behind a beautiful waterfall.

"Squeaks, take my hand," demanded Bubba, as the Team followed Lehonti toward the tunnel. "You have to stay with me now. I don't want you getting lost again."

Squeaks rolled her eyes and said, "I'm not going to get lost. I will be just fine."

Bubba reached for her hand anyway and said, "Come on. This is the only way you are going anywhere."

Hesitantly, Squeaks took Bubba's hand.

Runt took the lead, and the Team followed. As they walked behind the waterfall, Lehonti was waiting at the entrance of a small, diamond-shaped opening.

"Follow me, quietly," Lehonti said. "We are traveling through a bat cave."

He slipped through the opening behind the waterfall and into a small room. It was the size of a boxcar on a train, and grew larger from side to side and floor to ceiling as they moved further into the tunnel. They had traveled approximately a half-mile when Lehonti turned, put his fingers to his lips and motioned with his other hand to the top of the cave. As the Team looked up, they could see hundreds of bats.

Stick tapped Hero on the shoulder and whispered, "Bats are almost worse than snakes."

"Don't worry," replied Hero. "I am right here."

Cautiously, the Team continued to follow Lehonti through the bat cave.

"What is all over the floor?" KP whispered.

"It's crunchy like gravel," said Bubba.

"Well, it is slippery over here," said Bean.

"What ever it is, it's absolutely everywhere," said Runt.

Suddenly, Squeaks sneezed. The Team instinctively looked up at the ceiling. A few bats screeched and fluttered around, but most of them seemed to remain still. Everyone breathed a sigh of relief.

Bubba whispered, "Careful, Squeaks. Try really hard to hold those in, okay?"

"I tried. It's my allergies. If we don't hurry, I am going to sneeze again and again," Squeaks whispered back.

Suddenly, something dropped right in front of Bubba's face. "Whoa, what the heck was that?" Bubba quietly asked, looking toward the ground.

Hero laughed and replied, "Now I know what is on the ground. I don't know why I didn't think of it before."

"What is it?" asked Bean.

"Guano," Hero replied.

"Guano?" asked Runt. "Are you sure?"

"Look at all those bats. You bet I'm sure," replied Hero.

"Guano. What is guano?" asked Bean.

"It's bat dung," answered Hero smiling.

"Oh. How gross! And we're standing in it. I'm going to be sick," replied Bean, picking up one foot as if that would solve the problem.

Lehonti walked out of the bat room and motioned for the Team to hurry. Moving as quietly as possible, the Team followed him, glad to be leaving.

After the entire Team had moved several yards outside the bat cave, Lehonti asked, "What happened to Ole?"

"Was he the last person to find the treasure?" asked Runt.

"He was last," replied Lehonti. "Is he safe?"

"Mr. Jensen, his great, great-grandson, told us Ole was killed under very mysterious circumstances," Hero explained.

Lehonti was noticeably upset. "His family knows who killed him?"

"They do not know for sure," replied Hero. "His family thought that the person who killed him had also taken Moroni's map. Mr. Jensen was so excited when we found it."

"You found it?" asked Lehonti, obviously surprised.

"Yes, we did," replied Bubba. "And we did it as a Team."

"Bad men were looking for Moroni's map. Never let them know you have the map. Never allow the map to fall into the hands of anyone who will not follow the Lord," Lehonti stated.

"Do you know who these men are?" asked Tater. "Who are we watching for?" he wondered.

"I do," replied Lehonti firmly.

"Who?" asked Bean.

Lehonti stopped dead in his tracks, turned to the Team and asked, "Have you read the Book of Mormon?"

Shocked, KP asked, "How do you know of the Book of Mormon? It was written years after you would have come here."

"Ole brought me that book. I will tell you all, the Book of Mormon reveals exactly the way it happened," Lehonti said with great conviction. He turned abruptly and continued to walk through the cave.

"Lehonti, who is trying to get this map?" asked Stick. "We need to know!"

"It is the followers of Satan. They know the treasure will help to build the kingdom of God," Lehonti solemnly answered.

"Was Ole killed to prevent the building up of the kingdom?" asked Bean.

"He must have been, because the treasure has not been used since Ole died. When you find the treasure, you will have much work ahead of you, Team," answered

Lehonti.

"Work? What kind of work," asked Red.

"That is for the Lord to decide," said Lehonti.

"Didn't I read in the Book of Mormon that you had been killed, Lehonti?" quizzed Red.

"I was poisoned," Lehonti responded.

"Then how can you be here leading us?" asked Tater.

"I made restitution for my wrongs. The prophet Moroni sent me to this cave. I can help those who will build up the Lord's kingdom," Lehonti explained.

"Well, we are glad you are here to help us," said Squeaks smiling. "We could never find our way through these tunnels without you."

"Tunnels? They seem like mazes to me," said Stick. "And if we never have to see bats again, that is fine with me."

Lehonti smiled.

"I am sorry that you are here alone, Lehonti," said Bean.

"Don't feel sorry for me," Lehonti replied. "Remember, never let your guard down. Never give in. Satan will find a way to tempt you if you do."

The Team was quiet as long as Lehonti spoke, intrigued at every word he said.

Lehonti led the Team in and out of tunnels and up and down hills. The Team was unsure of where they were or how to get out of the cave.

"Are we getting close yet?" asked Red.

"We are here," replied Lehonti. He crawled onto a small ledge about four feet off the ground and then through a small gap in the wall.

"Finally, I don't think I could walk another step," Stick stated.

"If you can't walk, how in the world are you going to get back?" asked Red. "I'm not going to carry you."

Stick looked horrified. "I forgot that I would have to walk all the way back, too," he said. He took a deep breath and let out a long sigh of frustration.

"Don't worry, Stick. I will help you walk back," said Squeaks.

Everyone, including Lehonti, chuckled.

"Funny, Squeaks," said Stick.

Lehonti pointed to the far wall and said, "Choose a key. When you are ready, I will lead you back." He turned and left the room.

"He's not gonna show us the right key?" asked Stick.

"I guess not," replied Hero.

"We better get it right," said Butch. "I don't want to come back here.

The Team inched toward the back wall. As they moved closer, they could see five keys hanging side by side on the wall. Every key was plain, and each key seemed to be the same size and shape.

"Oh boy, which one do we choose?" asked Red.

"I'm really not sure this time," replied Hero. "Any ideas, KP?"

KP shook his head. As he picked up one of the keys to compare with another, he said, "I don't have a clue."

"Me neither," said Butch holding another key. "There is no difference between this one and the one next to it," he said as he compared the two.

Bubba stared at the wall. Suddenly, he yelled, "Wait! Put the keys back. Don't get them mixed up."

Both KP and Butch looked at Bubba. "What are you talking about?"

"Please put each key back in its correct spot. Don't mix them up," Bubba responded.

KP and Butch carefully replaced the keys and slowly moved back from the wall.

Bubba quickly stepped toward the wall and pointed to the silver-dollar-sized pictures beside each key. "If the keys are all the same, then there has to be something else special about them, right? The thing that is different is the engraved pictures next to the keys. Maybe the engraved pictures have something to do with the right key," Bubba surmised.

"Good catch, Bubba," said Hero. "I didn't even notice them. I was too busy looking at the keys."

"What do the pictures look like?" asked Squeaks.

"The first one is a picture of a man — maybe Christ," replied Tater, squinting his eyes to see the details of the engraving.

"The engraving by the second key is of three men," said KP.

The third picture is one of the heavens and clouds," said Butch.

"Look Team," said Stick. He was staring at the fourth picture. "Isn't this the picture engraved on the rock I brought back from the last clue?"

Eagerly, the Team moved closer to inspect the engraving.

"I think he is right," said Bean.

"Me too!" said Squeaks.

This has to be the right key then," said Butch. "One eye single to the glory of God."

"Isn't that what Cheri said?" asked Bean.

"For sure," responded Hero.

"What about the other pictures?" asked Bubba. "There is one of Christ, heavens and clouds, three men — probably the three Nephites and the last picture is..."

"It is a picture of books — probably the Book of Mormon," interrupted Runt.

"How will we know for sure?" Butch asked.

"We can't know for sure," answered Bubba.

"I'm not deciding alone," Hero declared. "So, which key does everyone vote on?" he asked.

"Why would we have found the same picture of an eye with the last clue, if it wasn't what we are looking for with this clue?" asked Bean.

"Let's not jump to any conclusions," said Red. "We don't have time for mistakes if we want to find this treasure soon."

"Let's vote!" said Runt.

Hero pointed at the key with the eye on it and asked, "All right, who votes this one?"

Everyone voted for the key with the eye engraved by it and Hero said, "Okay. We have our next clue. Let's get to the library and see if Cheri will translate it."

The Team crawled back through the small gap in the wall to where Lehonti was standing watch.

"Did you make your choice?" Lehonti asked seriously.

"We did," responded Bean, proudly holding up the key.

"Is it the right one?" asked Bubba.

Lehonti shook his head. "I cannot say. You have a long journey ahead."

He immediately turned and walked briskly back in the direction the Team had just come.

Bean took the key and placed it safely in the inside zipper pocket of her backpack, then ran quickly to catch up with the Team.

When she reached the Team, she patted her backpack and said, "Safe and sound."

Hero nodded at her, acknowledging her responsibility for the keys. To keep up with Lehonti they practically had to run. They had been traveling for about an hour when Lehonti abruptly stopped, crouched down on one knee, glanced left and then right. He sniffed the air.

"Danger," he whispered, holding both hands straight out to the side to stop the Team. "Stay near. Don't make any noise."

He jumped to his feet, held his bow and arrow in front of him and cautiously continued.

"I don't like this," said Bean, nervously looking around. "What do you think is out there?"

"Just stay close," said Hero. "Bubba, hold onto Squeaks. I don't want to lose her again. Team," he whispered, "stay close."

The Team anxiously continued to follow Lehonti. They had traveled nearly a mile when Lehonti's tense glare seemed to soften a little. This helped to put the Team at ease.

"Is everything okay now, Lehonti?" asked Butch.

"For now," Lehonti responded.

"What was it?" Tater asked. "I didn't smell or hear anything."

"I smelled a bear," Lehonti replied, still watchful.

"Oh, great. Now I get to worry about bears, too," complained Stick, looking over his shoulder.

"Are we out of the bear caves yet?" asked Bean.

"Yes, but one must be on alert in all caves," Lehonti stated.

"How much further before we get back to your cave?" asked Squeaks.

"I am taking you to where you fell through the mountain," Lehonti answered.

"Is this way faster?" asked Red.

"Yes, greatly," answered Lehonti.

"We go a mile," replied Lehonti. "Straight north through these caves."

"That doesn't sound too hard," said Stick, still a little uneasy.

Then out of the shadows lurched two enormous brown bears.

Petrified, Hero shouted, "Lehonti, what do we do?"

"Watch out! They are attacking as a pair," he replied, searching for a way the Team could escape.

The bears growled and approached the Team, shaking their heads furiously. Squeaks clung to Bubba tighter than she ever had before.

"Don't worry, Squeaks. I've got you," said Bubba, trying to comfort her.

As the bears continued to growl, Squeaks finally screamed as loud as she could.

The bears looked around in confusion. Lehonti had time to draw his arrow and shoot at one of them. The bear growled furiously as the arrow struck its chest. Seconds later, it dropped dead in its tracks.

The second bear pushed and tugged at the dead bear. Then it turned to the Team and growled in vengeance.

Lehonti frantically said, "This will only make the bear angrier. Hero, lead your Team through the tunnels. In one mile you will reach the opening. You will be safe. May Moroni's treasure bring you all that you desire. Go quickly, and I will fight this bear."

"We will stay and help," said Hero.

"No," commanded Lehonti. "You have a greater mission to fulfill. Go now. Go quickly, and don't come back," Lehonti demanded.

Hero turned to the Team and yelled, "Follow me, and stay together."

"What about Lehonti?" asked Squeaks, concerned for her new friend's safety.

"He is a great Lamanite warrior," responded Hero. "He has fought bears before."

Hero glanced back once to see Lehonti fire an arrow at the second bear, which now was standing on its hind legs. The bear looked twelve feet tall. Seconds later, Lehonti was out of sight.

"Lehonti said once we are through the caves and back to the tunnels, we will be safe. Keep moving as fast as you can," said Hero.

"I'm tired," said Stick. "And my feet hurt."

"Come on, Stick, just keep moving," said Hero.

The Team had been moving quickly for five minutes when they heard a terrible scream and an echoing growl. Squeaks began to cry.

"Is Lehonti all right?" she asked worriedly.

"He will be fine," reassured Bubba. "He knows what he is doing. How do you think he got all those bear skin rugs?" But Bubba was not certain that the noise had not been Lehonti being killed.

"Should we go back and check on him?" asked Runt.

"No," responded Hero firmly. "Lehonti said we have a greater mission to fulfill."

"How is finding treasure a greater mission?" asked Bean, panting loudly.

"I don't know. But Lehonti said not to come back," replied Hero with overwhelming certainty. "We have something so important to find with this treasure that Lehonti is willing to sacrifice his life for it."

"Hey ya'll, Lehonti died along time ago in the Book of Mormon, I'm sure the Lord's fixin' to keep him safe," said Tater. "Besides I'm sure the Lord has lots more for him to do still. Right Hero?"

"That's right, Tater," replied Hero. "I'm sure we will need his help again."

The Team continued through the caves, each realizing the gravity of Lehonti's decision.

"I think we are back to where the stalagmites are dripping water into beautiful little pools, remember?" Bean said, as she looked around.

"There is the puddle where I tossed a rock," said Runt.

"Can we walk yet?" asked Stick. "My feet aren't going to make it much longer."

"Do you think we are safe?" asked Butch, still glancing over his shoulder.

Tater, who was bringing up the rear, said, "I can't see or hear anything."

"Lehonti told me we would be safe when we reached the tunnels back at the opening," Hero said. "I think we can walk."

Even though they were excited about the new key, the Team was still worried about the fate of their new friend Lehonti. As they finally reached the entrance, the Team heard thunder and rain.

Hero flicked his flashlight on and looked at his watch. "Oh my gosh! It's one o'clock! Mom is going to be a nervous wreck," he said hysterically. "I didn't know we had been gone this long." Hero rummaged through his backpack looking for the walkie-talkie. As soon as he found it, he called home. "Mom, are you there?" he asked.

Mom instantly answered, "Team, is that you? Is everyone okay? Where have you been for the last six hours? I have been worried sick."

"Sorry, Mom. We have been searching in Paradise Mountain, and we had no signal on that side of the mountain," Hero replied. "Please don't be upset."

"I'm not upset, Hero. I've been very worried. Is everything okay with the Team? Is Squeaks all right?" she asked, with a worried, nervous tone in her voice.

"She is fine, Mom. She is just hanging out with the

Team. We are taking good care of her," Hero replied, eternally grateful that the bear had not killed Squeaks.

"Please take good care of her, and keep the Team safe, Hero. Okay?" Mom asked insistently.

"Don't worry, Mom. We have the situation under control," responded Hero. "I promise."

"Now that I don't have to worry anymore, are you any closer to finding the treasure?" she asked, ready for an end to their treasure hunting.

"Boy, do we hope so. That last clue was kinda tough, although we did find a lot of cool stuff," replied Hero. "We are just about to head back to the library. We have the next key that we need translated. When do you want me to check in again?" he asked.

"It's about one in the afternoon now. How about in three hours?" said Mom. "Right around four o'clock."

"All right. Love ya tons, Mom," declared Hero.

"Good luck, Honey. Stay safe. Love you, too. Over and out," Mom replied.

Hero smiled as he put the walkie-talkie back in to his backpack and thought, "She is so funny. What a nut!"

When the conversation ended. Tater said, "Is it really that late? No wonder I'm starving. Why don't we take a break and eat our lunches?" he asked.

"Any chance we could attract a bear?" asked Stick, anxiously glancing over his shoulder.

"I hope not, Stick," said Bubba.

"We still have a lot to do today," said Bean. "Shouldn't we keep moving?"

"You're right, Bean," said Runt. "I want to get this

next clue translated. We have got to be getting close to finding the treasure."

Butch grabbed the rope leading back to the opening of the cave and said, "Tater, will you hold this for me? I will get to the top and help everyone out."

Tater held the rope, and Butch scurried up. Just as he reached the top, a bright burst of light filled the sky above his head, and a loud crash of lightning cracked in front of him. Then rain poured from the sky.

Butch looked down from the rope and asked the Team, "How long do you think it is going to rain? We have had more in the last week than the entire last year." He slid down the rope and jumped the last few feet to the bottom of the cave. "I don't really want to go out in this rain," he continued. "I think we should stay here and eat our lunches."

"I agree, Butch," replied Bean, looking up toward the rain. "I don't want to go out in this rain and lightning either."

"I'm not sure if it is safer in here with the bears or outside with the lightning," said Hero.

Tater, who had been wanting to work on Team security issues anyway, smiled and said, "It's a great time to get our plan for the crooks set up and into motion before we get too close to the treasure."

"You're right, Tater. Let's make our plan right now," said Hero. "Everybody, pull out your lunches. We'll eat and listen to Tater's plan."

"We still have several hours before the library closes, anyway," said Runt.

The Team moved to a dry area in the cave, sat down

in a circle and listened as Tater took charge.

"I have been thinking about all of your ideas from the other night, and I think I have a plan that will land those crooks back in jail," said Tater confidently.

"Enough drama," said Red. "Let's hear it already."

Tater looked at Red, scrunched up his eyes and nose and said, "I'm getting there. Just a minute, Red." Tater then looked back at the rest of the Team and said, "We know that they are hiding above the Treehouse. And we know, thanks to Squeaks, how they found out and know about the map."

Squeaks beamed when Tater mentioned her name.

Tater continued, "We also know of their plan to take our treasure, and we can't let them do that. So, I have formulated an idea."

"Well, it is about time. We've already heard that part," interrupted Red sarcastically.

Tater ignored Red this time and continued, "I worked on this most of last night because I couldn't sleep," he said. He unzipped his backpack and carefully pulled out a rolled up piece of leather. He carefully removed the rubber bands that secured both ends. Then he slowly unrolled the piece of leather to show a perfect replica of Moroni's treasure map.

"Did you take the map when I wasn't looking?" asked Hero, pulling off his backpack to check.

"No," replied Tater. "This is a fake map that I drew last night. The crooks will never know it is not real."

"This is a fake?" asked Butch, looking closely at the map.

"Yep," replied Tater. "You can see that none of the mountains, streams or anything are in quite the right place.

However, I don't think the crooks will know that."

"So, what is your plan exactly?" asked Bubba.

"Well," said Tater, moving off one knee and sitting on the ground, "my plan is to have a meeting in the Treehouse when we know the crooks are up above us listening. We will talk about how we just don't have any more time this week to work on finding the treasure. Then we will receive a fake call from Squeaks confirming that Hero and Bubba's mom says we have no more time for treasure hunting because she saw their report cards and they have some studying to do or something like that. We officially take a break and exit the Treehouse, leaving the map and a few fake keys on the table for the prisoners to steal. If we pretend that the final clue is translated and that we have no idea where to search, the crooks will sneak down into the Treehouse when we are not there and steal it."

"And that fake clue can send them to where we will have the police waiting on an anonymous tip," Squeaks interrupted.

"That is a great idea, Tater. Good job," said Hero.

"I know it will take a little work, but I think we can pull it off," Tater said confidently.

The Team agreed.

Ready to get the key translated, and still a little nervous about the bear, Butch looked up through the broken wood and said, "The rain has slowed. We need to get moving."

Excited to put Tater's plan into action, the Team climbed up the rope. Looking back down into the cave, they vowed they would never forget their great friend Lehonti and all he had done for them, and especially for Squeaks.

Chapter Fourteen

Hiking to their bikes seemed to take forever. The slippery, wet conditions made climbing down the mountain treacherous and slow. Worried about Lehonti and unsure what the treasure might be, the Team did nothing but think most of the way back.

A few blocks from town, Hero finally broke the silence. He asked the Team, "Any thoughts or ideas on what the treasure is?"

"I'm not sure that it is money or jewels any more," said Bean.

"I'm still hopeful," chimed in Stick, smiling widely.

"Come on, Stick. How can money or jewels be valuable to the Lord?" asked Bean.

"Do you think it could be the golden plates, then?" Stick asked. "They are important to the Lord."

"No," said Bean. "I doubt the treasure is the golden plates."

"I'm still wishin'," Stick replied, smiling bigger. He took pleasure in knowing he was irritating Bean.

Bean just shook her head in disgust.

"Oh come on, Bean. I'm just kidding," said Stick. "I'm not that shallow."

"I hope not," she replied.

"So what do you think it is, Hero?" asked Runt.

"I'm not sure. Its value must be vast for Lehonti to be here protecting it for thousands of years," Hero responded.

"I think it is an old-time treasure that we are going to give to the prophet, to help build the Kingdom of God," offered Red.

"How will that build the Kingdom of God, Red?" asked Runt.

"Well, people would really have to believe in the Church if we discovered a real Book of Mormon treasure that everyone could see," he answered.

"That can't be it, Red," said Runt.

"Why?" asked Red, a little confused.

"Because, then people would have to believe, and the Lord would never take away their agency," said Butch.

"That's right," said Hero. "I agree."

"Why would they have to believe?" asked Squeaks.

"Squeaks, imagine we found the golden plates, for

instance, and we took them to the prophet who allowed everyone to see them. Everyone in the world would see they were real. Then they would have to admit Joseph Smith was telling the truth. At that point, they would not need to have any faith to believe," said Bean.

Squeaks thought for a minute and then asked, "Doesn't everybody already know that Joseph Smith was telling the truth and that he translated the Book of Mormon?"

"Not everybody, Squeaks," replied KP, with a smile gently spreading across his face.

"Why not?" she asked.

"Not everybody has your faith, Squeaks. Some people just don't believe Joseph Smith's story," replied Butch.

Squeaks thought about what Butch had said. Then she asked, "So what do you think the treasure is?"

"Not a clue," said Red.

"I'm sure it's gonna be great," said Bubba reassuringly.

Still contemplating all the things the treasure could actually be, the Team arrived at the library. They followed their new routine of locking up their bikes and then looking for Cheri. This time, she was watching for them. As the Team entered, she looked at them with an immense sense of relief.

"You're safe," she said with a sigh. "I was afraid I had sent you to the wrong place."

"Nope. We found everything just fine," said Tater. "And I haven't seen extra followers today."

"Great," replied Cheri.

"Should we go translate the key?" asked Red, pointing to the back area of the library.

"Yes, yes. Follow me to the back tables," she said, as she quickly turned and moved down the hallway. Once at the table, she asked, "Was that last clue hard to find?"

The Team looked at each other, and Hero responded, "Hard and dangerous, we even had encounters with bats and bears."

"Bats and bears? Did anyone get hurt or bitten? Do we need to go to the hospital?"

"No, Cheri. Everybody is okay. In fact, no one was hurt at all," said Runt.

"That's good," Cheri said, "So tell me all about it."

The Team looked at each other, and Hero asked, "Cheri, could we tell you about the entire adventure after we retrieve all of the clues?"

Cheri looked around at the Team. "Oh. You want to go out and find this next clue, huh?"

The Team smiled and nodded.

"So, you are in a hurry?" Cheri teased.

The Team smiled and nodded again.

"All right. Give me the key, and I will get it translated," Cheri said. "But when you have found the treasure, I want a full account of everything you saw and did. Fair?" she asked.

"Fair," replied Hero. "You will be the first to hear everything."

Cheri nodded and said, "Okay, key please."

Bean quickly opened the small hidden pocket in the bottom of her backpack. She located the new key and pulled it out of the pocket.

"Here you go," Bean said, holding out the key.

Cheri took the key and examined it for more than five minutes. Unable to wait any longer, Hero asked, "Is it the right key, or did we choose the wrong one again?"

When Cheri did not immediately respond, Stick got really nervous. "I can't go back to that cave, guys. I'm afraid of what is down there," he said. "And what about Lehonti? If he is hurt, what would we do?"

"SHHHH, Stick," KP said anxiously.

Cheri sensed everyone's fear. "Wait, Team. I think this one is good. I'm just looking it over to make sure I translate the clue correctly for you. Now who is Lehonti?"

"Someone we will have to tell you about sometime," said Hero, scowling at Stick.

"So is this key okay?" asked Bubba.

"The key is fine, Team. But you won't change the subject that easily. Who is Lehonti?" Cheri demanded, with a stern look on her face.

Hero took a deep breath and said, "You are never going to believe us."

"Sure I will," responded Cheri. "Who would have ever thought the map you found would have led to anything, let alone several ancient keys with Egyptian Hieroglyphs."

"You're right," Hero replied. "Please don't think we are crazy."

"Yeah. We met a really cool guy from the Book of Mormon," said Squeaks.

"Really?" she questioned, raising her eyebrows.

"Really," said Bean. "He was one of the warriors in the Book of Mormon. Heavenly Father allowed him to stay and protect the treasure," she said excitedly.

"Did he help you?" Cheri asked.

"He saved me," replied Squeaks fondly.

"Saved? I thought you said no one was in danger or got hurt," Cheri retorted.

"No one was hurt, but we did encounter a little danger," responded Butch.

"What was he like?" Cheri wondered.

"Just like a Lamanite warrior," said Red.

"He was so awesome with his bow and arrow. He looked just like an Indian chief or something," said Stick.

"Is he still there?" Cheri quizzed.

"We think so. We had to leave him fighting a bear, and we don't know if he is all right," replied Runt sadly.

"I'm sure a great warrior like that would have faired just fine against the bear. Don't worry, Team. I am sure the Lord has taken good care of him," Cheri said. "Now let's get down to translating this key. It looks like the right key to me," she said confidently.

"Are you sure?" asked Runt.

"I think so. Let's translate and find out for sure," Cheri said, turning the key in her hand. "This is so thrilling."

The whole Team was excited and relieved, especially Stick and Squeaks.

"Thank goodness," said Squeaks. "I would like to go back to the cave to see Lehonti, but I don't want to see the bats or the bears."

"I think I am ready," said Cheri. "Scribe, would you please get the paper and pen? I need you to write down the translation."

KP hurriedly dug into his backpack and pulled out his

pen and paper. He turned to Cheri and said, "I am ready when you are."

Cheri started,

"'Your final destination...'"

Hero looked at the Team. "It's our last clue! I told you guys we were close."

Cheri peered up over her glasses and asked, "Do you want me to keep going?"

"Yes, please. Sorry," said Hero.

Cheri looked back down through her glasses and continued,

"'Its sure Helaman 5:12 was started by
3 Nephi 28:2,
Alma 16:17 together to form a green canopy.
Inside of its strength lies a small opening
to the Mosiah 8:17.
When used with the 1 Nephi 4:6, will build
your testimony to Ether 5:4.
With his Helaman 5:8 in your hands, much
service is desired.
Serving with 1 Nephi 16:28 is a trait that's
admired.'

"Whoohooo! I can't believe how much harder each clue is getting," said Cheri, as she finished translating the clue. "Team, you have a lot of work ahead of you on this one. I will leave you to get started. Let me know if you need anything else. I would love to stay and help, but I know this is something you need to do as a Team. The Lord has helped you find this map for a reason, and I am excited for you to finally find the treasure. Good luck," Cheri said, as she pushed back her chair and stood up from the table. She turned and headed back toward the front of the library.

"Our final clue! We are on our final clue!" said Bean excitedly.

"Any idea where the clue is leading to?" asked a mystified Runt.

"This one doesn't really give us any great direction," replied Red.

"If this is our final clue, Red, it has to be the hardest by far," said Butch.

"Come on, guys. Let's not worry about what is hard and what isn't right now. Let's get down to business," said Bubba, who was rummaging through his backpack for his Book of Mormon. "KP, what is the first scripture reference?" he asked.

KP picked up the translation and said, "Helaman 5:12."

As Bubba started turning the pages in his Book of Mormon, Runt hollered, "Wait! Wait! Bubba, there are nine scripture references in the clue. Why don't we each take one to work on separately? We can try to determine on our own which word we think best fills in the blank. Then we will read the entire translated clue from everyone's effort."

"Good thinking, Runt. We can probably get it done faster that way," said Stick.

"Hey, wait. I would rather work together," said Bean.

"It might take longer, but then we can be certain we have chosen the right words. That way we can make sure we are going to the place that we're supposed to," she said

"I think you're right, Bean. Team, what do you think?" Hero asked.

"She's right. She is always right," said Tater, with a smile.

"KP, may I see the translation please?" asked Hero.

KP passed the paper across the table to Hero.

Hero picked up the paper and said, "Bubba, read Helaman 5:12 for us, please."

Bubba quickly thumbed through his scriptures and began reading. "'And now, my sons, remember, remember that it is upon the rock of our redeemer, who is Christ, the Son of God, that ye must build your foundation; that when the devil shall send forth his mighty winds, yea, his shafts in the whirlwind, yea, when all his hail and his mighty storm shall beat upon you, it shall have no power over you to drag you down to the gulf of misery and endless wo, because of the rock upon which ye are built, which is a sure foundation, a foundation whereon if men build they cannot fall.'"

As he finished reading, Butch exclaimed, "Hey, I think I remember this scripture from another clue."

"Yeah, I remember it, too," replied Bean elatedly.

"Wasn't the word *foundation* part of the clue from Ghoul's Gulch?" asked Stick.

"That clue talked about a sure foundation also," said Hero.

"Well, does the word *foundation* fit into the blank?" asked Runt.

KP read the first line out loud. "'Its sure foundation was started by 3 Nephi 28:2.'"

"That has to be it," stated Red.

"I guess we better make sure we have a sure foundation," said Tater.

"What is a sure foundation?" asked Squeaks, with a puzzled look.

"A sure foundation is a solid, strong testimony, Squeaks," responded Bubba, as he reached up and put his arm on her shoulder.

"Do we have that?" she asked innocently.

The Team looked around at each other, but Hero replied confidently, "We sure do."

Squeaks smiled and said, "What is the next scripture reference?"

Hero looked at the translation and said, "3 Nephi 28:2."

Squeaks responded, "I've got it. Let me read it."

Hero smiled at her and said, "Go ahead."

Excited to help, Squeaks read at a snail's pace, "3 Nephi 28:2, 'And they all spake, save it were three, saying: We desire that after we have lived unto the age of man, that our ministry, wherein thou hast called us, may have an end, that we may speedily come unto thee in thy kingdom.'"

"What does that mean?" she asked.

"Well, the clue says, Its sure foundation was started by something? What could a foundation be started by?" asked Bubba.

"The Lord, or people?" suggested Butch.

"Does the scripture refer to the Lord or people?" asked Runt.

"There is nothing, really," said Bean, a little confused.

"Nothing but the reference to three," interjected Runt.

"What does the number three have to do with people?" asked Stick.

"The scripture is talking about three people," declared Runt.

"What three people? What are you talking about?" asked Stick.

"If you read a few verses before and after this one, you can see the scripture is talking about the Three Nephites," replied Runt. "Do you think *three* would fit in the clue?"

"I don't know. Let's check it out," suggested KP. He read the first line of the clue. "'Its sure foundation was started by three.'"

"That works," said Stick, "and sounds good."

"Is it right?" asked Red.

"I think so," said KP. "I can't see any other word that fits better."

"Let's move on, then," suggested Bubba. "What's next?"

KP read, "'Alma 16:17 together to form a green canopy.'"

Tater, had already looked up the scripture and began to read, "Alma 16:17, 'That they might not be hardened against the word, that they might not be unbelieving, and go on to destruction, but that they might receive the word with joy, and as a branch be grafted into the true vine, that they might enter into the rest of the Lord their God.'"

"Well then, what is going to form a green canopy?" asked Bubba.

"Branches do," said Squeaks.

"And so can a vine," added Red.

"Yes, but how do they form a green canopy?" asked Bean.

"When there are lots of them. Duh!" answered Stick.

"Boy, Stick. You are really getting on my nerves today," retorted Bean.

"Come on. Come on, Team," said Hero. "Let's work together. Bean you have a good point. What else is in the reference that could fill this blank?" Hero asked.

"Can't trees be grafted together?" asked Tater. "I think that is what my mom does with fruit trees."

"Yes. And when you read the first line of the clue, the word trees seems to make sense," replied Bubba eagerly. "'Its sure foundation was started by three, grafted together to form a green canopy.'"

"The clue is not talking about three people, but three trees. Grafted together, they make a sure foundation," said Bean.

"Three trees would also make sense since Moroni's map has the very large tree right in the center, remember?" asked Bubba, holding up the map.

"I have never seen three trees grafted together around here, though," said Runt.

"Keep reading the clue, KP. Maybe the next line will give us a hint," said Hero.

KP grabbed the clue and read, "'Inside of its strength lies a small opening to the Mosiah 8:17.'"

"I've got it. Just a second," said Red, searching for the scripture. Then he read, "Mosiah 8:17, 'But a seer can know of things which are past, and also of things which are to come, and by them shall all things be revealed, or, rather, shall secret things be made manifest, and hidden things shall come to light, and things which are not known shall be made known by them, and also things shall be made known by them which otherwise could not be known.'"

"Oh, my goodness. I am not sure where this reference is going," said Bean.

"Don't worry. Let's break down the sentence," suggested Bubba. "'Inside of its strength' — that must mean the three trees grafted together, right?" he asked.

The Team nodded in agreement. Bubba went on, "'Lies a small opening to…what?"

"The scripture talks about the past, the future, secret things and hidden things. One of those could fill the blank, right?" asked Runt.

"Yes, but the Book of Mormon was written in the past. I think the *blank* in the clue is the word *past,"* said Tater.

"That's possible. But the Book of Mormon talks about all of those things," said Stick.

"I agree. However, we are searching the references for just one meaning, and it refers to the past first," said Bean.

"I agree," Hero interjected. "We are searching for treasure of our past, and the clue says, 'inside of its strength, or inside of the tree, lies a small opening to the past.'"

"Man, wouldn't that be cool? Time traveling to the past?" asked Bubba.

"Yeah right, Bubba. Like time travel is really even possible," laughed KP.

"I hope it's not possible. I don't want to go. That wouldn't be a good treasure at all," said Bean nervously.

"Come on. Let's keep going. I like the word *past*. Let's use that one," said Red, ready to keep moving.

"Fair enough," said Hero. "Everybody all right with that?" he asked.

The Team agreed, so Hero said, "KP, go on with the next scripture reference, please."

KP started from the beginning and read,

> "'Its sure foundation was started by three, Grafted together to form a green canopy. Inside of its strength lies a small opening to the past. When used with the 1 Nephi 4:6 will build your Ether 5:4 to last.'"

"Bubba?" said Hero.

"I'm already there," said Bubba. "1Nephi 4:6, 'And I was led by the Spirit, not knowing beforehand the things which I should do.'"

"This scripture is short and sweet," said Butch.

"Even better, it's easy," said Stick.

"Yep. 'When used with the Spirit, will build your Ether 5:4 to last'. Somebody look up that scripture," suggested Bubba.

"I've got it," said Butch. "Ether 5:4, 'And in the mouth of three witnesses shall these things be established; and the testimony of three, and this work, in the which shall be shown forth the power of God and also his word, of which the Father and the Son, and the Holy Ghost bear record — and all this shall stand as a testimony against the world at the last day.'"

"This one is going to be harder," said Stick. "I was hoping this entire line of the clue might just be easy."

"It is easy, Stick," said Bean with a grin. "We could have figured it out without the scriptures."

"How?" asked Stick.

"In Church, what are you doing when you build something?" she asked.

"Building your testimony," answered Squeaks proudly.

"See, we didn't even need the scriptures for that one," Bean smugly said. "What's next?"

KP, excited to keep moving, continued with the clue.

> "'Its sure foundation was started by three, Grafted together to form a green canopy. Inside of its strength lies a small opening to the past. When used with the Spirit, will build your testimony to last. With his Helaman 5:8 in your hands, much service is desired.'"

"Okay, who has this one?" asked Bubba.

Hero calmly said, "Yo, I'm ready here. Helaman 5:8, 'And now my sons, behold I have somewhat more to desire of you, which desire is, that ye may not do these things that ye may boast, but that ye may do these things to lay up for yourselves a treasure in heaven, yea, which is eternal, and which fadeth not away; yea, that ye may have that precious gift of eternal life, which we have reason to suppose hath been given to our fathers.'"

"I know this one," said Red.

"What is it?" asked Stick.

"I think it is *treasure,"* replied Red.

"Me, too," responded Stick.

"I think they are right," said KP.

"That's a scary thought," teased Runt.

"I knew they would find something about treasure," said Tater, smiling.

"Treasure works in the sentence," said Bubba. "'With his treasure in your hands, much service is desired.' Sounds right to me."

"Okay. Let's go on," said Bean.

KP, still holding the clue, read the last line. "'Serving with 1 Nephi 16:28 is a trait that's admired.'"

"My turn," said Runt, scanning though the pages of his scriptures. 1 Nephi 16:28, 'And it came to pass that I, Nephi, beheld the pointers which were in the ball, that they did work according to the faith and diligence and heed which we did give unto them.'"

"There are two words that work well in the line," said Bubba.

"I think so, too," said Bean. "Both *faith* and *diligence."*

"I like *faith* in the sentence," said Butch.

"If we have the treasure, I think we have to have faith to keep it. I agree with Butch," said Runt.

"Good, I think that's it," said Red.

"KP, would you read the entire clue now?" Hero anxiously asked.

"You betcha," he replied.

"'Its sure foundation was started by three,
grafted together to form a green canopy.
Inside of its strength lies a small opening to the past.
When used with the Spirit, will build your testimony to last.
With his treasure in your hands, much service is desired.
Serving with faith is a trait that's admired.'"

"Perfect," said Tater. "Where to? Any ideas?"

Suddenly, everyone jumped as the walkie-talkie buzzed. Bubba somehow ended up on the floor and the Team laughed. Hero, still laughing, answered and said, "What's up, Mom?"

"Just wondering if you knew what time it was, Team?"

Hero glanced at his watch and panicked, "Sorry, Mom. I didn't realize it was this late. We are on our way home right now."

"Dinner is waiting for you and the Team. I figured you must be getting close to finding the treasure. Soooo, I called all of the Team's parents, and you are all okay to sleep over tonight."

"Wahooo! Good job, Mom," whispered Bubba.

"Thanks, Mom. You're the greatest! We are still at the library, but we are leaving right now. See you in a few minutes," Hero replied.

"I'm starving. What great timing your Mom has, Hero," said Tater, slapping Hero on the back.

"I think we are all hungry this time, Tater," replied Hero.

"Let's go, Team," said Bubba. "We can decide where the next clue is after we get rid of those crooks."

The Team agreed. They quickly gathered up their belongings, waved at Cheri and left the library.

Tater, the last to leave, turned to Cheri and said, "With any luck, tomorrow will be the day. Keep your fingers crossed."

Cheri held up both hands with her fingers crossed.

The ride home was quick, and Tater was grateful. He did not think he could go one more minute without food.

Chapter Fifteen

After an exhausting, exhilarating, scary day, the dog-tired Team sat down to dinner.

"So, tell me about your day, Team," said Mom, as she passed out hamburgers.

"It was so cool, Mrs. M.," said Butch.

"Really?" she answered.

"We went to the north side of Paradise Mountain," said Bean. "Do you know how pretty it is over there?"

"I don't," replied Mom. "What did you find?"

"We found a new cave. We found more clues. We even found...," Runt paused and looked at the Team.

"Found what?" asked Mom.

Runt watched as Hero softly shook his head.

"…a bat cave," he answered.

"A bat cave? Are you serious?" Mom asked. "Did anyone get hurt?"

"No. We were all very careful," replied Bubba.

"Hero, did you really find a bat cave?" Mom asked.

Relieved, Hero smiled at Mom and said, "Yep. We found a bat cave."

"With thousands of bats," Squeaks added.

"And guano everywhere," added Bean with a disgusted look.

"I'm glad you didn't get hurt," said Mom. "What else did you find?"

Nervous that the Team might tell her everything, Hero said, "We did find the last clue. Cheri, the librarian, said it is our final one."

"Great! Your last clue? I bet you are glad you cleaned Mr. Jensen's attic. You have had a great adventure because of that map," Mom stated.

"You're right," said Butch. "We wouldn't have had anything to do the last several days without the treasure map."

The doorbell rang. Of course, everyone jumped up to answer the door. Mom immediately said, "Whoa, Team. I will get the door."

Disappointed, Squeaks said, "Mom, I want to see who it is."

"Sit up and eat, Squeaks, or you won't get to go on any more treasure hunts with your brothers and the Team."

Hero smiled at Squeaks and said, "Yeah, Squeaks. Sit down or you can't go with us any more."

Squeaks looked at Hero, scrunched up her eyebrows and sat down at the table.

As Mom answered the door, the Team could hear two men's voices. Mom returned after several minutes, sat down and, without a word, went back to eating her hamburger.

"Who was that, Dear," asked Dad, as he walked in with another plate of hamburgers.

"Yeah Mom," said Bubba, "So, who was it?"

Mom looked up casually. "Two policemen," she said. "One was named Officer Cahoon, and the other was named…," she thought for a minute and then said, "Oh yeah, Officer Nelson."

"What did they want?" asked Hero.

"Those prisoners are still at large, and they were wondering if we had seen anyone suspicious in the neighborhood. They left their phone number in case we saw anything. I've put it by the phone."

Bean nervously asked, "Have you seen them anywhere?"

Mom replied, "I haven't. Have you?"

"No. We have been gone all day. We haven't seen them," responded Tater, through a mouth full of chips.

"You would be sure to tell us if you did see them, right?" asked Dad.

"I can't believe the police haven't caught them yet," said Bean, avoiding the question.

"Me neither. I can't believe they ever escaped. According to the news, Warden Willard, is offering a reward for any tips leading to their capture," Mom said.

"A reward?" responded Red.

"I guess so," said Mom. "The Officers said the reward was twenty thousand dollars. Can you believe that?" she asked.

"The warden must really want to catch those two crooks," Dad concluded.

"Twenty thousand dollars?" repeated Stick in disbelief.

"Man, it's too bad we don't have any idea where they might be," interjected Bubba. He knew that if the Team turned in the crooks, Eddie and Earl would tell the police about the treasure map.

"I sure wish I knew where to find those crooks," said Stick. "I would love to have that reward money."

"Now, that would be a big treasure for you, Team," Mom said smiling.

"Should we start looking for them, for real Mom?" asked Squeaks.

"No. And don't get any ideas, Team. These are bad guys that won't let you get in the way of their freedom. Do you understand?" she asked sternly.

"We have other things to find right now, Mrs. M.," said Tater cheerfully.

"That's right, Mom. We would much rather find Moroni's treasure than those crooks," said Bubba.

The Team finished eating, swiftly cleared their plates and headed to the basement. They were eager to determine where to go to look for the next clue. They were also ready to set into action their plan of tricking the two crooks. With Tater's plan already laid out, they practiced their parts to perfection. They rehearsed for nearly three hours before Mom finally sent them to bed.

The next morning, the Team was anxious and excited.

They opened the sliding-glass door and headed out to the Treehouse.

"We can do this. No worries," Hero whispered to the Team. They casually walked toward their Treehouse, just as they had every morning so far this summer. They knew they were being watched from the shadows of the leaves and branches above them.

Tater reached the ladder, firmly grabbed the bottom and steadied it for the Team. One by one, the Teammates climbed into the Treehouse. Just as the Team had planned, Tater was the last one to climb up the ladder. As he reached the top, he said in a booming voice, "I will pull up the ladder. Let's hurry and figure out what to do next."

"Here we go," said KP quietly, through an enormous grin.

Hero called the Team to order as usual. "Well, we are almost there, Team. I'm sorry we are having so much confusion on this last clue. Should we try reading it again?"

"Read it again? Are you serious? We have already read it about a thousand times," said Red.

"I'm not sure how many times we have to read the same words. We still can't figure out where this last clue might be," said Runt, following their script perfectly.

"All right. What great ideas do you have, then?" asked Butch, acting irritated with Runt.

"I'm sure I don't know, Butch," said Runt.

"I'm getting tired of looking for a treasure. We are not even sure it exists," said Butch.

"It better exist!" declared Stick. "I hope I didn't go through all of this for nothing."

"Why don't we take a break," suggested Tater.

"A break?" asked Bubba.

"We have been working on this treasure non-stop for days. Let's take a break," responded Tater.

"I agree," said Bean.

"How is taking a break going to help? That will only delay us from finding the treasure," said Bubba.

"We're starting to get frustrated with the map and each other. If we take a break, maybe when we come back, we will be able to figure out what we are missing," responded Bean.

"What do you think, Team?" asked Hero. "Should we take a break?"

Bubba groaned loudly and said, "Do we really need to vote? Let's just stop."

"Do we have to stop looking?" asked Stick.

"No. We don't have to stop," said Hero. "But it might be good for us."

"What are we going to do?" asked Red, sounding obviously disappointed.

"Yeah, the rain hasn't stopped. We can't play ball yet," replied Stick.

"Guys, let's go do something else for a day. We can come back to this tomorrow," Bean said, as she laid the fake keys on the treehouse table.

"I agree. Here is the map, Bean," said Tater, as he placed it on top of the keys.

"And here is the last translated clue from Cheri," said KP, as he handed it to Tater.

"Will everything be safe up here?" asked Bubba.

"It will all be fine," said Hero. "No one even knows that we have the treasure map."

"And if no one knows it exists," said Butch, "How would anyone know that we have left the map up here?"

"Come on. Everything will be fine. Let's go see a movie. I heard *The Best Two Years* is in theatres. Let's go see it," said Hero. "It will be a fun break."

Tater threw down the ladder and said, "With any luck, Squeaks doesn't know we are taking a break."

"Oh man, I hope not," said Red.

"She doesn't know anything. She went shopping with Mom," said Hero. But Hero knew she was hiding, ready to watch and listen to the crooks after the Team left the Treehouse.

"Let's get this break over with so that we can continue looking for the treasure," added Bubba loudly.

The Team climbed out of the Treehouse and back down the ladder. They hoped their acting had convinced the criminals to steal the fake map. The Team hurried into the house and waited to see what the duo would do next.

Once they were inside, Butch asked. "Do you think our little skit convinced them?"

Hero shrugged. He lay on the floor in the kitchen and intently watched the Treehouse through the slits in the blinds.

"I hope so," replied Tater, lying next to Hero. "Only time will tell."

Above the Treehouse, Eddie and Earl were shocked.

"What is going on?" asked Earl.

"Looks like they gave up," said Eddie. "Just like kids to give up. I knew they couldn't do it."

"You did?" asked Earl.

"Yes," answered Eddie. "Now we can take the map and find the treasure ourselves."

"They couldn't find the last clue. How will we?" asked Earl.

"Are you joking? They are just a bunch of kids. We are so much smarter than they are. This is going to be a cake walk," said Eddie.

"Yeah. We are smarter than them," responded Earl. "So, what do we do now?"

"Well, we go get that map and stuff," Eddie said.

"How?" said Earl. "I don't want to get caught."

"We're not gonna get caught. Those dumb kids are going to the movie. They won't know for hours, that their stuff is missing. When they find out, they will think the little kid did it," said Eddie.

"Yeah. They won't know nothing," agreed Earl. "Let's go get the map."

Earl began to climb down the tree.

"Wait," said Eddie. "We want to be sure they're gone."

The duo sat and watched for nearly thirty minutes.

"Come on, I'm tired of waiting," said Eddie. "Let's move."

"I'm ready," Earl replied.

Eddie and Earl climbed out of their hiding spot, moving very carefully. The weather had not improved, and the tree was wet and slippery. Its branches swayed wildly in the wind. They climbed from the top of the Treehouse, down the side to the window. Then they slid through the window and slithered like snakes along the Treehouse floor.

Tater, who had not taken his eyes off the Treehouse, informed the Team, "They are on the move!"

The Team lied down in a line on the floor, spanning the width of the sliding-glass door. They watched as the two men maneuvered themselves into the Treehouse.

Once he was far enough inside the Treehouse, Earl stood up and asked, "You think anyone saw us?"

Eddie peered over the windowsill. "I don't think so. I can't see anyone."

"Good," replied Earl. "What do we do next?"

Eddie crawled over to the table. He reached up and grabbed the map and keys. Then he said, "It's treasure huntin' time."

"Let me see! Let me see!" demanded Earl, as he joined Eddie under the table and grabbed for the map.

"Now, let's see where we will be going to find our treasure," Eddie said, as he carefully studied the map. He pushed Earl's arm away, not allowing him to see the map. "Earl, read me the clue they had translated," he demanded. He held out the paper, but never took his eyes off the map.

Disappointed, Eddie refused to let him see the map, Earl took the clue and read,

"'The treasure is near, your journey's almost done.
Let the corn, chicken and eggs lead you to the final one.
This next clue is hard, but will be found under the three boards.
Look at the farm, and you'll get your just rewards.'"

"What do you think that means, Eddie?" asked Earl.

"I think it says to go to a farm and look underneath three boards. That doesn't sound hard," said Eddie. "What is those kids' problem?"

"They're dumb," replied Earl. "You said so."

"Yeah," said Eddie.

"So, I think we need to go to the farm. Should we try the one that's not very far from the library?" suggested Earl.

"The one those kids stopped at a few days ago when the wind and rain was bad?" stated Eddie.

"Yeah, that's the one. Let's go," Earl said.

"As soon as we get the treasure, let's disappear somewhere in Mexico, okay?" suggested Eddie.

"Perfect," replied Earl. "I'm ready. Let's do it," he said.

Eddie picked up the map and the clue, grabbed a few of Tater's fruit snacks and headed toward the Treehouse ladder.

"Have you seen those kids at all, Earl?" asked Eddie.

"Not for the last hour," Earl replied, looking out the window and helping himself to a few fruit snacks.

"Okay, let's get moving," said Eddie, as he started to climb down the tree.

"What about these keys? Do you think we need them?" Earl asked, holding one up to show Eddie.

"Probably," responded Eddie. "Bring them."

Earl quickly picked them up and followed Eddie down the ladder. Once out of the tree, the duo quickly headed right for Mr. Cahoon's farm.

As soon as the two men were out of sight, Squeaks climbed out of her hiding spot and ran into the house. She was very excited to tell the Team what she knew. Tater opened the kitchen door just as she arrived.

"They are on their way to Mr. Cahoon's Farm," she said.

"It worked! It worked!" said Stick, victoriously.

"The police don't have them in custody, yet," said Hero.

"Let's not count our chickens before they hatch!" said Runt.

"Do we call the police yet?" asked Red.

"No, not yet," replied Bubba.

"Okay, remember the plan?" asked Hero. "Tater, take Bubba, KP and Butch. Stay out of sight. Follow the convicts to the farm and then call us on the walkie-talkie when they get there. As soon as you call, we will call the police. All right?" he asked.

Tater agreed, and the boys quickly scurried on foot to follow the prisoners. They moved cautiously toward the farm. About a half mile from the farm, Tater spotted the prisoners.

"There they are," Tater said, pointing toward the barn.

"They are almost there. Should we call in yet?" asked KP.

"No, not yet. Let's make sure they are in the barn and searching, before we call for the police," said Bubba.

They watched as the duo crawled along the edge of a newly-planted wheat field, and headed straight toward the barn. Once they entered, Tater turned to Bubba and said, "Now. Call Hero, and have him call the cops, quick."

"Remind him to say 'No sirens'," prodded Butch. "I don't want to follow them if they run away."

Bubba quickly called Hero and said, "It's working. They are in the barn. Call the police, and remind them 'No sirens'."

Hero, picked up the phone. His heart was racing. He dialed *67 to make his call anonymous, and then dialed the number Officer Cahoon had given his mother the night before.

Trying to speak in a deep voice he said, "Officer Cahoon?"

"Yes, this is he," replied the officer.

"The two prison escapees are at your dad's farm. They are in the barn, right now. Go quick, and they will still be there." If you turn off your sirens, they won't know you are coming. Hurry!"

Officer Cahoon asked, "Who is this?"

"That doesn't matter," responded Hero.

"It does if you want the reward," demanded Officer Cahoon.

"I don't. I just want you to catch those two men," Hero insisted.

"Is this a prank call? We don't have time for jokes," Officer Cahoon said angrily.

"No! This is not a prank call," replied Hero, suddenly worried.

"You better not be messing around, kid," replied Officer Cahoon, and hung up the phone.

He turned to Officer Nelson and said, "We just got an anonymous call about a possible location for the escaped convicts. Should we check it out?"

Officer Nelson responded, "We have nothing to lose. Let's go look. Where to?"

"My Dad's farm," said Officer Cahoon.

The two men hurried to their patrol car and sped off toward Mr. Cahoon's farm.

"If we catch them, I bet I could be 'Officer of the Year'," Officer Cahoon said aloud.

"You mean, we could be 'Officers of the Year'," Officer Nelson corrected him.

"Yeah. That's what I meant," responded Officer Cahoon.

"Should we call for back up?" asked Officer Nelson.

"Do you want to share credit?" asked Officer Cahoon.

"Not really," Officer Nelson responded.

"Then I guess we are on our own," Officer Cahoon concluded.

As they neared the farm, Officer Cahoon turned off all the lights and sirens. He used a small back road to get to the barn. About a hundred yards away, he parked and turned off the car. He looked at Officer Nelson and said, "Let's sneak up on them from here."

Officer Nelson nodded. Quietly, the two men opened their doors and got out of the car. Once outside, they drew their weapons. They slowly approached the barn, moving cautiously toward the rickety, old structure.

"What now?" asked Officer Nelson, when they reached the door. "Should we scream 'Police. You are surrounded!' Or should we just go in after them?"

"What will be more heroic?" asked Officer Cahoon.

"Probably going in after them," replied Officer Nelson.

"Well, let's do that. I want Warden Willard to be extremely impressed with our fugitive-capturing abilities," boasted Officer Cahoon.

Quietly, they pulled the barn door open and looked inside. Officer Cahoon was immediately hit in the forehead with an egg.

"I've been hit! I've been hit!" he yelled, as he ran out the door and fell to the ground.

He was in serious pain. Officer Nelson frantically rushed to his side. He smiled as he reached down and wiped the sticky substance off Officer Cahoon's face.

"It's egg yolk," said Officer Nelson. He held up his hand for Officer Cahoon to see the sticky mess. "You're not dying."

Officer Cahoon looked at Officer Nelson and said, "That really hurt. Those convicts are dead when I get my hands on them. You take the front. I'll climb to the barn's hay door and get them from above."

He wiped away the egg. Then he quickly jumped up and ran toward the hay door of the barn. "You dirtbags are surrounded. You better give up!" he screamed.

Officer Nelson stayed at the front door and waited for Officer Cahoon. The prisoners watched the officers through cracks in the wood. Realizing they had nowhere to run.

"We can at least hold them off for a little while with these eggs," said Earl. He took aim and hit Officer Nelson as he peeked around the front door.

"I'm not going back to prison," said Eddie, suddenly frantic. "How did they find us?"

"Warden Willard is going to kill us if we go back there. We will be in isolation for six months," said Earl nervously. "I really don't like to be by myself."

"I'm not going back," stated Eddie.

Earl just rolled his eyes. Returning to prison was now just a matter of time. And being taken back into custody could just be a matter of minutes.

"You already said that, Eddie," reminded Earl.

"Surrender," the officers yelled.

Eddie yelled back, "Not a chance. We could stay in here for days."

"We are going to have to come in after you, and someone is going to get hurt," yelled Officer Nelson.

"Well, that someone is going to be you!" Eddie yelled back.

"We will see about that," said Officer Cahoon, climbing to the hay entrance on the second floor of the barn.

"I'm gonna get you convicts," yelled Officer

Nelson. He tried to distract the two escaped prisoners by opening the front door again.

Earl threw several eggs and plastered the door.

"Nice try convict. You missed me!" Officer Nelson yelled, distracting their attention from Officer Cahoon.

Earl, became infuriated. He suddenly ran full speed toward the door. He threw it open and jumped at Officer Nelson like a six-year-old boy.

"I hate you!" he yelled. Earl knocked Officer Nelson to the ground. He swung his arms wildly, but never really connected with anything.

Then Earl came to his senses. He jumped to his feet and ran back into the barn, slamming the door behind him. From behind the door he yelled, "You can't get me!"

Completely dumbfounded, Officer Nelson picked himself up off the ground. He found his gun in the dirt and wiped off the mud. Then he yelled, "I can't wait to get you back to prison. You're going to have bathroom duty for a year."

Earl ran back to where Eddie was hiding and said, "We are in so much trouble. What are we going to do?"

"Everything is going to be fine. We will be out of here shortly," Eddie responded.

"Come on, Eddie. How are we going to get out of here? We are surrounded," cried Earl.

"Look what I found," said Eddie, pointing to a tractor. "We will get the tractor started, and break out of the barn. Then we will head for the border and disappear into Mexico — treasure or not."

"Great," said Earl.

The two men started creeping toward the tractor.

"Stop, you two!" yelled Officer Cahoon, as he came flying down from the hayloft. Eddie and Earl looked up and saw the airborne officer above them. At the last second, they stepped aside and Officer Cahoon crashed into the barn wall. He knocked several boards loose, and his gun went flying twenty feet across the barn floor.

Earl ran over and grabbed the gun. Then he held Officer Cahoon at gunpoint as Eddie pulled more boards free to reveal an escape route.

"Come on. Let's go Earl!" yelled Eddie.

"What do I do with him?" asked Earl, waving the gun at the officer.

"Leave him," said Eddie. "Let's go."

Earl told Officer Cahoon, "If you try to follow us, we will hurt you."

He hit Officer Cahoon on the back of the head with the gun, and then he ran to follow Eddie out the side of the barn.

Officer Cahoon moaned, and slowly reached for the back of his head. He felt the giant lump left by his gun.

"Officer Nelson, help!" he hollered.

"What happened?" Officer Nelson asked, as he threw open the door. He rushed over to help Officer Cahoon off the floor.

"They're getting away!" Officer Cahoon replied. He held his head with one hand and pointed to the missing boards with the other. The two men raced out of the barn and scanned the fields for movement.

"We better not have lost them," said Officer Nelson.

"That will really make Warden Willard mad," answered Officer Cahoon, still searching.

From the cornfield, Bubba, Tater, Butch and KP watched the two officers in utter disbelief.

"How could the cops let them escape again?" asked Butch. "We gave them a prime set up."

"They are coming our way. We better do something," said Tater. "I'm not sure they will fall for another trick if they get away now."

"What do you have in mind?" asked KP. "One of them now has a gun."

"Do they even know how to use it?" joked Bubba.

Tater said, "They don't have any idea that we are here. Right?"

"As far as we know," answered KP.

"Why don't we try to catch them?" said Tater.

"Yeah, if we startle them, we might be able to catch them off guard," said Bubba.

"How?" asked KP.

"We should be able to move in front of them unnoticed. When they get close, we knock them down and tie them up," replied Tater.

"Tie them up with what?" asked Butch.

"I still have some rope in my backpack," answered Bubba.

"I do, too," said KP, opening his backpack and rummaging for the rope.

"Okay. Let's make this work. Bubba, you and KP get the tall guy, and Butch and I will get the short guy," instructed Tater.

"Let's get 'em," said KP.

"Here they come," said Tater. "Watch out for that gun."

As Eddie and Earl ran through the six-foot-tall corn stalks, they never expected the boys to jump out at them. Tater hit Eddie's knees, knocking his feet out from underneath him. In seconds, Tater and Butch were sitting on top of him, tying his arms behind his back.

Earl saw Bubba and KP lunge toward him. He instinctively raised his arm and pulled the trigger.

Butch screamed, "Bubba, look out!"

Tater heard the shot. He jumped to his feet and raced over to help his friend. He ferociously tackled Earl from behind, knocking the gun from his hand. KP grabbed the rope and tied Earl's arms.

Then Tater turned toward KP and Bubba and screamed, "Have you been shot? Are you hurt?"

"No. We are both fine," replied KP.

"I see blood. Were you hit?" Tater asked Bubba.

Bubba sat up, holding the right side of his head and replied, "The bullet just grazed me. I'm okay. No worries. It's just a little blood," he said.

Tater moved over to get a closer look at the wound. He breathed a huge sigh of relief when he could see that Bubba had only been scraped by the gun's bullet.

Butch, still sitting on top of Eddie, said, "I'm sure the cops heard the shot. We have got to get out of here, quick."

"Butch is right. We have to move," said Tater. "Are the crooks tied up tight?" he asked.

"I just checked them. The ropes are nice and tight," said KP, giving them a final tug.

"Good. Let's get out of here. Bubba can you walk?" Tater asked helping him off the ground.

Grabbing Tater's hand, Bubba stood up slowly. He was a little wobbly on his feet. "I'm fine," he said. "We need to get out of here. I can hear the cops coming."

Bubba, KP, Tater and Butch left the crooks tied up on the ground. They quickly disappeared into the tall, dense field of corn stalks.

Moments later, Officer Nelson and Officer Cahoon burst through the small, open patch to find the tied up criminals.

"What's happened here?" asked Officer Cahoon. "How did you two get tied up?"

Neither of the men said a word. Who would want the cops to know that they had been caught by a bunch of kids?

"As far as I am concerned, we caught them," said Officer Nelson. "You two aren't talking, are you? So, who will ever know?"

Officer Cahoon agreed. "It's our chance to be heroes. Let's go turn them in!"

Officer Nelson untied the rope from around Earl's hands. He grabbed his handcuffs off his utility belt, yanked both of Earl's hands behind his back and cuffed him, as he read him his rights. Officer Cahoon followed suit and placed Eddie under arrest as well. The Officers walked the convicts back to the police car. Earl dropped his head in despair. He knew Warden Willard would be merciless.

"So much for time off for good behavior," he thought, as Officer Nelson opened the back door and pushed him inside the car.

Officer Cahoon walked Eddie to the other side of the car and opened the door. He pushed him in and said, "Officer Nelson, today is going to be a great day."

Officers Nelson and Cahoon drove back toward the prison, anxiously anticipating the smiling face of Warden Willard. The boys watched from the shadows as the only two men who knew about their treasure map were taken back to jail — hopefully for a very long time.

"I guess there is one good thing about prison," Earl said.

"What's that," scoffed Eddie.

"We won't have to go hungry any more," replied Earl.

"Zip it," said Eddie.

Chapter Sixteen

Tater, Bubba, KP and Butch raced back to the Treehouse, excited to tell the rest of the Team what had just happened. By the time the boys made it home, the rest of the teammates were watching the breaking news on television.

"They got 'em!" screeched Squeaks in delight.

"Our plan worked!" yelled Tater, as he ran into the house, panting heavily and trying to catch his breath.

"We can see. Look," said Hero, as he pointed to the television.

The Team watched in silence as Warden Willard spoke. "Due to the diligent efforts of these two men," he said, pointing to Officers Nelson and Cahoon just arriving at the prison, "we have apprehended the two escaped convicts. These two officers risked their lives. They have single-handedly protected this community from two dangerous men. We owe them a sincere debt of gratitude and a big hand for a job well done." Warden Willard took a deep breath before continuing.

Tater interrupted, "I guess we are nobodies."

The Team smiled at Tater and turned back to the television.

Warden Willard continued, "To honor them for their dedicated service as they tracked these fugitives, Governor Storrs and I will have a special ceremony tomorrow night at the new City Hall. We will award each of them with a medal for bravery. The community is invited to join us. Thank you."

Warden Willard stepped back from the podium and turned toward the waiting police car. He quickly walked over, reached into the back seat and grabbed both men by their ill-fitting clothes. Then he personally escorted them back into the prison.

"Oh, I would hate to be either of those guys tonight," said Hero.

"Yeah, that Warden Willard looks like he's pretty tough," said Bubba. He rolled on the floor and laughed as the news replayed the men's faces when the Warden grabbed their arms.

"So what happened to Bubba's head?" asked Bean.

"He was struck by a bullet," said Tater.

"What?" asked Hero, running to his brother. "Are you all right? What happened?"

Bubba said, "Oh, it's just a scratch. Don't worry."

Obviously shaken, Hero told the Team, "Finding the treasure has been pretty dangerous. Does everyone still want to continue?"

"Are you crazy? We are almost there," said Red. "I don't want to give up now."

"I agree," said Stick. "We are so close, I can feel it."

"And the crooks are out of the way," Bean added.

Hero said, "Okay, let's all be really careful. I don't want anyone else to get hurt."

"We need to get moving. We have wasted half the day on those crooks," said Bean.

"I'm ready to find the treasure," said Squeaks excitedly.

"The Team grabbed their backpacks, the real clues, maps and keys, and headed for the Treehouse.

"I am still not sure where to start," said KP.

"I don't know either. Where is there a clump of three trees growing together?" asked Bean.

"What if you can't tell they are three trees growing together?" asked Squeaks.

"Squeaks, you're too little for this. Just wait and you can help us when we figure out where we are going," said Red.

Squeaks sat quietly and listened to the Team's discussion. This was the first time the Team had ever allowed her to be inside the Treehouse with them, and she wanted to stay.

"Mrs. M. said she was not aware of three trees growing together anywhere in the valley. The biggest tree she knew of is the one with our Treehouse," said Runt.

"Our tree is the biggest one I know of," said Tater.

"Let's read the entire clue one more time," suggested Hero. "Bean, would you please read it?"

"Good idea. I need to have it fresh in my mind, too," Bean said, as she carefully took the real clue from her backpack.

"'Its sure foundation was started by three.
Grafted together to form a green canopy.
Inside of its strength lies a small opening to the past.
When used with the Spirit, will build your testimony to last.
With his treasure in your hands, much service is desired.
Serving with faith is a trait that's admired.'"

"Anyone have any great ideas where we are supposed to go?" asked KP.

"The clue doesn't really give any specific direction the way the last clues have," complained Butch.

"Talking about a sure foundation again and a green canopy has to mean something," reasoned Bubba.

"I agree," said Runt.

"What do you think Moroni meant when he talked about a green canopy?" asked KP.

"Could it be a green tarp?" asked Stick.

"No," said Hero. "The clue says it is grafted together. The only things I know of that are grafted together are trees and vines."

"Right, Hero. But, if it is a tree, what tree is it? Thousands of trees grow around this area," asked Bubba.

"Do you think it could be a tree over by Mr. Jensen's house?" asked Stick.

"Excellent question, Stick," said Runt. "But I think it could be a tree anywhere."

"There has to be more in the clue than we are seeing," said Red, looking over the clue again.

"You're right, Red. But what?" asked Tater.

"What about *foundation* and *started by three*. What do those words mean?" asked Bean.

"I think they have something to do with three trees," said Squeaks. "Wouldn't three trees make a sure foundation?" she asked.

"Well, then the clue says there has to be three trees growing together, and inside of the tree is a small opening," said KP, re-reading the clue.

"Who might know of three trees growing together?" asked Runt.

"What about Mr. Jensen? Do you think he might know of a big tree like that?" asked Bubba.

"Great idea," said Butch. "Bubba, I can't believe you can still think with a bullet coming that close to your head. Good job," he said.

Bubba smiled, rubbing the scratch on his head.

"Let's go ask Mr. Jensen," said Hero.

"Squeaks, do you want to go with us to Mr. Jensen's house?" Bubba asked.

Squeaks sat up tall on her chair and smiled. But then she responded, "I will wait for you here."

"Is that what you want to do?" asked Bubba, a little surprised.

"Yes," she replied.

"Are you sure, Squeaks? You have wanted to be with us every time. Why not now?" asked Stick.

"Well, you will be coming back to the Treehouse pretty soon. I don't want to go to Mr. Jensen's house, just to come right back here," she said.

"The tree might be somewhere far away. We might not come back here soon," said Tater.

"Yes you will," responded Squeaks.

"Okay," said Tater, shaking his head in disbelief.

The Team threw down the ladder and climbed out of the Treehouse. They grabbed their bikes and headed straight for Mr. Jensen's house.

As they arrived, Mr. Jensen was carrying groceries from his car into the house. Excited to see the Team, he set the groceries on the porch and asked, "Did you find the treasure?"

"Not yet," replied Hero.

Mr. Jensen looked sad and asked, "Is finding the treasure just too hard?"

"No," responded Bean. "We are to the very last clue, and we need some help."

"Help?" asked Mr. Jensen. "Maybe I can help. Follow me," he said, excited for the opportunity to assist. The Team picked up the groceries and followed Mr. Jensen into the house.

As Mr. Jensen put the groceries away in the kitchen, he asked, "Tell me all about your adventures so far. Have you found anything that suggests the treasure still exists? How can I help you?"

"Wait, wait! One question at a time," said Bean.

"Our adventures have been great," said Butch. "You won't believe all of the really neat places we have found."

"And," said Red, "we have even met a person from the Book of Mormon."

"A person?" questioned Mr. Jensen. "Who?"

"This really neat warrior, Lehonti," said Runt.

"A warrior? So the treasure really exists," said Mr. Jensen, shaking his head. "I wish I could have gone with you."

"Lehonti even knew your great-grandfather, Ole. Lehonti was sad to learn that Ole had been killed," said Bubba.

"Lehonti knew him?" asked Mr. Jensen excitedly. "This is so wonderful. Tell me more."

"We have found all the keys to the clues. The only thing left is the treasure," said Bean, pulling the keys out from her backpack. "Look at these," she said, as she handed them to Mr. Jensen.

He solemnly took the keys and said, "I have seen these before."

"You have? When?" asked Runt.

"I saw them when I was a boy. After Ole's funeral, my grandparents and parents pulled out all of his photo albums for us to look through. I saw pictures of these; I am positive of it," Mr. Jensen said.

"Do you still have the albums?" asked Bean eagerly.

"I'm sure I do. They were up in the attic. I think you

brought them all down when you cleaned."

"Hey, we looked at some of those albums. I remember seeing pictures of really cool stuff," said Hero.

"Just a minute, Team. Let me go look," said Mr. Jensen, as he hurried to the back bedroom. He returned with two very large albums. "If I still have the picture, it will be in one of these two photo albums."

Hero reached over and took one. Bubba, Tater, Red and Bean started scanning through the pictures in one album, while Runt, Butch, KP and Stick looked through the other with Mr. Jensen.

They had only turned a few pages when Bean yelled, "That's Lehonti! That's him. I am sure of it." The Team looked at the black and white picture and agreed. The photo was Lehonti for sure.

"Why didn't we look at this earlier?" asked KP. "It might have helped us."

"I'm sorry, Team. I forgot these even existed until now," replied Mr. Jensen.

"Look. This picture shows the cave of bats," said Stick, all nervous again.

"You were in there?" asked Mr. Jensen.

"We sure were," answered Runt.

"Team, you are braver than I thought," Mr. Jensen stated.

"Hey, there is a picture of the volcano and lava house," said Bubba. "I almost fell into that," he said.

"What?" asked Mr. Jensen. "This looks too dangerous for you young kids."

"The People in the pictures really look like Nephites and Lamanites. I wonder if they still lived there when your great-grandfather was looking for the treasure," said Butch.

"Did you meet any other people besides Lehonti?" asked Mr. Jensen.

"No. He was the only one," replied Bubba.

"Why are there so many pictures of the tree in our backyard, Mr. Jensen?" asked Hero.

"Because your home is where my great-grandfather Ole used to live," he replied.

"He lived in our house?" asked Bubba, obviously shocked.

"He sure did," said Mr. Jensen. "The house has been remodeled, but it's the same tree."

"Cool," replied Bubba, intrigued at the idea that people from the Book of Mormon could have been in his house.

"What are you looking for now?" asked Mr. Jensen.

"We are not sure," said Bean.

"That is why we have come to see you," replied Hero.

"Is there a clue that leads you to where you need to go?" asked Mr. Jensen.

"Yep. Just a second and I will read it to you," said KP, unzipping his backpack to pull out the clue.

"'Its sure foundation was started by three,
Grafted together to form a green canopy.
Inside of its strength lies a small opening to the past.
When used with the Spirit, will build your testimony to last.

> With His treasure in your hands, much service is desired.
> Serving with faith is a trait that's admired.'"

"We think that the clue is talking about three trees being grafted together. But we have never seen a tree that big," said Bubba.

"Have you ever seen a tree that big, Mr. Jensen?" asked Runt.

Mr. Jensen sat quietly, thinking for several minutes. Then he finally replied, "The biggest tree I have ever seen is the tree that holds up your Treehouse, Team. Have you checked there yet?"

"We haven't because it is just one tree — not three," replied Red.

"Are you sure?" asked Mr. Jensen.

"It looks like just one tree," replied Tater.

"Trees that are grafted together, grow together," replied Mr. Jensen.

"Are you serious?" asked Stick. "You mean, the treasure could actually be in the Treehouse?"

"Well, probably not in the Treehouse itself. But it seems logical to me that the tree could have something to do with your treasure — especially since my great-grandfather used to live in your house," Mr. Jensen replied.

"That's not good," said Bean quietly, but barely loud enough for Mr. Jensen to hear.

"Why isn't that good?" asked Mr. Jensen.

"The crooks were up in the tree," blurted out Stick. "I hope they didn't find anything."

"The crooks? What crooks?" asked Mr. Jensen.

"Oh, nobody," said Hero.

"Well, I think it is somebody. And if you don't tell me, I will call your mom right now and end this treasure hunt," warned Mr. Jensen.

"Those two prison escapees," answered KP quickly.

"The inmates that broke out last week?" Mr. Jensen asked.

"That's right," replied Butch. "They were hiding out in your attic and were here when we found the treasure map," he said.

"Until earlier today, they had been following our every move," added Runt.

"I can't believe this, Team. This treasure hunting is much too dangerous," said Mr. Jensen.

"Not anymore," said Tater. "We devised a plan and set up the prisoners to be captured. And it worked!" he said triumphantly.

"The escapees were captured just a few hours ago," said Bubba.

"Oh, good. I hadn't heard yet. But Team, I am still concerned that this treasure hunt is too difficult," said Mr. Jensen.

"Well, we have had some scares," said Butch, "but all we have left to find is the treasure."

"Team, what if the treasure is dangerous?" asked Mr. Jensen.

"How could it be? It's just a treasure," reasoned Stick.

"I don't want to see any of you get hurt. Please be very careful," Mr. Jensen said slowly.

"We will. We promise. None of us has been hurt too badly, Mr. Jensen," said Runt.

"Mr. Jensen, could we borrow those two albums?" Hero asked, pointing to the books on the coffee table.

"These albums contain the only pictures I have of my great-grandfather. But if you promise to be careful with them, I will let you borrow them," he replied.

"We will. Thank you, Mr. Jensen," replied Hero.

"I wonder if we will find anything in here that helps us locate the treasure," Hero said, as he picked up the two albums and placed them in a plastic grocery bag.

"Possibly," responded Mr. Jensen. "Just remember to be very careful."

The Team grabbed their belongings. Bean picked up the keys and put them back into the zipper pocket of her backpack. Then the Team filed out the front door and onto the porch.

"The rain and cold weather are going to stop any day now, right?" asked Butch, as he quickly zipped up his windbreaker and pulled on his hat.

Excited to head back to the Treehouse, the Team jumped on their bikes. With a quick wave goodbye to Mr. Jensen, the Team raced for home.

As they pedaled down the driveway, Red suddenly remembered the puddle prank he tried to pull the last time the Team was at Mr. Jensen's house. Seizing the moment, he carefully avoided the puddle that contained the hidden rock, and he aimed his bike and speeding tires for a different puddle. To Red's shock and horror, the bike again stopped, but he did not.

He launched over the handlebars. He fell hard and rolled head over heels for about ten feet. Mr. Jensen had again placed a rock in the puddle to avoid getting his car stuck in the mud.

The Team was not able to control their laughter. As Red sat in mud, trying to figure out what went wrong, Bubba fell off his bike again from laughing so hard.

"I can't believe this," muttered Red. "Two times. This never happens. This is almost like déja'vu."

Stick was still laughing as he pulled Red's bike out of the puddle. He walked it over to Red and said, "Come on. We've got work to do."

They peddled anxiously back toward the Treehouse, while Red nursed his sore ego one more time.

Chapter Seventeen

The Team returned to the Treehouse, planning to search through Mr. Jensen's photo albums for clues that would help them figure out their final destination. They climbed back up the ladder and found Squeaks waiting patiently.

"I told you that you'd be back," she smugly said. She brushed her hair off her face and pulled it into a ponytail.

"Why is that, exactly?" asked Hero, bugged by her attitude.

"Do you know something we don't know?" asked Bubba, as he carefully removed the photo albums from the plastic bag.

"Maybe," she replied.

"Be quiet, Squeaks. We have a lot to do," Hero curtly said. He sat down at the table and got ready to look at the photo albums again. "Come on, Team. We've got to find this treasure."

The Team gathered around the table and searched the photos for anything that might give them an idea about where to look.

"There are some really neat photographs in here," remarked Red, as he turned page after page.

"Do you think these people could be real Nephites and Lamanites?" asked Butch.

"Who else would they be?" asked Bean, pointing to the picture of Lehonti. "We know that this picture is real."

"I don't know," replied Butch. "It's just kind of hard to believe that Ole could really have known Nephites and Lamanites."

"I agree," replied Bubba, looking up from the photo album. "All we have ever seen before are sketches of what people think the Nephites and Lamanites looked like."

For several minutes, the Team scoured the photo albums, completely entranced by the pictures. Squeaks, who had quietly been looking at the album over Hero's shoulder, scared the Team half to death when she yelled, "Look! It's a picture of Lehonti!"

Hero glanced at the picture and asked, "I wonder who he is standing with?"

"Do you think it could be Moroni?" Squeaks asked.

"I guess it really could be anyone from the Book of Mormon," replied Runt.

"I wish I knew who any of these men were," said Butch, pointing to one of the pictures.

"Men? They look more like boys to me," replied Bean. "I don't think they look much older than you guys do."

"Well, in John Bytheway's, *Righteous Warriors* CD, he said many of the warriors in the Nephite armies were young — maybe about fifteen," said Bubba.

"That's right," said Hero. "They are the same age as me."

"That is so cool. They were only a few years older than I am," said Red.

"I am not sure how cool that is. I wouldn't want to be leading or fighting an army in just a few years," said Stick.

"I could do it," interjected Tater. He stood up to flex his muscles for the team.

As the Team laughed at his not-so-bulging muscles, Bean picked up a baseball from the floor, and tossed it at Tater. Then said, "Sit down. You are making us all sick."

Bubba snatched the baseball out of the air just before it hit Tater. "Come on, guys," he said. "Let's find the treasure. I would love to have my picture taken with some of these guys," he said, pointing to the pictures in the album.

"If they really are Moroni, Nephi, Alma, Ammon, or Mormon, or any others from the Book of Mormon, I definitely want to meet them," Hero said eagerly.

"The men you are talking about have all been dead for thousands of years. How would you be able to have your picture taken with them?" asked Stick.

"Maybe Mr. Jensen's great-grandfather was able to travel in time, back to Book of Mormon days," suggested Bean.

"How do you travel back in time?" asked Runt.

"I definitely do not have a clue," replied KP. "I don't think it is really possible."

"Maybe it has something to do with the treasure?" suggested Runt. "I wish I knew where to look or what to look for," he said.

"I don't know how to help, either. I am really not sure what we are looking for," said KP.

"I'm not sure either," added Hero. "Other than we know it is a tree. I was hoping these pictures might tell us something."

"Not only a tree, but a tree you can get inside of," responded Butch.

Squeaks' eyes widened at Butch's comment. "A tree you can get inside of?" she asked.

"That's right," Tater responded. "A small opening to the past lies inside of this giant tree."

"I know the tree," Squeaks said assuredly.

"Really, Squeaks? What tree?" asked Hero.

Sure she knew the answer, she replied, "This tree — the Treehouse."

"Come on, Squeaks. Just be quiet, will you? The Treehouse is one big tree — not three. And it doesn't have a small opening or anything in it," said Red.

"But…," she started.

"Squeaks, if you can't just sit here and be quiet, we will have to ask you to leave the Treehouse," interrupted Hero.

Angrily, Squeaks turned and headed toward the ladder. She muttered under her breath, "You won't have to ask me to leave. I will leave on my own and go find the treasure for you."

With that, she furiously stomped down each step of the ladder, making sure that the entire Team heard every step.

"You two sure made her mad," Tater said to Red and Hero.

"So what?" Red retorted.

Hero, squirmed a little and said, "She has really helped us. We could have been a little nicer."

Red just shrugged. The rest of the Team quietly continued to look through the photo albums for some sign of a tree.

Bubba, realizing Squeaks might have some important information, decided to follow her. He reached the ground, just in time to see her walk around to the backside of the tree. He tiptoed around the tree, only to be surprised by Squeaks. She was leaning against the base of the tree with her arms folded.

"I knew you were coming," she said matter-of-factly.

"Well, it's not like you to leave an invitation to stay in the Treehouse if you don't have a really good reason," responded Bubba.

"Why won't Hero believe me?" she asked angrily.

"He does. He just has to worry about the whole Team's feelings," Bubba replied.

"I really know where this tree is," Squeaks insisted.

"How do you know for sure?" Bubba asked. "Have

you seen the tree?"

"Seen it? I have been inside it!" she declared.

"Then why haven't you found the treasure?" Bubba asked.

"I didn't know what I was looking for," Squeaks said.

"Okay, Squeaks. I believe you. Why don't you and I go look at this tree and see if it really is the one that the clue said to look for? If it is, we will come back together and get Hero and the Team. Does that sound fair?" asked Bubba.

Squeaks looked at Bubba. She took three steps away from the tree. Then she turned around and pointed at it. "Very well. We are here," she said.

"What?" asked Bubba, "What are you talking about?"

"I guess it is about time you find out how I learn everything that your Team is doing, Bubba," Squeaks said.

She carefully pushed aside a basketball-size rock and a few branches. "If you wiggle between the dirt and the crevasse in the tree, you will find a small opening that leads all the way to the top, inside the tree," Squeaks explained.

"Are you serious, Squeaks?" Bubba asked, as he walked toward the opening.

"That is why I waited for the Team to come back. I knew that you would. There were a lot of pictures of this tree in Ole's albums, weren't there?" Squeaks asked.

"I didn't really look as close as I should have. I was more interested in the people," Bubba said.

"Well, I don't know who they were. But I do know that the clue has something to do with our tree," replied

Squeaks.

Bubba crouched down on his knees. As he prepared to poke his head into the small opening, he said, "Squeaks, I really hope you are right."

"Bubba, I know I am," she declared.

With that, Bubba laid down flat on his stomach and wiggled back and forth until he was inside the opening of the tree. Squeaks, was excited for Bubba to see her secret place.

She whispered, "So, what do you think? Am I right?"

From inside the tree, Bubba answered, "Squeaks, how long have you known this was here?"

"Since last summer when the Team was building the Treehouse and you wouldn't let me help," she replied.

"You little sneak. I really think you might be right! Go get Hero, quickly," Bubba demanded.

Squeaks ran to the ladder and climbed up to the Treehouse in record time.

"Hero! Hero! Come quick. Bubba needs you and the Team fast," she screamed.

"What are you squawking about?" Red asked, as he poked his head out the Treehouse door.

"Get Hero, Red. Bubba needs him and the Team right now," Squeaks demanded.

Red turned to relay the message to Hero, who was walking toward the Treehouse door.

"I heard her. What is it, Squeaks?" Hero asked.

"Grab the clue, the keys and the map, quick. Bubba found the tree," she yelled. She knew they would not follow her if they thought she was the one who had found the tree.

Ecstatic, Hero turned and called to the Team. "Quick, throw me my backpack, and get the clue. Bubba has found something."

The Team followed Squeaks to the bottom of the ladder, and KP said, "All right, Squeaks. Where to?"

Calmly, she walked to the other side of the tree.

Frustrated, Red put his hands on his hips and angrily asked, "Squeaks, where do we need to go?"

She looked over her shoulder at the Team, and then said, "Follow me."

"You better not be messing around, Squeaks," threatened Hero.

Squeaks, already behind the tree, did not even respond. The Team walked around the tree to find Squeaks pointing to the small opening.

"What is this?" asked Hero.

"I told you I knew where the tree and the small opening were," Squeaks said confidently.

"Where is Bubba, Squeaks?" Hero asked.

"Already inside," she answered.

"Are you serious?" he asked, as he knelt at the opening and called for Bubba. "Bubba, are you in there?"

Bubba surprised Hero when he replied, "I'm right here, Hero. This is the coolest thing I have ever seen."

"Can you see the treasure?" Hero asked.

"No, but I think I might have found something. There are hieroglyphics all over the place in here," Bubba said.

"Is there enough room that I can climb in?" Hero asked.

"I actually think you, and maybe two others, might fit

— right here at the bottom," Bubba answered.

Hero dropped down on his stomach. He poked his head inside and wiggled his body through the opening. Once inside, he called for KP and Bean to carefully crawl inside with them.

"Please push my backpack inside first, KP," Hero said. "And bring the keys with you, Bean."

As the rest of the Team formed a half-circle around the back of the tree, KP and Bean followed Bubba and Hero's lead, wiggling into the small opening.

Once inside, the four were completely amazed at what they saw. Bulges and ledges had formed where the three trees were grafted together. The tree was beautiful on the outside, but on the inside, it was gnarled and twisted. Huge knots and mounds of wood had formed everywhere.

"It is not very pretty in here," said Bean, as she looked around.

"What have you found?" asked KP, as he stood up and look at his new surroundings.

Bubba replied, "There are some Egyptian looking writings just above us on one of the ledges. And pictures are all over the place in here."

"Should we go check it out?" Hero excitedly asked.

"Sure," answered Bean.

"I think as each of us climbs up to one of the ledges, we will free up some room here at the bottom. Then, we could probably get the rest of the Team into the tree," Hero said.

"I think so, too," replied KP. After he surveyed their

surroundings one more time, he leaned over to the small opening in the tree. He called to the remainder of the Team and invited them inside.

As the rest of the Team crawled into the opening, Hero, Bubba, KP and Bean maneuvered eighteen feet straight up into the tree.

"What do you think?" Bubba asked, as he pointed toward the hieroglyphs. "This has to mean something, right?"

Just a foot hold behind Bubba, Hero continued to climb over the ledge. He poked his head over the top to see where Bubba was pointing. Energized by the prospect of finding the treasure, Hero said, "Bean, hurry and get up here. Let's try to draw these symbols and get them to Cheri quick."

Just a second or two behind Hero, Bean squished her way onto the same twisted, gnarled ledge. She unzipped her backpack and frantically searched for paper. Upon finding it, she was ready to draw the pictures.

"What are the symbols?" asked Bean.

"First there is a tic-tac-toe box, then the letter B," said Hero.

"Okay. Go on," she said excitedly.

"All right, next is a rectangle box, curved inward at either end. Then the next symbol is a box with three straight sides, and a fourth side that curls in half way," Hero explained.

"Like this?" asked Bean, holding up the paper to show Hero the picture.

"Yep, just like that," Hero responded.

Finishing her drawing she called, "What's next, Hero."

"Next is a little stick figure holding out his hand, followed by what looks like a bull's nose ring. And the last symbol is a "B" shape again."

"Just a second," Bean said.

"Is there more?" asked Bubba.

"Yes," replied Hero. "Two more shapes just below that. First, the man stick figure again, and then the tic-tack-toe-box.

Bean was silent a moment as she tried to draw what Hero described. "Anything else?" she asked.

"Yes. One more series just below that," Hero answered.

"What are the symbols?" shouted Squeaks.

Hero paused and looked back down toward the base of the tree. "Give me a minute," he said. "I'm hurrying." After several seconds, Hero said, "Bean, the first figure is a duck. The "B" shape follows and then two small flags."

Bean frantically drew what Hero described.

Anxious to know what was next, Runt hollered, "Is there anything else, or is that all of it?"

"Just a diamond shape, with a peg sticking out of each corner," replied Hero.

"What do you think that is?" KP asked.

"We have seen diamond shapes at every clue," Stick answered, as he listened from below.

"Let's hurry and get these clues to Cheri," suggested Bubba. "I'm ready to find the treasure."

Nervous and excited, the Team slowly crawled out of the Tree. Hero, the last to wiggle out, stood up and brushed off the dirt from his shirt and said, "Come on. Let's get to the library."

The Team ran full speed to the front yard, picked up their bikes off the lawn, and retraced their steps to the library one more time. They locked up their bikes and ran into the library to find Cheri.

"Cheri," called Hero, as he entered the back room, startling her.

She gasped, and grabbed her chest. Then she answered, "Oh, you scared me."

"Sorry," replied Hero. "We found it — the location of the treasure."

"So, what is it?" she asked, smiling eagerly.

"We are not sure yet. We need you to translate this for us," replied Bean, handing Cheri her drawings.

"What is this?" Cheri asked.

"Inside the tree were these engravings. We couldn't bring the tree to you, so I had to make a sketch. Hope you can translate the pictures," Bean replied.

"Let's have a look," Cheri said, sitting down at their usual table. Quiet for a moment, she studied the pictures. "These drawings are letters."

"What letters are they?" asked Tater.

"Wait, let me write this down," said KP.

"No need to do that KP," said Cheri. "You should be able to remember this. These drawings spell out *S, E, R, V, I, C, E."*

"Okay. The first word is service," said Red. "Next word."

"Next word is *I, S,"* replied Cheri.

"I know that word," said Squeaks. "That spells *is.*"

"Right you are, Squeaks," smiled Cheri. "The last row spells *K, E, Y.*"

"Key," said Stick.

"Service is key?" said Runt. "What does that mean?"

"Please don't tell me that is the treasure?" said Stick.

"It could be," responded Cheri. "Learning service is important, and will benefit you throughout your entire life."

"Cheri, are you serious?" asked Red.

Cheri shrugged her shoulders, smiled and said, "It's not a bad lesson."

"What about the diamond shape with the pegs at each corner, back at the treehouse?" asked Squeaks.

"Could those pegs mean something?" asked Butch.

"A diamond shape and pegs?" asked Cheri. "How many keys did I translate?"

"Four. You translated four of them," squealed KP.

"I'm not sure, Team, but I think the saying *'service is key'* might be something you need to know. But the diamond shape and pegs might reveal the true treasure," replied Cheri, grinning.

Eager to return to the Treehouse, Bean said, "We've got to see what those pegs are for. Come on. We have to get back fast."

Tater grabbed Cheri in a bear hug and whispered, "Thanks, Cheri. You're awesome."

The Team ran out of the library, unlocked their bikes and rode frantically back to the Treehouse.

"Move it! Faster!" called Tater, as he waited for Hero, Bubba, KP and Bean to crawl back inside the tree. "Don't you do anything until I get in there," he called impatiently.

"We won't," replied Bubba, already sitting on the ledge.

"We want to see, too," whined Squeaks. "This is my secret hideout."

"We'll wait, Team. Don't worry," reassured Bean.

As Runt, the last teammate to squish through the opening was finally inside the tree, Tater asked, "So, do the pegs move?"

"No. They are solid," answered Hero, pushing on them. "I don't think we are going to find a secret door this time," he replied, chuckling.

"Those pegs have to mean something," said Butch. "We haven't seen them at any of the other clues."

"They look like the thing Mom hangs her keys on at home," said Bubba. "Do you think we need to hang the keys on it?"

"What good would that do?" asked KP.

"I don't know," replied Bubba. "But they have to be for something."

"Let's try that. We have nothing to lose," suggested Tater.

Hero agreed. "Let's try it," he said. "Bean, hand up all the keys, please."

Bean dug around in her backpack for a minute. She gathered all the keys from the zipped pouch in the bottom.

One by one, she handed them to Hero. Hero carefully hung each key on a separate peg and waited to see if anything happened. After several tense minutes of silence, Squeaks finally blurted, "Nothing is happening."

"I can see that, Squeaks," Hero sharply responded.

"Do you have them all in the right place?" Squeaks asked.

"How am I suppose to know if they have their own special peg, Squeaks?" asked Hero.

She shrugged as she looked up at Hero and said, "I am just trying to help."

"I know," said Hero. "Sorry. I was just excited for this to be right. What should we try now, Team?" Hero asked.

The Team was quietly pondering the next move, when Bubba squealed, "Look!" He pointed to very small, engraved symbols under each peg.

"Bubba, you're gonna kill me doing that. Quit, scaring me please!" said KP, still holding on to his chest.

"What is it?" asked Hero.

"Right under each peg is a small symbol. What are they?" he asked trying to get a better look.

Hero leaned over and looked at the pictures. He squinted his eyes tightly and said, "The top one is an eye. That peg must be for the last key." He quickly switched the keys around. "The peg on the right side of the diamond is the Egyptian number twenty-two," he said. He quickly moved that key to the correct spot. "The left side of the diamond is a...sun or a light."

"That must be the key I found in the rock," shrieked Stick.

Hero changed the last two keys around carefully, and then said. "Well, I guess we will see if anything happens."

Seconds later the tree started shaking violently back and forth. Squeaks, was scared to death. She screamed at the top of her lungs. The rest of the Team tried to brace themselves by holding onto anything they could grab.

"What was that?" asked KP.

"An earthquake," answered Runt.

"Oh sure. We have those so often here," said Runt.

"Are the keys okay?" asked Bean.

Hero, caught up in the shaking, had completely forgotten about them. He quickly turned and poked his head back over the ledge just high enough to see them. Then he squealed, "The treasure! It's here!"

Quickly, he climbed up high enough to pick up the football-sized box. He carefully moved it off the small ledge to an area where KP, Bean and Bubba could see it as well. Then he started opening the box.

Red shouted, "What is it? What is it?"

"Hang on a second, Red. I've almost got it open," replied Hero. Hero slipped his backpack onto his back to free both hands. He grasped the box firmly with his left hand. Then held it close to his body as he pried open the small latch. He looked down at the Team and said, "This is it. We've done it."

"Just open it already," Tater demanded.

Hero smiled and lifted the heavy stone lid. As he laid the lid back as far as it would go, a blinding flash of light filled the space in the tree. The light was brighter than anything they had ever seen. Everyone had to look away and cover their eyes.

"What is it, Hero?" asked Bubba, still shading his eyes.

"I can't see either, Bubba. I don't know," Hero answered.

As the Team waited for Hero to regain his sight, Squeaks said, "Earthquakes, bright lights, rain and thunder. What is next?"

"Don't ask!" said Runt superstitiously. "If you say things like that, something bad is bound to happen."

Squeaks just smiled, "All right, already. What is it?" she asked.

Hero finally looked in at the contents and answered, "I don't know. I have never seen anything like this."

"Well, show us," said Butch impatiently.

Hero handed the box to KP and said, "Hold this, and I will take the treasure out."

KP quickly took the box. As Hero picked up the object, KP set the box down on a lower ledge. Hero held up a small, round ball. Delicate engravings covered its entire outer shell. Hero thought it might be made out of brass. As he looked down at the ball from the top, he could see two spindles inside. On the side of the ball was a small, screen-like area that was blank. Hero had absolutely no idea what he was holding.

He showed it to Bubba, KP and Bean and asked, "Have you ever seen anything like this before? Any idea what it is?"

"Hey, I have," said Bubba. "In Sunday School last week, my teacher showed a picture of it."

"What is it, then?" asked KP.

"If I didn't know better, I would say it is the Liahona," said Bean.

"That's what I thought," said Bubba. "I have read about it several times in the Book of Mormon."

"The Liahona doesn't flash numbers on the front," said Hero, pointing to the screen.

"When did those start flashing?" asked KP. "I didn't see those a minute ago. The screen was blank. Plus I don't think the Liahona had a monitor. Technology was a lot different back then, you know."

"This can't be the Liahona. Lehi's description in the Book of Mormon is similar, but I don't ever remember reading about flashing numbers," said Runt.

"Look. It flashed the number again," said Bean, pointing to the ball.

"I agree with KP and Runt. The people during that time didn't have this kind of technology," said Runt from below, still trying to see the ball.

"But it looks like the Liahona, and the clues say it would be a great treasure from Book of Mormon days," said Bean. "This would definitely be a great treasure."

"I was sure wishing for money and jewels and stuff," said Stick, sounding disappointed.

"Could we turn this in for money?" asked Red.

"Real funny, Red," said Hero. "The clues all hinted that this wasn't going to be a treasure of money."

"Even Lehonti told us that," said Squeaks.

"Well," said Butch, "How can we do the Lord's will with a little ball that flashes numbers?"

"I'm sure we will learn," said Bubba. "The Lord wouldn't help us find this if he wasn't going to tell us or show us how to use it," he said.

"I guess you're right," said KP. "Do you think this is another one of those tests of faith?" he asked.

"I do," said Bean. "What kind of faith are we showing right now?"

"Hey, the numbers stopped flashing," interrupted Bubba.

"What happened?" asked Tater. "Those numbers have to mean something; so why would they disappear?"

"We need to figure this out," replied Hero.

"Can I see the Liahona, Hero?" asked Squeaks.

"Well, Squeaks, we don't know for sure that this is the Liahona. It's kinda tight quarters in here. But if you give me a minute, I will try to get down to give you a closer look at the treasure," Hero said. Slowly he started moving down the ledge. Carefully holding the delicate ball up for everyone to see.

Suddenly Bean exclaimed, "The number 73 BC just flashed again. Does that mean anything?"

"I don't know. I hope nothing scary," said Hero nervously.

Hero stopped climbing down the gnarled interior of the tree to look at the flashing number. Suddenly the number flashed again. But this time, a burst of bright light shocked the Team, and instantly everyone turned away.

"Hero, is it a bomb?" asked Runt, still looking down at the ground.

With no response from Hero, Runt rubbed his eyes

and looked up to make sure they were all okay.
"Where did they go?" he asked, totally confused.

"What do you mean, 'Where did they go?'" panicked Squeaks, looking up to where Hero, Bubba, KP and Bean had just been sitting.

"Are they dead?" asked Red.

"How would I know?" replied Tater, climbing up to check the area. "They just disappeared," he said. He swiftly snatched the box off the ledge and anxiously looked inside.

"How could they just disappear? And if they did, where did they go?" asked Runt.

Bewildered and confused, the Team searched for almost an hour, but found absolutely no trace of their missing teammates.

"What am I going to tell Mom?" asked Squeaks, panicking.

Tater, now the senior member of the Team, took charge.

"Ya'll aren't goin' to say nothin'. Listen up! Let's get out of here and go back up to the Treehouse. We need to see if those old photographs give us any idea where they went."

The Team wiggled slowly out of the small opening at the base of the tree.

Tater yelled, "Move it! Get up the ladder to the Treehouse. I want to find them before we have an even bigger problem."

Chapter Eighteen

"Where are we?" asked Bean, as she slowly searched the unfamiliar surroundings.

"I have no idea. But we are no longer inside the tree," said KP.

"I can see that," responded Bean, grabbing Hero's arm. Tears welled up in her eyes.

"Don't worry, Bean. Everything will be fine. I'm sure we are where the Lord needs us to be," Hero said reassuringly.

"In the middle of a field, in the dead of night, with no lights, streets, phones, or anything around as far as the eye can see?" she yelled angrily.

Bubba grasped Bean's hand and said, "Let's try to find out where we are."

Hero and KP agreed.

"Where should we go?" asked KP.

"We could follow the North Star like the shepherds did," said Hero, pointing to the sky.

"Real funny, Hero," said Bean. "I'm just hoping that I am dreaming, and that I will wake up from this nightmare any minute."

"If we follow the North star, maybe it will lead us somewhere. Right?" suggested Bubba.

"Wait! What about this ball? If it is the Liahona, didn't that guide Lehi and Nephi in the wilderness?" Hero asked, holding up the ball to look at it again.

"We don't even know for sure if it is the Liahona," reminded KP.

"Let's pretend that it is," suggested Bean. "Maybe it can show us how to get out of here and back home." She grabbed it away from Hero.

As they stared at the ball, the number 73 BC was still there, but no longer flashing.

"That number has to mean something. What is it?" Hero asked.

"Wouldn't it be funny if the Liahona took us back in time?" KP said, laughing.

"NO! It wouldn't," said Bean. "I don't want to travel in time. Especially backwards."

"Why?" said KP. "I think that time travel would be a lot of fun."

"Thank you, no! I know what happened in the past. The people in ancient times lived through a lot of wars, long journeys and scary stuff. I'm still living at home with good food, clothing, a roof over my head, and I kinda like it there," she replied abruptly.

"Don't worry, Bean. Everything will be all right," said Bubba calmly.

"And why are you so calm?" she asked. "Do you know something we don't?"

"No," Bubba replied, walking toward her.

Suddenly something whizzed past his head. Everyone instinctively dropped to the ground.

"What was that?" Hero asked.

"I have no idea," said KP.

"It made a buzzing noise — kinda like an arrow," suggested Bubba.

"Who would be shooting an arrow?" asked Bean. "Could it have been a Frisbee or ball?"

"Maybe it was a bird," suggested Hero.

"It didn't look like a Frisbee. It looked like an arrow," said KP emphatically. "I wish I could have seen it better. The sky is just too dark."

"What kind of an arrow?" asked Bean.

"The kind from Book of Mormon days," said Bubba, holding up the arrow he found on the ground.

"Book of Mormon days? What do you mean?" Bean asked, starting to panic.

"I think we have traveled back in time to the year 73 BC during Book of Mormon days," Bubba responded coolly.

"Oh, I am going to be sick," Bean exclaimed. "My mom is going to be so mad at me."

The four huddled together, and hoped that whoever shot the arrow would not find them. Seconds later a large, burly man appeared. He towered above them. He had broad shoulders, tan skin, leather bands around his arms and a shaved head. He carried a spear and had a machete tied at his waist.

"Who are you, and why are you on the king's land," he demanded, in a deep, booming voice.

Too afraid to say anything, the four children sat motionless and silent.

"Answer me," he yelled.

Bean shuddered in fear.

"We are lost," answered Hero, shaking feverishly. "We were trying to find the city. We've never been here before," he answered.

"What is your business here?" he demanded.

"We are travelers from the north," KP answered.

"The north?" he asked. "Nephites?"

"Yes,"

"The city is that way," the man stated, as he pointed to the east. "This is not a safe area. Move quickly. You have exactly three minutes to be off the King's land, or you will die."

Not sure what else to do, Hero, KP, Bubba and Bean ran eastward as fast as they could. They were suddenly in a race for their lives.

The Titan's have a date with destiny… Where will they end up next?

About the Author

Although born in Provo, Utah, Tina spent most of her life in San Diego, California. Her writing is strongly influenced by her hometown experiences and her large family whose flair for story telling never ends.

As a direct descendant of Heber C. Kimball and Orson Pratt, the stories told to her by her parents about them encouraged a fascination with the Book of Mormon, Church history, and the adventures of the early saints.

Tina Storrs Monson currently lives in Draper Utah, a suburb of Salt Lake City. She attended Brigham Young University where she met her husband, Kreg. They have been married for sixteen years and have four children.